FOR THE LOVE OF A COMANCHE WOMAN,
HE WOULD BREAK A TRIBAL LAW . . .

"Little Green Frog," Pitalesharo called, his voice suddenly thick. "Please, do not go."

She turned and walked back to the warrior, her eyes still lowered. "Grey Bear has told you how to speak my name in Spanish. You see, I know some of the Spanish words that you two use. What does the chief's son wish?" she whispered.

"I did not send Grey Bear, but I have wished for you to come to me since the first time I saw you."

"I too have wished for nothing else, Man Chief." She looked up into his face and was almost overcome by the tenderness and desire she saw there. "Perhaps it is with you just as it is with me. . . ." She breathed in deeply then, amazed at her own words.

They embraced suddenly. Pitalesharo pulled Little Green Frog tight against him and they stood that way for a small eternity. His hand stroked her hair, ran down her back to the curve of her derrière, lingered there. She felt the hardness of his desire against her belly and shuddered, moving sinuously against it. He let go of her and pulled her dress up over her head, freed it from her arms and dropped it to the ground. . . .

PAWNEE MEDICINE

PAWNEE MEDICINE

BILL HOTCHKISS & JUDITH SHEARS

A Dell/Banbury Book

Published by
Banbury Books, Inc.
37 West Avenue
Wayne, Pennsylvania 19087

Dell ® TM 681510, Dell Publishing Co., Inc.

ISBN: 0-440-06855-4

Printed in the United States of America

First printing—October 1983

For Merle and Goldie

Chapter 1

The grizzled old mountain man reined up his pony on a rise above the Republican River and raised his long-barreled Virginia flintlock over his head. The lumbering procession behind him staggered to a dusty halt.

"Juan Antonio," he shouted. "Get your ignorant hide up here. They's something on ahead."

Termite Joe Hollingback wasn't sure what was out there, but a startled flock of vultures had risen from behind a hill on the other side of the shallow river and now circled lazily against the pale blue sky of late summer.

In this country at this time, it paid a man to be cautious, to use all his instincts and senses to keep his hide intact and his scalp in place.

Antonio Grey Bear Behele, who had been riding at the rear of the procession of twenty-five loaded pack mules, pulled up his spotted stallion beside Termite Joe. He gave Hollingback a skeptical look, then scanned the horizon himself.

"I see nothing," the tall Spanish-born Pawnee said in Pawnee. "Perhaps your pony smells buffalo and grows frightened."

"If you'd been raised as a white man instead of a red devil, you'd sense things better," Hollingback replied irritably. "I tell you, they's something up ahead. See them vultures? They just went up over the far rise like something startled 'em. We got company, maybe."

"Coyotes have chased the carrion birds from a carcass, Joe. You've been worrying about Kiowa and Kaw Indians ever since we left St. Louis. We're in Skidi lands now. Only very foolish Kiowa would approach this close to our villages unless they came in a full-scale war party. And there has been no sign."

"Something up there, I tell you," the buckskin man insisted.

"Then it must be one of our own. We have been so slow that they have come to search for us."

"Maybe," Hollingback grunted. "Check your load anyhow, coon. I ain't even sure you know how to shoot that fancy Kaintuck that Pilcher give you."

"Did I miss the deer this morning, Juan José? No, I did not miss—even though your rifle misfired."

"Wagh! Damp powder was all." Termite Joe chuckled as he continued to scan the low ridge to the south of the river. "And a lucky shot to boot. Ain't one nigger in a hundred could snap a deer's neck at that range, and you know it, too."

"Perhaps the deer died from fright," Behele suggested. "She was looking straight at you, I think."

"Likely, likely," Hollingback agreed. "Look up there, Juan Grey Bear—what did this child tell you?"

A lone figure on horseback appeared atop the rise, an Indian wearing the bonnet of a war chief.

Behele studied the figure for a moment before speaking. "It's Pitalesharo. My blood brother has come to meet us, Joe. The Kiowa will not take our scalps this day."

"Wal, I figgered it was some such. But I seen the buzzards, coon, and you didn't. Now ain't that a fact?"

Antonio Behele yipped out the Pawnee war cry. Within a moment the sound was returned by the solitary rider atop the crest and the warrior galloped his pony down the incline toward them.

"Grey Bear and Termite Joe," the rider called out. "I came to find you. We have trouble in the village."

"Hold on to your bonnet, Man Chief," Hollingback laughed as the powerfully built Pawnee warrior drew up to them. "The Cheyenne ain't stole all the horses, has they?"

"What is it, Pitalesharo?" Behele demanded.

"We must hurry back, my friends," the Pawnee answered. "Two days from now the shaman intends to sacrifice to Morning Star. My father and I will need your help to stop this thing."

"Burning up a few intestines ain't going to bother nothing, is it? What's all the fuss?"

"Not that kind of sacrifice," Pitalesharo said grimly. "Wounded Man believes that Morning Star is angry with our people because we have not followed the old ways. He intends to burn a young Comanche woman Hawk Foot captured during a horse-stealing raid while you were gone. He must not be allowed to do this thing. She is a fine woman, my friends. She should be given to one of the warriors as a wife, not burned to death. In truth, Wounded Man hopes to sway the loyalties of our people away from my father so that Hawk Foot can become the new head chief of the Skidi. Already he has many who side with him, and my father's words are not heard. The people think only of war now, and Hawk Foot encourages them. He says we must kill all the whites who come into our lands. Come—you can tell me the news from St. Louis as we ride. There is no time to waste."

"He wants to burn an Indian gal alive?" Hollingback was astounded.

"It is the old way," Pitalesharo sighed. "But it has been many winters since such a sacrifice was made. Grey Bear and I were just boys then."

Behele nodded vigorous agreement. "I was fortunate not to be the one burned. At first I was a slave to Lacheleshoro, but when Pitalesharo and I became blood brothers, the chief adopted me. I was ten years old at that time and I was very lucky."

"Yes," Pitalesharo agreed, "lucky the shaman's warriors had captured a Cheyenne in battle. When my father was a boy, Termite Joe, the people sacrificed white men whenever they could. It would not have been safe for you in those days. Whites were believed to make the best sacrifices, especially the ones who wore iron suits. My people thought they were only half human. That's what the old stories say."

"Goddamned heathen devils," Hollingback snorted. "Ain't no hope for the lot of you, none at all. The Pawnee start up that sort of thing again, and we'll have more damned bluecoats out here than you can shake a stick at, I'll tell you."

"There are not enough bluecoats in St. Louis to harm the Skidi," Antonio Behele said. He hoped that would end the discussion.

"Damned fools," Hollingback persisted. "Ain't I got it through your thick skulls yet that St. Louis is just a little place? Enough bluecoats and we could wipe out the last one of you. So far the government's just been taking it easy with you."

"Your government, not ours," Pitalesharo pointed out. "But that is of no matter. Right now Wounded Man intends to burn the Comanche, and I would like you two to help me. My father has already spoken strongly against the sacrifice, and now it is a matter of the people choosing sides. If Wounded Man is able to go through with what he has planned, then even greater trouble will follow. It is possible that my father and all of our clan will have to split away from the village and form a village of our own.''

''Wounded Man does not want the whites to travel through our lands,'' Behele said after a moment. ''He wishes to mount attacks against whatever supply caravans move back and forth between St. Louis and Santa Fe. That is what he has always said, and now he uses the sacrifice as a test for the loyalties of the people.''

Pitalesharo nodded agreement.

''Got you,'' Termite Joe Hollingback said. ''Lachelesharo's friends with Pilcher and Governor Clark, and the old shaman don't want no part of it. If the chief makes some kind of truce and gets rifles in exchange, then Hawk Foot ain't never going to be head chief. Damned Indians is just as conniving as civilized white men, by God.''

''If we go on talking,'' Pitalesharo suggested, ''the Comanche will be nothing but bones and burned flesh. Were you able to get the firesticks and powder, Joe?''

''Fifty rifles and damned near as many pistols,'' Hollingback replied. ''But that's on agreement that the chief will keep his word and come north to St. Louis in the spring to work out a proper agreement—and leave the damned mule wagons alone in the meanwhile.''

''Red-haired Chief knows my father will keep his word if he is able to do so,'' Pitalesharo answered. ''Now we must get these weapons into the hands of those who are loyal to my father. If Saynday is with us, there will be no need for them.''

Hollingback shouted his string of mules into motion and Behele sang out, ''Let's get moving.''

The animals grudgingly started forward up the trail that led along the south fork of the Republican toward the Skidi village. Two or three of the beasts brayed their protests as they resumed their journey.

Shortly before nightfall Termite Joe led the mules up and away from the river across a low rise covered with bunch grass and occasional clots of sagebrush to a large spring that issued from beneath a cap of dark sandstone. It was a place that had seen many encampments, and it was less than one day's journey from the permanent village of the Skidi.

From the rise above the grove of cottonwoods close by the spring the long line of the Rocky Mountain front range a hundred and fifty miles to the west was dimly visible, a ragged black shadow low to the horizon. The highest peaks glinted faintly beneath the crimson of summer sundown.

Hollingback halted for a moment, cupped his hand above his eyes and stared toward the mountains. He reflected that if a man didn't know the mountains were there, he might suppose they were nothing more than bands of running clouds along the horizon.

For the preceding week she had been kept under constant watch and restricted to a small lodge separate from the shaman's. Wounded Man's Cheyenne slave, Hummingbird, attended her and stayed close beside her even when it was necessary to walk away from the village to relieve herself. Her captors' attitude toward her seemed to have changed. The Pawnee women, at first more or less friendly and even solicitous, had grown silent and aloof. They looked away when she passed them.

Even Hummingbird, whom she considered her special friend and would-be protector, now seemed distant and sad. When Little Green Frog asked what was wrong, the

Cheyenne only shook her head and gave the hand signal that indicated that she could not or would not speak of the matter.

Now, with the dropping of the sun beyond the far mountains, Little Green Frog was ushered back into her solitary lodge. For the first time two warriors were stationed outside as guards.

She had made no attempt to escape. She had done nothing to anger these Skidi Pawnee since the day of her capture a full moon past. Why should they now, after all this time, decide it was necessary to guard her?

On the day of her capture she went alone to the little stream that ran beyond the broad meadows where the horses grazed. She wanted to be alone to think about Six Feathers, the handsome young warrior who wished to pay court to her and who sometimes contrived to meet her when she walked out away from the village to pick the shiny blackberries that grew in a profuse tangle along the stream.

But Six Feathers did not come to join her that day.

Instead the Pawnee poured yipping and howling upon the grazing herd of horses. Their arrows and pistol fire made quick work of the young boys set to tend the animals, and while Little Green Frog watched in horror, the Pawnee cut out more than two hundred horses and drove them directly toward where she was hiding beneath the thorny hedge of berry vines.

The leader, who she later learned was named Hawk Foot, turned aside, dismounted, hacked his way in among the berry vines and dragged her out, his knife at her throat. He bound her wrists and ankles and slung her onto his horse.

For a week now there had been much discussion within the Skidi village, but what it was about she did not know. Not even Hummingbird had told her anything, and she had decided it was best not to ask. Whatever the issue was, it was clear that tempers were beginning to run high. Even Pierre Papin, the jovial French trader, seemed upset. Several times she had heard him cursing at one warrior or another from within the big mud lodge where he lived and conducted his trading post.

Little Green Frog lay down on her rough pallet, her face toward the rounded adobe wall of the small lodge that had become her prison.

For a time shortly after her capture she had been kept in the lodge of Hawk Foot's immediate family, and the young war chief had treated her kindly. He had not forced his sexual attentions upon her. Several times he had suggested they might lie down together, but she had smiled and declined and he had respected her wishes. Other young men came to the lodge, and though at first she understood little of the Pawnee language, she nevertheless realized that the men were attempting to impress her.

One or two, she understood, wished to persuade Hawk Foot to give her to them as a wife. But Hawk Foot seemed to be in no hurry to part with his captive. Then he had taken her to the lodge of his uncle, Wounded Man, the wifeless shaman who kept Hummingbird as a servant. After that it seemed she was to take her place as another slave. The shaman did not seem interested in either of them in the way of a man and a woman, for which Little Green Frog was grateful. She and the Cheyenne rapidly became close friends, happily working and talking together when the shaman was absent. Little Green Frog was learning the language of the Pawnee from Hummingbird and bits and pieces of the Cheyenne tongue as well.

Another of the warriors showed interest in her. His name, Hummingbird told her, was Pitalesharo, Man Chief, the son of the head chief. Whenever he came near, she felt terribly shy. She could not help herself. Hummingbird had laughed and teased her about it.

She knew that the chances of the head chief's son taking a slave for a wife were almost nonexistent. Her salvation, she had long since concluded, lay not in staying with her Pawnee captors but in making her escape. With a fast pony and a small supply of food, she would flee the Skidi village when the people were asleep and ride toward the south. The journey would be difficult without a weapon. But many edible plants and roots and berries grew along the stream bottoms that intersected the otherwise endless sea of grass, the hills of rounded stone, the bluffs of salt and gypsum. She would not starve to death, she told herself. Comanche women knew how to fend for themselves. She had memorized the salient details of the long ride north from the lands her own people roamed to this permanent village of rounded domes of mud.

Pitalesharo: a handsome face, powerful arms, a slim waist. It was good to know that such a warrior watched her at times and seemed to take pleasure in the watching.

She heard voices outside the lodge and sat up. It was Hummingbird. The Cheyenne was speaking with the men who guarded the entrance. They were teasing her and making rude jests.

"I would force you to lie down with me," one of the male voices said, "but Hawk Foot will have you instead. He will convince Wounded Man to part with you. Probably he will cut your throat when he has satisfied himself, Cheyenne. But I will buy you for a wife and treat you well."

Hummingbird laughed. "I will not have either of you. No one will cut my throat. There is someone else who will give many ponies for me. Move away now, and let me take this food into the lodge."

"Cheyenne women smell funny," the second male voice said.

"You smell nothing but your own breath, Mad Crow. That is what I think. Move aside now, or I will have to tell Wounded Man that you refused to let me enter."

Hummingbird entered the dark lodge. "I have brought food for you, Little Green Frog. Why do you sit here in the darkness? I will light the oil pot for you."

"Why am I being kept here?" Little Green Frog blurted out. "You have been my friend. You must tell me now."

Hummingbird struck steel and flint several times before she was successful in igniting the wick in the earthen pot, and then she signaled that they were obliged to speak in whispers.

"It is something bad," the slave said. "But I do not think it will really happen. Lachelesharo, the head chief, wishes to save you."

"Save me from what?"

"You really do not know?"

"How could I know anything?" Little Green Frog protested. "No one will speak to me now. What have I done to offend the shaman?"

"You have done nothing," Hummingbird replied. Her finely chiseled features were shadowed by the flickering light of the small lamp as she turned her eyes away.

"Then what is it? You are the only friend I have here, Hummingbird. You must tell me what I can do so that Wounded Man will forgive me."

"That isn't it. No, listen. You must not cry out if I tell you. They are all talking about it, but Lachelesharo says no. Do you promise?"

A terrible sensation of fear ran through Little Green

Frog, and memories of horror stories about the Pawnee flashed through her mind.

"Do they intend to kill me, then?" she asked.

Hummingbird forced herself to look directly into her friend's eyes. "My people are called the Morning Star People. We honor the great god and we believe that he favors us. We make offerings to him sometimes, but never like this. If we kill a captive, it is not because the god wishes us to do it. But the Pawnee are different. That is what Wounded Man says."

"The shaman wishes to sacrifice me to Morning Star?" Little Green Frog asked. Her voice clotted in her throat.

"Eat the food I have brought you," Hummingbird replied, "and I will tell you everything I know. Eat quickly so that I can return the basket to Wounded Man's lodge. He would have me whipped if he thought I had said anything to you. He told me that."

Fear was like a rope around Little Green Frog's neck and she could eat nothing. She pushed aside the woven basket filled with chunks of cold buffalo meat.

"What is going to happen to me, Hummingbird? If we have ever been friends, then tell me."

Hummingbird coughed softly and cleared her throat. She would have trouble speaking the terrible words.

"Wounded Man wishes to sacrifice you to Morning Star because he says the god is displeased. In the old times the Pawnee made human sacrifice, and Morning Star is angry that they have stopped doing this. Wounded Man says you are to be burned alive. It won't happen, though; I know it. The chief will never allow it."

Flames licking at her, her hair burning, more pain than she can stand, her clothing afire. She had seen a Ute prisoner burned alive at the hands of her own people, the

*body arching, convulsing in the fire, the long screaming
and then silence except for the hissing and popping and
bursting of something that was no longer a human being.*

"When?" Little Green Frog asked.

"Two dawns from now," Hummingbird replied. "At
the sacred time when Morning Star rises, just before it is
light."

"Take this food away. I cannot eat now. But when
you come in the morning, you must bring me a knife. The
small, sharp knife we use for cutting stew meat. I do not
wish to die in the fire, Hummingbird. Will you do that for
me?"

"I will. I will give the meat to one of the camp dogs
so that Wounded Man will not guess what I have told you.
Be brave, my sister."

Then she was gone. Little Green Frog could hear the
clucking of the guards' tongues, the slap of an open palm
against flesh, the hissing of Hummingbird's scornful voice.

Somewhere a wolf howled, a long, drawn-out wail in
the night.

Chapter 2

Pitalesharo, Antonio Grey Bear and Termite Joe ate quickly
and waited for the dawn. By forcing the mules ahead at a
somewhat faster pace than the long-eared beasts were accustomed to, they would reach the Skidi village, still some
thirty miles distant, by nightfall—granting that nothing
unforeseen happened to slow their progress.

At first light they moved up the south branch of the
little river the white men called the Republican toward the
meadows where two tributaries joined the main stream and
the Skidi village stood. It consisted of more than two
hundred earth lodges with rounded roofs.

There were nearly four thousand Skidi, as Termite
Joe calculated, the most powerful of the Pawnee groups.
And now, if Pitalesharo was correct, they were a people
divided in their loyalties between the head chief and the
bitter and envious old shaman. On the one hand was
Lachelesharo, Two Axes, as he was known to the whites,
Knife Chief if the name were rendered accurately. He had

befriended William Clark some years earlier and was more or less willing to coexist with the white trappers and the merchant trains that passed through his lands. Clark had been convinced that Lachelesharo might in time actually be willing to have a Christian missionary come to live among his people.

Termite Joe realized plainly enough that this had been a problem of communication between white and Indian. What Lachelesharo was primarily interested in was the acquisition of Long Knife medicine, the magic that gave the whites their power. Clark, on the other hand, seemed convinced that the Indians were hungry for the white man's religion. Well, it was a misunderstanding that could lead to some real good if it meant that the trappers and traders and others might be a mite safer in Pawnee lands.

But Wounded Man was a different matter altogether. The shaman saw his own influence over the people being threatened by talk of the white man's God. Perhaps in his own way Wounded Man actually had the best interests of the tribe in mind. Perhaps the shaman even foresaw the implications of white traffic through Pawnee lands for the danger that it was.

Hollingback thought of the condition of the red men east of the Mississippi River—half civilized, driven into lands not valued by the whites, occasionally even hunted for sport—more or less powerless to control their own destiny. There had even been serious proposals for extermination of the Indians. Here on the High Plains, on the other hand, the savages were free to live essentially as they always had, their lot altered only by the acquisition of firearms and whatever whiskey they could get their hands on, and the prevalence of lung disease and smallpox, two afflictions to which the Indians seemed to have no resistance whatsoever.

There was an old Pawnee tale about how the Skidi

acquired medicine dogs, horses, from the Spanish long ago. Saynday, Old Man Coyote, appeared in a shaman's vision and told him that the Pawnee could have the horses but that everything would change after that.

"And by God, it did, too," Hollingback whispered to his grey pony, rubbing the barrel of his Virginia rifle along the horse's neck as he did so. "Ain't no cure for it, neither. And that's what these boys don't see, horse. But you and me, we *do* see. Well, right now we got troubles. Old Papin's not going to like it, putting guns in the hands of the red devils, and maybe it won't come to that after all. There's been other times Pitalesharo's got riled up about one thing or another that didn't amount to nothing. Guess we'll just have to see what happens."

They entered the Skidi village just as the evening shadows were welling up out of the basin of the confluence. Smoke from the cooking fires lay heavy in the air. The smell of rich food was thick in the motionless atmosphere and the people were eating and talking. There was nervous excitement among them.

At the center of the village a young woman was tied to a large, crooked box elder. Piled about her feet were clumps of dead sage and dried buffalo grass, piles of chips and a few short sections of limb wood.

Some of the children, standing back at a distance, yelled insults at her, but her face was without expression as though she could not hear their words. Another young woman was squatting nearby, her shoulders bent, her head lowered in a gesture of helplessness.

Pitalesharo directed Termite Joe to take the mules around to the far side of the village, avoiding conspicuous entry.

"Couldn't do nothing without checking in with Papin first anyhow," the mountain man replied. "You figgering to send your warriors over to the post a couple at a time, then?''

"Exactly," Pitalesharo said. "Grey Bear and I will speak with our father. Then I will send him to meet with you and Papin at the post. We will have plenty of time to get everything arranged. Wounded Man will not begin the sacrifice until just before dawn, the sacred time when the star rises.''

"Two Axes is going to have to make his mark on a note for Papin. The company won't go for anything less. In fact, if we don't pull in a good take of pelts, me and Pierre are going to be in worse shape than that leetle squaw that's tied to the tree. Wagh! This here's irregular business, I'll tell you.''

"Juan José Termite came into the world talking," Behele said, shaking his head, "and he's never stopped since. The white man's company will have its furs.''

"You want her done quick like, I'll need some help getting the goods into the post, lads.''

"We'll be there to assist you as soon as possible," Pitalesharo assured him. "Get going now, and stay back away from the firelight. No doubt we've already been detected, but that could not be helped. How much whiskey did you bring from St. Louis, Joe?''

"Winter's supply for every white nigger in the woods, just like regulations say.''

"Enough for you and Pierre Papin?''

"A mite more than that, a mite more. A Pawnee buck brings in a good take of furs, he tends to get white in the face, you might say.''

"Yes. Tell Papin I said to drag a few kegs out to where the people are assembled. He can make some money selling drinks. Many of the men will have extra buffalo robes to part with.''

"A leetle diversion, you might say?''

"Soon our friend will begin to think like a Pawnee," Behele chuckled softly. "There is still hope for this one, Pitalesharo."

"That will keep Hawk Foot and the others away from the post," Pitalesharo agreed. "That will work well, I think."

Pitalesharo and Behele proceeded directly to Lachelesharo's lodge. They found the chief engaged in conversation with three of his counselors. Half a dozen of Pitalesharo's warriors were there as well, and his mother, Raven Quill, sat on a leather-bound bench beside the cooking fire tending to a pot of venison stew. The lodge smelled strongly of smoke and was uncomfortably warm despite the open entryway.

Raven Quill embraced Pitalesharo and Behele, her adopted son, and then returned to the stewpot without speaking.

"You have brought the St. Louis supplies with you?" Lachelesharo asked.

"Termite Joe has taken the mules to Papin's trading post." Pitalesharo glanced around the room as if to assure himself that all present were loyal to their chief and then continued, "Fifty rifles and the same number of pistols, according to Joe. As many firearms as there are in the village already. Papin will hand them out to those who follow your words. Is that what you wish, Father?"

The chief's face, half revealed in the glow of the cooking fire, appeared for the moment as if it were a mask of sadness. The prospect of arming some of his people against the others did not sit well with him, but at length he nodded.

"It is perhaps the only way," he said. "See that the weapons are given only to those who know how to use them. Listen to my words, all of you. There must be no shooting. We will not spill the blood of those who are one with us no matter what happens. If a show of force is necessary, the rifles will look good. The pistols are not to be handed out. Do you understand me, Pitalesharo?''

''It is understood, Father.''

''Yes. It is better for the Comanche to die than one of the Skidi. What chief would wish to be responsible for such a thing? I will address the people one more time. They may yet hear the wisdom of what I say, though it will be hard for them now to change their minds. Have they brought the woman out yet?''

''She is tied to the box elder,'' Pitalesharo answered. ''Grey Bear and I must go quickly now to help Hollingback unload the weapons and get them safely into the post.''

''Papin will take whiskey to the warriors,'' Grey Bear Behele added. ''That will keep them busy for a time.''

''I ordered it,'' Pitalesharo said. ''Does that meet with your approval, Father?''

Lacheleshoro nodded and grinned. ''Men who drink the alcohol change their minds more quickly, but sometimes for no reason at all. Later I will make a strong speech, and many of those who follow Wounded Man and Hawk Foot will hear what I say and will agree with me. . . .'' The head chief let his voice trail off before continuing. ''But then Wounded Man will speak also, and he has strong speech medicine. What will happen this night is very important to our people. Perhaps I should have agreed to the sacrifice in the first place, but—''

''You could not do that,'' Pitalesharo said.

''No, I could not do that. It is wrong to kill anyone in such a way. She should be saved also because she is strong and comely and should bear sons to a warrior.''

For a moment Lacheleshoro stared quizzically at his son and then shrugged his shoulders. ''You and Grey Bear go to the post. In a few moments I will send Buffalo

Runner and Two Boulders after you. My counselors will search out the others and direct them to the post also. Then I will need to be alone for a time. Perhaps something in my medicine bundle will tell me the right thing to do next.''

The whiskey that Papin doled out, sometimes in exchange for furs and sometimes for nothing more than a warrior's promise, had done its work. A few of the Pawnee warriors had passed out. These men, Papin reflected, would be in a nasty mood in the morning whether the Comanche girl was burned alive or not. *Quel dommage!* Too bad.

In the lodges the children were asleep, while around the great firepit at the center of the village men and women alike feasted on buffalo and venison, roots and berries, fish and small game. A great quantity of ear corn from the garden places along the river had been roasted as well, and melons, tomatoes and squashes were piled high in woven baskets.

For a time the captive at the tree sagged against her bonds and slept, then awoke, her eyes wide with terror. Close beside her sat Hummingbird, granted permission to do so by Wounded Man himself in deference to the bond that had developed between the two women.

It was well past midnight when Lacheleshavo strode into the area between the great cooking fire and the box elder and began to speak.

''People of the Skidi Pawnee, hear my words, the words of him who has led you in peace and in war for more than ten winters. You fear the displeasure of Morning Star and so you wish to burn this woman to death. Do you believe Morning Star will take pleasure from a few minutes of screaming? You have listened to the shaman and he has misled you. Wounded Man has powerful medicine, yet even a great medicine man can be mistaken. Has he told us what dream visions Morning Star has given to him? Perhaps he is fearful that we would read these dreams differently than he does.''

Pitalesharo and Behele and Termite Joe, standing apart from most of the others, noted the responses of the people. Some were nodding agreement with the chief and some were expressing their displeasure and annoyance.

"She don't look good, gents,'' Hollingback muttered.

"Morning Star is a god of war,'' Lachelesharo declared. "If he is displeased with us, then we must uphold our honor against those who are our enemies—the Cheyenne, the Ute and the Comanche—those who steal our horses and kill our warriors.

"But is this woman one of them? Do we slaughter women and children, like our enemies? It is easy to kill this prisoner, but it is not so easy to strike coup upon an enemy who is strong and who has his weapons in his hands.

"If Morning Star is unhappy, then we must strike at the Ute, for they have stolen our horses and killed two of our men. Hawk Foot was supposed to lead a raid against them, but he did not do it. Instead he brought us some Comanche ponies and one of their women. That is why Morning Star is displeased.

"To sacrifice this young woman will not help us. She must be returned to her own people or taken as a wife by one of our warriors. We have made sacrifices in the past; some of us remember them. But have we ever tortured women? Such a thing has always been wrong. Can any of you remember when we did it? No, because we never have, not for so long as any of us here have been alive.

"We must take revenge upon the Ute. I myself will lead you. Look at my arms, warriors! Do they appear old and weak? What man among you would be willing to wrestle with me when it is time for the fall buffalo hunt? I have wrestled many times and always I have won. Many times I have led you in battle, and we have come back to decorate our lodges with the scalps of our enemies.

"Now hear your chief's words! Unbind the Comanche and I will appoint a party to return her to her own people. Then we will make a war party against the Ute. This is what I have to tell you, warriors!"

The Pawnee, many of them caught up by the energy of Lachelesharo's harangue, began to voice their approval, and for a moment Pitalesharo was hopeful that his father's appeal had succeeded. But Wounded Man and Hawk Foot together came forward, and the shaman held out his hands as a signal that he too would address the people.

He was a tall, spare man of perhaps forty-five winters, nearly the same age as the chief. A jagged scar down the left side of his face shone livid in the pulsing firelight. The wound, long ago taken in battle against the Comanche, ran from his forehead through his eyebrow, blinded him in one eye and continued across his cheekbone nearly to the chin.

Termite Joe stared at the shaman and concluded that he looked like the figure of death itself. In the firelit darkness not even the crimson and white markings the shaman had used to accentuate the scar would be necessary. Hollingback felt a chill along his spine. He drew his Virginia rifle closer against his belly for comfort.

Beside the shaman even the powerfully built Hawk Foot seemed somehow dwarfed. From a distance Hawk Foot might easily have been mistaken for Pitalesharo except for the shaved head with the roach across the crown.

"Skidi," the shaman cried out, his harsh voice like the screech of an owl. "Knife Chief misleads you. His heart has turned from the old ways and he listens to the white men more than he does to the fathers of our people.

I have indeed told you of the vision in which Morning Star came to me as a chief with a headdress of shining golden feathers. He told me not only who he was, but also that I was to sacrifice the slave in my lodge.

"He declared that we must not allow the whites into our lands, for they are our enemies. It is all right to trade with them, for they provide us with weapons. But their words are false; we must not believe anything they say to us.

"We must return to the old ways, for otherwise Morning Star may trail fire once again, just as he did in the stories of the ancient ones, and destroy the earth with flood and fire. These are the stories we pass on from generation to generation, and we know they are true.

"Knife Chief forgets that the Comanche is my slave, given to me by my nephew, who captured her in battle. She is mine to do with as I please. Knife Chief has no say in the matter. And it is Morning Star himself who has told me what I must do.

"Warriors! You follow Hawk Foot in battle and he leads you to victories. You hear my words and you know that I am right. Morning Star has spoken and we must not anger him!" Wounded Man gestured toward the east.

Morning Star was already above the horizon.

Wounded Man gestured to the four sacred directions and to the earth and the sky. He raised his right hand toward Morning Star and then turned back to face Hawk Foot, who handed him a pitch-pine torch. The shaman lit it at the fire and began to walk slowly toward the prisoner.

Hummingbird rose and rushed forward. She threw herself down at the feet of Little Green Frog, scattering clumps of sage and tumbleweed as she did so. Hawk Foot strode to the prone Cheyenne, pulled her to her feet, slung her over his shoulder and walked away from the pyre.

Little Green Frog stiffened but did not close her eyes. She stared at the shaman.

The Pawnee were utterly silent, gazing in dull fascination at the shaman and his victim. Then someone leaped forward, brushed past Wounded Man and placed his back against the Comanche girl bound to the box elder. He had a pistol in either hand and the weapons were leveled at the shaman.

"Wounded Man, you will be Dead Man if you do not back away," Pitalesharo hissed. Then he raised his voice and shouted. "Pawnee! You know me, all of you. I too have led you in battle many times. I am Pitalesharo, son of Lachelesharo and leader of the Rarispahat, the Red Lances. I am the one with the pipe and the four rattles and the four drums.

"People of Wolf-Standing-in-Water Village! I claim this woman on behalf of my warriors. I claim her so that we may return her to her people. I too have spoken with Morning Star, and that is what he has told me to do.

"Any who wish to oppose me, come forward now. We will wrestle. If I am defeated, I will leave this village forever. But if I win, then the loser must likewise leave and never return."

A wave of muttered anger and surprise swept through the Skidi. Some looked to Wounded Man while others sided with Lachelesharo, who strode out and stood beside his son.

Then Behele and Termite Joe Hollingback and nearly thirty of the Red Lances moved forward to form a circle about the box elder. Each one held a rifle above his head.

Chapter 3

The party rode south, pushing the horses as hard as they dared in the dim predawn light over uncertain footing. Hawk Foot and a few of his Thunderbird Lance warriors had pursued them a short distance, shouting challenges and insults but staying out of rifle range. But the shaman's nephew had stopped his pursuit less than half a mile from the village. Perhaps he planned to mount a larger party when more of the warriors had sobered up from the Frenchman's whiskey or perhaps he did not want to push the intratribal conflict further.

Little Green Frog rode behind the chief's son, her arms wrapped as tightly as she could manage around the muscular midsection. Her hands were completely without feeling from the long hours when they had been bound with rawhide thongs. Her legs also were weak and partly numb, and she was afraid that if she loosened her grip, she would fall off the horse.

She was desperately tired and wished she could sleep,

but whenever she closed her eyes, she saw again the Pawnee village, the orange firelight, the looming figure of Wounded Man chanting to the assembled people. Even with her eyes open she did not completely believe that she was no longer bound to the crooked elder tree awaiting death.

The night had been longer than her whole lifetime, had seemed to become her lifetime, with everything that went before less convincing than a dream. Perhaps even now she was only dreaming. Perhaps the flames were licking about her ankles; perhaps her body was screaming while her mind thought she was riding horseback behind the handsome son of the Pawnee chief.

She had been determined that she would not show fear before the enemies of her people, and as the night wore on in its eternity of pain, something had happened within her. The pain and the fear had fled to some distant place in her mind and she had watched with a strange, crystalline calm everything that went on.

Perhaps this is what the young men feel, she remembered thinking, when they torture themselves and fast and drag buffalo skulls about by skewers through their flesh so that the spirit people will pity them and send them a vision.

And then the Pawnee camp disappeared and she saw a shallow pool along a stream, a place thickly curtained by trees and wild cucumber vines. On a wet stone at the edge of the pool a small green frog sat smiling. It sang a song to her:

> "This one is brave;
> She does not cry out.
> They are bringing good things for her.
> The spirit people are laughing."

The magic animal opened its mouth again and children tumbled out, many children, giggling and shoving each other. And then the vision dissolved.

The Comanche suddenly laughed aloud, remembering the funny, squeaky voice of the frog and the way it had looked with all those children jumping out of its mouth. She realized that her eyes had closed after all and that her cheek was resting against Pitalesharo's shoulder. She could feel the hard muscles working smoothly beneath the soft leather of his shirt.

He is strong, she thought drowsily, feeling for a moment almost like a little girl sleeping in her father's lap. He is strong and warm and he smells good, even though he is a Pawnee—the realization made her pull upright and as far away from the chief's son as she could manage.

"Where are you taking me, Pawnee?" she demanded loudly. "If you stole me from the shaman so that you and your warriors can lie with me, then you must take me back and let them burn me. I am Comanche and the daughter of a great chief. I will not shame my father Fox Shirt."

Several of the warriors guffawed, and the tall Spaniard who dressed like a Pawnee and was called Grey Bear said, "It's just as I told you about women, amigos. Two hairbreadths away from sizzling like a buffalo haunch, and already she is thinking of sex." Little Green Frog blushed and glared straight ahead as the warriors laughed even more loudly.

Pitalesharo seemed less amused than the other men. "My father is also a chief. I do not wish to shame him either. Perhaps the Comanche should ride with Grey Bear."

"Don't worry, pretty one," called a short, heavyset warrior with a wide comical mouth. "If Man Chief does not wish to lie with you, Two Boulders is willing."

"You'd lie with a sagebrush if you thought there

might be a snake in it, Two Boulders,'' Behele called back.

"All of Two Boulders' dogs keep their tails tucked between their legs," remarked a thin-faced young man. "I used to wonder why that was."

The bantering went on for some time and Little Green Frog keenly regretted her words. She kept her gaze fixed resolutely on the back of Pitalesharo's shirt and tried not to listen to the men's coarse jokes. The numbness was beginning to go out of her hands and she began to feel as if needles of fire were running beneath her skin.

The sky had grown very light now and streamers of pink cloud burned in the east. Little Green Frog could no longer keep her eyes open. Her head drooped once again against Pitalesharo's shoulder. His muscles tensed and for a moment she was afraid he would shrug her away from him.

"Sometimes Comanche women speak too hastily," she whispered so that the others wouldn't hear. "That is what our men say, anyway."

"I think the Comanche men are right," Pitalesharo grumbled, but his back eased.

He will like me again later. Why do I want him to like me?

Her eyes closed and she slept. The rhythm of the horse's movements and the shiftings of the man's warm body in her tightly clasped arms incorporated themselves into her half-conscious dreams.

The party traveled steadily throughout the morning. As the sun rose higher, it became a relentless force, glistening off the long vistas of grass and rock. The monotonous procession of ridge top and valley was broken only by occasional stream beds trailing a band of lush green trees and brush and tangles of wild roses.

Frog rode quietly, half dozing some of the time, at other times wide awake. But she did not speak, and Pitalesharo could tell only by the shifting of her weight against his back whether she was sleeping or awake.

As the heat of the day grew more intense, the entire party lapsed into silence. Pitalesharo could not have told with complete confidence whether he rode waking or dreaming most of the time as the land rolled endlessly before him.

However much he tried to turn his thoughts to other matters, he was keenly aware of Frog's presence, of the soft weight against his back, the thighs pressed against his own. When she shifted against him, he could feel the tug in his loins. But his desire was tempered by a feeling of tenderness, a wish to protect her that he had never felt toward any woman other than his mother.

He fought against the feeling, recounting to himself again and again the arrogance of her words, her accusation against him and his Red Lance warriors. After all, they had risked their own lives and jeopardized their standing in the tribe in order to save her. But he knew it was a losing battle and he tried not to think of the time when they would leave her with her own people. Would she miss him as he would miss her? It seemed not.

"Do you know what her name is?" Antonio Grey Bear asked in Spanish. Pitalesharo had learned it from his friend and they had used it since boyhood to communicate secretly.

"*La Ranita Verde*, Little Green Frog," Pitalesharo replied. "She has a very bad tongue."

"*Sí, es verdad.*" Antonio Grey Bear kept his gaze fixed on the horizon ahead.

"Ranita Verde," Pitalesharo repeated after another

period of silence. "That's not a very good name for her. She should be named after something beautiful, a flower or a pretty bird, no?"

"Perhaps that is why she has such a bad tongue, my brother," Grey Bear speculated.

"Perhaps," Man Chief agreed, "perhaps."

The Red Lances rode steadily throughout the day, stopping once at midday to rest the horses before they left the stream they were following to the southwest. They didn't stop again until they had crossed to the drainage of Big Sandy Creek, where they made camp near sundown.

Pitalesharo and Little Green Frog had not spoken to each other at all since the exchange of the morning. After the midday rest she had ridden behind Thin Cloud, for the burden of carrying double had taken its toll upon Pitalesharo's roan.

Throughout the afternoon Pitalesharo had made an effort not to look at the Comanche woman, and yet time and again he had found his gaze fixed on the slight figure clinging to the young brave. Despite his resolution he felt a fierce pang of jealousy.

When the party halted to camp, the chief's son busied himself with his horse. He led the roan downstream to graze, hobbled it and turned it into the lush grass of a meadow where the creek banks widened.

As he was thus engaged, he heard Two Boulders bellow from behind the willow brush that screened off the main campsite. "Hi, hi!" the stout warrior shouted. "You, woman without sense, what do you think you're doing?"

Pitalesharo pushed through the willows and saw Little Green Frog sitting flat on her backside holding an armload of deadwood. Two Boulders stood over her glaring. For one wild moment Pitalesharo thought that the warrior had attacked the Comanche and a red haze of unthinking rage flared behind his eyes. He leaped forward.

Two Boulders continued to fume, but Pitalesharo saw now that the bearlike man was pulling the firewood from Little Green Frog's arms and lifting her gently to her feet. "You should not be doing this. You are just a thin little thing, not much good for anything anyway, and now you are trying to kill yourself. Is that how the Comanche treat their women?"

"I was only trying to make myself useful," Frog stammered. Her eyes were very large and bright and Pitalesharo could see that she was on the verge of tears. "I do not know what happened, only my legs went out from under me."

"Humph." The next moment Two Boulders had hoisted her up as easily as if she were a child. He stood for an instant, looking one way and then the other, as if uncertain what to do with his burden now that he had it. To cover his confusion he began to bluster again.

"You," he shouted at the warriors who were standing and watching with amusement. "You all look like a bunch of foolish prairie dogs. Don't grown men have anything better to do? Thin Cloud, I think your mother mated with a porcupine and hit you over the head with a stick when you were born. That must be why you have no sense. Go spread a robe, now, and hurry—over there, under that tree where the grass is soft."

"Put me down, Two Boulders," Little Green Frog said. "I can walk now. I do not wish to be carried like an infant."

The big man ignored her protestations and carried her over to where Thin Cloud had hastily spread the robe. He laid her down very gently, still grumbling, and ordered her to remain.

Antonio Behele, who had moved up to stand at

Pitalesharo's shoulder, broke out laughing. "Who would
have guessed that the brave Two Boulders is actually a
mother bear?"

Pitalesharo managed to smile though his thoughts and
feelings were still in an uproar. "Yes, Antonio, he is like
that. Perhaps Two Boulders needs a new name—Mother
Bear."

Several of the Red Lances were laughing; Pitalesharo
knew they would give Two Boulders no peace that evening. "I think I had better go over there and make sure she
is all right," the chief's son said.

"I think that is probably a good idea," replied his
Spanish brother with a trace of a smile.

Pitalesharo strode over to where Little Green Frog lay
on the buffalo robe, protesting while Two Boulders still
hovered and fussed over her. The warrior chief stood with
his arms crossed, trying to decide what to say.

Two Boulders glanced at him. "I think the little
Comanche will be better after she rests for a night. I will
go see that the boys hurry with the fire. We need hot food.
Especially this one," the barrel-chested warrior added,
kicking playfully at the sole of Little Green Frog's moccasin. "She needs to get fat and grow big breasts so a real
warrior will wish to make love to her. But maybe the
Comanche braves like boys instead?"

"At least the Comanche do not burn women," Frog
retorted.

Two Boulders only grinned and swaggered off toward
the group of braves, where Thin Cloud and several of the
youngest Red Lances had gotten a fire burning and were
spitting chunks of venison from the deer that Spotted
Wolf had killed earlier in the afternoon.

With his garrulous friend gone, Pitalesharo felt more
tongue-tied than before. "You will be able to ride tomor-

row?'' he asked abruptly, realizing as he spoke that his tone was harsh.

Little Green Frog glanced up at him and then quickly away. ''Yes,'' she murmured. ''It is just that my legs were tired, I think.''

He remembered again the small body tied to the tree, the ankles swollen above and below the thongs that cut into them so cruelly, the slender arms stretched too high above her head. The memory made his throat knot painfully, and he wanted nothing more than to kneel beside her and take her into his arms and hold her against him. But he realized that it was foolish to think such thoughts, so he spoke again, and again his words came out harsher than he wished.

''Stand up,'' he demanded. ''I want to see if you can stand now. If you have been hurt, we will have to think what to do, for we have no medicine man with us, and your people will probably kill us if we bring you to them injured.''

''If you will give me a horse, I will ride back to my people alone,'' she snapped, her temper flaring again.

''I did not mean that,'' Pitalesharo said more gently. ''Here, give me your hand and I will help you to stand up.''

She was able to rise, but she could not hide the trembling of her legs. ''I had better sit down again,'' she said after a moment. ''I will be well in the morning, Man Chief. I will be able to ride a horse by myself if you have one for me.''

Pitalesharo helped ease her down to the blanket and for a moment remained kneeling beside her. He looked into her face, saw the lines of exhaustion, the circles like bruises under the eyes, and felt another wave of tenderness. She glanced up at him and smiled tentatively.

"Ranita Verde . . . Little Green Frog," he began and then stopped.

"What do you wish, chief's son?"

He stood abruptly. "That is not the right name for you." He turned and strode away.

As Pitalesharo approached the group at the fire, Behele called out, "Ho, chief! I feel lucky tonight. Let's wrestle for horses. Your roan nag against my magnificent paint."

Pitalesharo waved his hand absently, seeming not to have heard his blood brother's challenge. He moved to the fire, looked about as if uncertain what he was doing there, and then drew his knife and sliced a chunk of nearly raw meat from one of the haunches of roasting venison. He took his food down to the stream, where he sat on a boulder and looked out over the water.

"Lovesick," Two Boulders called, rolling his eyes and clutching with one hand at his chest and the other at his groin so that the warriors laughed uproariously.

Pitalesharo heard the laughter as if it were coming from another world. It didn't matter to him at all. The moon was nearing the full, and now with the twilight almost completely melted into night, its pale light filtered through the leaves of the alders that lined the creek and glinted in the water. In the distance a screech owl called, a trilling mating cry answered by another and then another. In the solitude and the comfort of the familiar night sounds of the prairie, the son of the chief of the Skidi Pawnee tried to make sense of a world that seemed suddenly to have shattered in a bewildering and frightening way.

He didn't hear the footsteps until the last moment, but he knew before he turned that the intruder was Antonio Grey Bear. The newcomer squatted on his haunches beside Pitalesharo and gazed in silence at the gleaming water.

Something splashed, a fish or a frog, and the owls continued their mating chorus.

"It is a pretty night, my brother," Behele ventured at length.

Pitalesharo didn't answer; the two remained in silence again for a time. Antonio waited quietly for his friend to speak of what was troubling him.

"Everything is changed, Grey Bear," he said at last.

"This is true, *mi hermano*," Behele replied. "There is a saying that only the mountains remain forever. Perhaps even that is not so."

"Our tribe is no longer a tribe. I do not know what it will be like when we return. I never thought that I would defy the priest and tear my village apart. I never believed that would happen. Perhaps it is not the same for you because you were not born among us. . . ."

Here Pitalesharo's voice faltered as if he was unsure how to continue. He stood and hurled a small stone far downstream. "I feel like a crazy man, my brother. I am a stranger to myself. I think the Pitalesharo who lay down to sleep two nights past is not the same Pitalesharo who awoke. Perhaps the night spirits sucked my soul and I am a night spirit too but do not know it."

Behele caught the edge of panic in his friend's voice and made his own words calm and light-hearted.

"Sit down, hermano," he said. "Come, let's enjoy the moonlight a little longer. I think Pitalesharo is Pitalesharo. I think my brother is in love with the little Comanche. Sometimes love makes a man feel like a stranger to himself."

"Do you know this feeling, Grey Bear, hermano? Yes, we are brothers."

"I think I do," Behele answered. "You feel as if you have found someone you have always known, one who is *a-tat*, sister, but also one you desire. It is as if you will be complete only so long as you are looking at her face. You feel you have found a part of yourself that was lost, but there is no way that you can keep it with you. You will not be able to live alone anymore, but yet you must.''

Antonio Behele's voice had taken on a tone of sadness, and Pitalesharo for a moment forgot his own troubles in discovering his friend's.

"Ah, Grey Bear. I did not know. Who?"

"It does not matter, Man Chief. There is nothing to be done about it. I promised all I had and was turned down. I have spoken with Lachelesharo about it. It is something I have lived with for a long time."

"The shaman's Cheyenne slave—the one for whom you offered a bride price?" Pitalesharo asked. "I did not know you felt so deeply for her."

"One does not die," Behele answered.

"I have thought that I would take Little Green Frog and we would go away from the others and live alone. I have destroyed my village. Maybe the wound could heal if I were not there."

"Yes," returned Grey Bear, "and then Hawk Foot will become chief when the shamans depose Lachelesharo. And the people will go back to the old ways of sacrificing captive girls to Morning Star, and Hawk Foot will lead the braves in raids on the wagon trains of the whites.

"Then the bluecoats will come in and easily kill all the people, since the whites won't trade with the Skidi and so the men will have no lead or powder for their rifles. No, perhaps the people could protect themselves with arrow and lance, and yet I think this is an idea worth considering. You have seen the soldiers at St. Louis. There are many places like St. Louis, Man Chief. There are many bluecoats and they all have rifles and ammunition."

Pitalesharo did not reply for a long time. The screech

owls broke off their calling as a chorus of coyotes began to yip and trill nearby.

"It is a very hard thing, my friend," he said at last.

"That's the truth," replied Grey Bear.

Little Green Frog, despite her best intentions, dozed for a time after Pitalesharo walked away. She awoke to find Two Boulders kicking at the soles of her moccasins again, grinning and bearing a pile of steaming venison slices on a piece of rawhide. She sat up and pushed her hair back from her face. The warrior squatted down beside her and offered her the food.

"Two Boulders," she said, still trying to wake up, "that is three times as much as I can eat."

"This? Why, this is only a snack. After you have finished this, I will bring you your real meal."

She smiled and picked up a chunk of the roasted flesh. She had not thought she was hungry, but the taste of the meat made her suddenly ravenous. The hot food released something else in her and she paused, tears suddenly filling her eyes again. "You are a very kind man, Two Boulders," she whispered.

"Ho," the round-bellied warrior laughed, "don't tell my wife that. She's terrified of me now, and I would have no peace otherwise."

"You are married, then?"

"You know her, Little Green Frog. The woman called Foolish Hen. She's nice and fat, and now she's pregnant besides. Some men like skinny women. Pitalesharo, for instance.

"I could not marry you because you are too thin. Foolish Hen is just right and she has a younger sister like her. Soon I will ask her to marry me also. It is better when a man marries sisters. The women do not fight, since they are used to sharing. After that I will get other women also. Why do you think I'm called Two Boulders?''

Little Green Frog laughed, blushed and reached for another piece of meat. Two Boulders also bit off a mouthful, and the two sat chewing together in companionable silence.

''Two Boulders?''

The warrior grunted, his mouth once again full of venison.

''Why does the son of Lachelesharo not like me? He will hardly talk to me. I know that sometimes I have a sharp tongue, but I sort of told him I was sorry. Am I too ugly, do you think? You said I was skinny,'' she finished in a rush.

Two Boulders laughed uproariously. ''So the Little Green Frog wishes to lie with the Man Chief.'' The warrior wiped the tears of mirth from his cheeks. ''I thought that all along. I am very good at figuring these things out.''

''I did not say—''

''You do not know Pitalesharo very well, Comanche. He would not run away from a hundred enemy braves the way he ran away from you. Nor would he run so from a hundred ugly women. He is a strange one. Once I offered to let him lie with Foolish Hen because I knew she would give him a good ride. But he would not do it, even though he was afraid of hurting my feelings. No, he thinks too much and has too much dignity. Do you not know that right now he is sitting by the water brooding over you?''

Little Green Frog mused upon these words and chewed at another piece of roast venison.

''If you wish to lie with the Man Chief, pretty one,'' Two Boulders added, ''I think you had better tell him so. He is very smart in other ways but oh, so stupid in the ways of a man and a woman.''

"I do not particularly wish to lie with him," Little Green Frog said, choosing her words carefully. "I do not even know what that is like, although the other women say it is pleasant. I just want to be with him always. I have not felt this way before, not even with Six Feathers in my own village. He is the one who wishes me to marry him."

"Man Chief spends too much time thinking," Two Boulders said again. "Perhaps he has never lain with a woman; I do not know. But listen. One night is better than nothing, or at least that is what I think. I had better go get some more meat before those coyotes eat it all up. The Red Lances are always very hungry." He rose and walked back toward the fire.

Chapter 4

Little Green Frog slept more soundly that night than ever before, and in the morning she found that indeed much of her strength had returned. The party made a quick meal of cold roast meat and headed out shortly after dawn. The Comanche rode alone now on a grey mare, one of the spare horses.

They traveled steadily for the next few days, always breaking camp early and riding until sundown or nearly sundown, with very few stops during the day. In spite of the grueling routine, Little Green Frog quickly regained her strength, for like all of them, she was accustomed to travel. The tired lines disappeared from her face and her natural good humor returned as well, so that in spite of what seemed a hopeless desire for the chief's son, she smiled easily and laughed often. Several of the young warriors flirted openly with her, and the others showed off shamelessly, performing tricks of horse-manship or marksmanship for her benefit, apparently unaware of the dark looks their leader occasionally shot at them.

Two Boulders most frequently rode by her side, and the two kept up a good-natured raillery in which the young Comanche gave as good as she got. The exchange lightened the tedium of the long days of monotonous travel, and Little Green Frog grew very fond of this man with the body of a bear and the face of a toad.

She frequently caught Pitalesharo looking at her, but he hardly spoke to her. This was extremely wearing on her nerves. Sometimes she thought perhaps her savior hated her after all, while at other times she was certain he desired her as much as she wanted him. Almost every night in her dreams she would imagine the two of them alone together, and he would speak words of love and touch her body in ways that caused her to awaken gasping.

They had been traveling almost due south for many days, following the base of the mountains. Behele called them the Sangre de Cristos.

One day, riding alongside her and Two Boulders, the Spaniard tried to explain to her about this Christ for whose blood his people had named the big mountains. But Little Green Frog could only shake her head, while Two Boulders laughed uproariously at the idea of worshipping a god who would let himself be nailed to a tree. Not even Old Man Coyote was that foolish, he concluded.

The Comanche had other concerns, however, for the many creeks they had been crossing during the past few days, she knew, were the headwaters of the Red River, the stream the whites called the Canadian. It would not be long before the party encountered her people.

That night she lay in her buffalo robes in an agony of indecision. What could be done? They could not marry, she and Pitalesharo. Two Boulders had said that one night was better than nothing, but perhaps one night was in truth worse than nothing. And perhaps after all the chief's son did not want her.

She was still wide awake long after the moon had risen. The pale light excited her, made the need to do something more urgent. She had almost decided to go and force Pitalesharo at least to speak his heart when a figure appeared from the shadows of the trees by the stream. Little Green Frog sat up, her heart pounding.

"Do not scream," the figure whispered. As he approached she recognized Grey Bear. He knelt beside her. "My brother sent me to get you. He wishes you to come to him. He says his heart is on fire for you and he will die if you do not come."

"Where is he?" Little Green Frog whispered urgently.

"Shh. He is up on that ridge, alone. He is a sentry tonight. I will take you to him if you wish to go and take his watch while you are there."

She rose, put on her moccasins and slipped away from the camp behind the messenger. Her heart was pounding so hard she feared it would crack her ribs.

The silver sheen of moonlight cast an aura of unreality on the sage-pocked hills. They climbed the ridge, stopping before they reached the crest. Grey Bear drew her close and pointed out the figure of Pitalesharo. He sat against a juniper so that his shadow was indistinguishable from that of the tree. Behele urged his brother's love forward a little and disappeared along the ridge.

She climbed hesitantly, feeling very shy and awkward. When she was almost to the ridge top, someone grabbed her around the waist from behind, pinning her arms to her sides. A hand covered her mouth, jerking her head back. As moonlight fell on her face Pitalesharo gave a surprised grunt, and still holding her tightly by the arm, turned her around to confront her.

"You," he whispered. "What are you doing here?"

"Your brother brought me," she replied in confusion. "Grey Bear said you wanted me to come to you."

"I did not say such a thing to Grey Bear," Pitalesharo said. Then he burst out laughing. "Hah! I think *i-ra-r-ri* is playing the matchmaker, but he is very clumsy at it."

Little Green Frog kept her eyes on the ground, her face hot with shame.

"I will go back, then," she whispered. She turned and began making her way down the ridge.

Pitalesharo made no move to stop her, but when she had stepped into the shadow of a clump of junipers, he called out, "Ranita Verde."

She waited.

"Little Green Frog," he called again, his voice suddenly thick. "Please, do not go."

She turned and walked back to the warrior, her eyes still lowered. "Grey Bear has told you how to speak my name in Spanish. You see, I know some of the Spanish words that you two use. What does the chief's son wish?" she whispered.

"I did not send Grey Bear, but I have wished for you to come to me since the first time I saw you."

"I too have wished for nothing else, Man Chief." She looked up into his face and was almost overcome by the tenderness and desire she saw there. "Perhaps it is with you just as it is with me. . . ." She breathed in deeply then, amazed at her own words.

They embraced suddenly. He pulled her tight against him and they stood that way for a small eternity. His hand stroked her hair, ran down her back to the curve of her derrière, lingered there. She felt the hardness of his desire against her belly and shuddered, moving sinuously against it. He let go of her and pulled her dress up over her head, freed it from her arms and dropped it to the ground.

He stared at her nude form in the moonlight, his gaze

running over the small firm breasts and the slim curve of her belly to the dark triangle where her legs joined. Everywhere his eyes lingered, she felt as if little fingers of flame rippled over her until she feared she would die if he didn't touch her soon. She grasped his hand and pressed it against her breast. She held her breath when he began to run his hands gently everywhere his eyes had been.

He led her to his place under the juniper, where his robe was spread, and lowered her onto the soft skin. He removed his loincloth.

She melted as she saw him in the moonlight, straight, hard, strong. "I have never lain with a man before," she whispered.

"I thought that might be so," Pitalesharo answered. "We do not need to make love if you do not wish it."

At that she pulled him against her and wrapped her legs around his waist, giggling deep in her throat.

"No, Ranita Verde, that is not the way to do it the first time." He pushed her back and knelt above her. He touched her everywhere, then at the center of her desire, moving his hands in such a way that she felt she would burst from the mounting waves of pleasure. Her body began to pulse as rivers of icy fire spread out from the center of her. She had to bite back cries of joy so that they came as little whimpers, and when they had subsided she threw her arms and her legs around her man and held him to her as tightly as she could.

He entered her then, moving slowly, slowly. The pain was intense for a moment. But then it subsided and he moved again, filling her completely at last. Even with the pain this was a new pleasure. They moved together, the ancient rhythm building, until he gasped and shuddered and then relaxed against her. They lay tangled in one another's embrace and she moved her cheek against his chest to feel the slickness of his sweat, tasting it with her tongue.

Just as she felt herself dropping into a wonderful, soft fog of sleep, the warrior suddenly groaned and pushed himself away from her. He stared at her in the moonlight as he touched gently at her face. "Beautiful one," he whispered. "Mountain Lily. Green Willow. Grass Bending in the Wind. Those are your names. But look what we have done. Your people could have come in and killed all my warriors while we were making love. I am supposed to be watching. Now I must do that."

She yawned drowsily and sat up. "Grey Bear is watching down the hill. He said he would. But I will go now, and tell him you are alert again."

"Do not go. Watch with me," he pleaded. "We can talk. We have not talked much, and there is much to say."

"I will dress, then, so we will not be distracted from watching." Then she cried out, "My dress! We left my dress on the ground down there. How will I ever find it in the dark? What will I do? I can't go down there in the morning wrapped in your robe. The Red Lances will all make fun of me."

Pitalesharo threw his head back and laughed and laughed.

The two lovers talked until dawn. They exchanged stories about their childhoods, each recalling events they had not thought they remembered. They told of dreams, of wishes, of foolish beliefs, of sadnesses and pleasures.

The next day they rode together, sometimes talking, sometimes merely gazing at one another. Two Boulders and Antonio Grey Bear teased them unmercifully for a while but lost interest when the lovers seemed not to hear them. The tall Spaniard and the barrel-chested warrior rode side by side rather disconsolately, both feeling somewhat usurped by the lovers' exclusive absorption in each other.

That night Little Green Frog and Pitalesharo made

love, slept in each other's arms and woke to make love again before dawn. For the next two days and nights they followed the same pattern.

On the third day, however, everything changed.

In midmorning Thin Cloud, who had been scouting ahead, discovered the Comanche village they sought, and Pitalesharo resumed his function as leader of the party, seeming almost to have forgotten Little Green Frog in the business of consulting with his warriors and making plans.

As for the Comanche, her heart felt like a cold stone in her chest. She had known this time would come, but its actual arrival was far worse than she had anticipated. Sometime this day, she knew, she would be reunited with her father and her mother and the rest of her family. Of course she loved them all, but sometime this day also the Pawnee warrior whom she loved more fiercely and desperately than anything else would ride away back to his people. She would never see him again.

While the Red Lances talked excitedly, making their plans, she sat to one side and tried to keep a brave face. After a time Two Boulders came and sat beside her and touched her shoulder gently. She looked at him and saw that for once his wide mouth was not smiling. His face was grave with understanding and sympathy, and Little Green Frog could no longer hold back the tears. They poured down her cheeks and for a moment she sobbed brokenly. Two Boulders put his arms around her and clumsily patted her on the back. He helplessly looked about, wishing someone would come to his rescue.

It was late afternoon when the party came down to the Comanche encampment on Ocate Creek. Pitalesharo rode a short distance in front of the others, Little Green Frog with him.

Just before they came into view of the village, he whispered, "We can be married, Mountain Lily. We can go live by ourselves. I don't want you to go back to your people. Let's turn around now and ride off. We don't need the others. I can take care of you."

Little Green Frog felt the tears starting again but blinked them back. "You know we can't do that, Man Chief. Nobody can live alone that way."

"Then I will become a Comanche."

"My people would find some reason to kill you," she replied, struggling to keep her voice even.

"My beautiful one, my Green Willow, I don't know if I can live without ever seeing you again."

His beloved was unable to reply.

As they came into sight of the Comanche tepees, a large war party rode out to meet them. The braves shouted and brandished their bows and rifles and lances as they encircled Pitalesharo's warriors. The son of Lachelesharo gave a signal and the Red Lances all discharged their rifles into the air as a sign that they came in peace.

Little Green Frog called out in Comanche, explaining the nature of Pitalesharo's mission. The warriors from the village encircled the newcomers nonetheless, still holding their weapons at the ready.

One young Comanche brave pulled his horse up in front of Pitalesharo and called out what obviously was a command. He held a Spanish rifle loosely pointed at Pitalesharo.

"Little Green Frog, what is this warrior saying?"

She hesitated. "He tells you to give me to him at once or his warriors will kill all of you. This is Six Feathers, Pitalesharo. He is the one who wishes me to marry him."

Pitalesharo's hand involuntarily moved toward his knife.

"I will not marry him now, Man Chief," Little Green Frog hastened to add. "I will never marry anyone now. Don't do anything foolish. I could not live if my people killed you."

Pitalesharo moved his hand away from his knife, but he made no move to comply with Six Feathers' demand. The two men sat glaring at one another and Pitalesharo tightened his hold on Little Green Frog.

Antonio Grey Bear moved up beside his brother and two Comanche warriors came up behind Six Feathers. At this moment of impasse an older man intervened.

He was well past the age of a warrior. His long white hair trailed behind him and his face appeared to have been carved from dried leather. The ancient one pushed his pony forward and began to berate Six Feathers. Then he turned toward Little Green Frog and opened his arms, his face cracked into a gap-toothed grin as he spoke to her in Comanche.

She replied and Pitalesharo could detect the affection in her greeting even if he couldn't understand the words.

"It's all right now, my beloved," Little Green Frog said in the tongue of the Pawnee. "This is my grandfather. You must allow me to go with him."

Pitalesharo dismounted and helped her down.

Six Feathers moved to dismount and Pitalesharo whirled toward his rival, his hand once again moving toward the knife. Little Green Frog called out sharply to the Comanche brave and he settled back onto his horse, his expression a mixture of hatred and confusion.

The former captive moved toward her grandfather. The old man dismounted and he and Little Green Frog embraced. The young Comanche woman was crying openly now.

The old man spoke loudly to the Comanche warriors

and then turned to the Red Lances and repeated his words in the Pawnee language.

"Hear what Whistling Bird says! I have seen many moons, many winters. I am not foolish like the young men. When the Pawnee visited us last time, they stole many horses and took my granddaughter as well. They came in war. But now they come in peace and bring Little Green Frog back to her people. The Comanche will forget about the horses, for we have borrowed others from the Kiowa. That is how it is with horses. For a while they belong to one man, then to another. But now our hearts are glad because the beautiful one has been returned to us."

Then Whistling Bird turned and spoke briefly with his granddaughter in Comanche.

"He wishes you to come share in a feast of celebration," Little Green Frog told Pitalesharo and the others. "He says his heart is overflowing with gladness because I have come back. He says many things like that. But I think it is best that you go now," she added, barely mouthing the words. "It will only be worse for us later."

Pitalesharo nodded. "Tell the Comanche that we are grateful for the offer of hospitality. Tell Chief Fox Shirt that Pitalesharo of the Skidi Pawnee, the son of Lachelesharo, sends him good wishes. Tell Six Feathers—"

"I will speak to all of them," Little Green Frog interrupted.

Pitalesharo stared into her eyes for a long moment. "Goodbye, Mountain Lily, Ranita Verde, beautiful Little Green Frog," he said softly.

A number of Comanche warriors escorted them out of this enemy territory. Pitalesharo and the others were aware of yet another group of warriors who trailed behind, staying out of sight but watching their movements for an additional day or so. But the son of Lachelesharo was not interested. He rode like a man in a dream, hardly speaking to his men at all.

For a time Antonio Behele left his brother alone, understanding well enough how he felt. But on the third day of their return journey, he moved up to ride beside Pitalesharo. For a short while he still didn't speak.

At length Grey Bear said musingly, as if addressing the air, "Amigo, has it ever occurred to you that Saynday, Old Man Coyote, is the god of love? When he smiles on you, he does it with his other end."

Pitalesharo stared at Grey Bear, looking for a moment as though he might strike him. Then Man Chief's face contorted and he laughed in spite of himself.

"I suppose it's better than if he never smiles at all, Juan Antonio. I only know that I feel very sad, very empty."

Chapter 5

Pitalesharo and the Red Lances camped early because they were now within a few miles of Wolf-Standing-in-Water Village and they wanted to make their entry by full daylight the following day. Indeed, if the Skidi were properly vigilant, a scout would detect their presence and bear word of their arrival to Lacheleshoro. Not only would a welcome of some sort be certain, but the chief would be able to send someone out to inform his son as to the situation within the village.

"Perhaps we should take no chances," Behele suggested. "I will ride on to the village and slip into our father's lodge after dark. That way there will be no surprises for us."

Pitalesharo dismounted and turned his roan free to graze on the bunch grasses and young willow brush that grew along the banks of the small stream. "Good idea, my brother. Spotted Wolf likes to bear messages, and besides, he's been sleeping all afternoon. Once or twice

I was afraid he would fall from his pony and break his neck.''

"I was not asleep at all," Spotted Wolf protested. "I think you were asleep, Pitalesharo. The Man Chief only dreamed the Spotted Wolf was dozing. I do not need to rest at all."

Behele laughed.

"Good," Pitalesharo said. "Then you will be glad to ride on to the village and tell my father that we will arrive by midmorning. But do not spend so much time making love to that little wife of yours that you fall asleep and forget to ride back to tell us what Lachelesharo says."

"He doesn't sleep, remember?" Behele grinned. "He's a good one for this venture."

"Of course," Spotted Wolf agreed. "I will be back before the night is half over. There will be plenty of time later for me to lie with my wife." Pitalesharo slapped the warrior's horse on its rump and Spotted Wolf rode off toward the north.

The Red Lances built several small fires and set to roasting portions of an antelope that Behele had taken with his Kentucky rifle earlier that day. The Pawnee were glad to be back in their own lands once again, and the conversation that night was jovial and animated. Soon it would be time for the great buffalo hunt, and the warriors who proved most successful would be much in demand among the young women of the village. There would be many buffalo robes to sell to Papin the trader, and quantities of dried meat would be put into storage against times when game proved scarce.

Pitalesharo, Behele and Two Boulders sat together about one fire and ate great quantities of meat. When they were contentedly gorged, Pitalesharo filled his pipe with long-stemmed tobacco, lit it, puffed and passed it to Behele.

Several times the pipe made its circuit among the three men, and yet no one spoke.

At last Two Boulders said, "It is very strange."

"What's strange, amigo?" Behele asked.

"It is all very strange," Two Boulders continued. "I did not think our leader would actually return Little Green Frog to her people. Even when we drew close to the Comanche village I still did not believe it. Is it not true that you are in love with that one, Pitalesharo?"

The leader of the Red Lances replaced the pipe in its sheath, appeared thoughtful for a moment and then nodded.

"Yes, old friend. If she had been one of our own people, I would have wished her to be my wife. That is true."

"What difference does it make that she is Comanche?" Two Boulders persisted. "Many Pawnee women came from other villages and even from other tribes, and yet they are Skidi now. I think Little Green Frog would have been happy to be a Skidi. No one would wish to be a Comanche if he had a choice."

Behele grinned and whistled.

"Perhaps the Comanche say the same thing about Pawnee," Pitalesharo suggested.

"No," Two Boulders insisted. "That would be very foolish. Not even Comanche are that foolish. Only white men are."

"I am a white man," Behele pointed out.

"That is not true, Grey Bear. Once you were Spanish, but not now. I was just a child, but I remember. The Comanche killed your parents as they were on their way to the Santa Fe villages. After that Lacheleshakó found you. You were very skinny when you first came to live with us, and we had to teach you how to talk because you didn't know how."

"I knew how to talk my own language," Behele

protested. "By now I have forgotten most of it, but I knew then."

"That does not matter," Two Boulders went on. "We had to teach you to talk, Pitalesharo and I and Buffalo Runner. We taught you. And after that the head chief took you as an adopted son instead of a slave because you and Pitalesharo had made yourselves into blood brothers. Even Hawk Foot helped to teach you how to talk."

"Hawk Foot," Pitalesharo mused. "We were all friends then, weren't we? In those days he was the only one I couldn't always beat at wrestling. Do you remember when we all rode off on our ponies and nearly got captured by the Kiowa? We were lucky to get away. Or perhaps the Kiowa felt sorry for us and let us outride them. Maybe that is what happened."

"Our ponies were too fast for them!" Two Boulders was scandalized that his friend should entertain such a thought. "That was a long time ago, but it doesn't seem very long, does it? I do not really feel any older than I did then."

"That's because he isn't any older," Grey Wolf laughed. "Not in his head. Two Boulders, you're a man-child who will never grow up. You will still be ten winters old even when you're as bald as Papin the trader."

"Only white men go bald," Two Boulders said.

"Is that true?" Pitalesharo asked. "Are none of our old men bald?"

"Maybe a few," Two Boulders admitted, "but I will never lose my hair."

"Not until the Cheyenne scalp him," Behele suggested.

"Not even then. But I still do not understand why you gave Little Green Frog back to the Comanche, Pitalesharo. I think she loves you too. So why didn't you keep her and make her your wife? All of us should have wives. I have one and Spotted Wolf has one; some of the others do too. Why is neither of you interested in having a woman to sleep with? When the winter comes, you keep each other warm.''

''Two Boulders would die if he had no woman,'' Behele laughed. ''His testicles are so large that he must have a woman every night or they will explode and kill him.''

Pitalesharo burst out laughing and Two Boulders' wide mouth spread even wider as he grinned, apparently pleased with Behele's assessment. ''That is not what my name means, you dog of a Spanish. Still, it is true that the sack between my legs is larger than anyone else's. If I am successful at the buffalo hunting and after that at trapping the beavers and the otters, maybe I will take a second wife. One woman is not enough for me.''

''How could I have married Little Green Frog?'' Pitalesharo demanded. ''If I kept her with me in the village, there would always be hard feelings between my father and Wounded Man. Perhaps there will be in any case. Besides, I do not think the other women would ever have accepted her, not after they had seen her bound to the tree and nearly burned to death. A man is often gone from the village, and a woman must have friends. Who would be willing to be friends with Little Green Frog after what happened?''

''Hummingbird was her friend,'' Behele said, gazing off into the night sky.

''Yes, she proved that. Hummingbird was the only one who was willing to care for her and to stay by her. I think she meant to allow herself to be burned alive along with Little Green Frog.''

''Then Hawk Foot carried her away. Hawk Foot wants her, but Wounded Man says his nephew must not marry a Cheyenne, only a Skidi. I suppose such a marriage would also make Morning Star angry.''

"She doesn't want Hawk Foot?" Two Boulders asked. "You used to meet with her down by the willows before you went with Termite Joe to the white man's villages. Perhaps you are the one she wants, Grey Bear."

"Two Boulders is very observant," Pitalesharo chuckled. "He keeps track of who meets whom, just like an old woman."

"Someone has to keep track," Two Boulders complained.

"The fire has died down, my friends," the Red Lance leader said. "I think it is time to sleep now. I just saw Buffalo Runner walk off toward the crest to stand watch."

The three men unrolled their buffalo robes and within a few moments Two Boulders was snoring loudly. "The wolves will not eat us, at least," Behele said into the darkness. "They will think we have a white bear sleeping next to us."

"Tomorrow we will be home again," Pitalesharo answered.

Spotted Wolf got back to the camp about midnight with word that the village was still in a state of agitation, with Wounded Man continuing to berate the people for their failure to make sacrifice to the powerful god Morning Star. He was still calling for one. However, Spotted Wolf told the others, Lachelesharo had the village in hand at the moment and would welcome his son's return the next day.

The coyotes had been crying in the distance when Spotted Wolf returned and Antonio Behele relieved Buffalo Runner at watch. Now it was nearly dawn and the coyotes once again were setting up their yipping and yowling on the crest above the Red Lance encampment.

"What's disturbing them?" Behele wondered.

The adopted Pawnee worked his way down along the

crest in the general direction of the noise. The endless sea of short grasses and rocky outcroppings that spread out toward the east was only faintly visible in the silver grey light of false dawn. The morning star, low over the far horizon, glowed in the east.

Behele discovered nothing unusual but at last came face to face with a pair of coyotes sitting on their haunches beside a great worn boulder that jutted from the grassy crest.

"Good morning, brothers," Behele greeted them. "I came to see what was wrong."

The coyotes did not move.

"Perhaps you were just playing games with me, then? Or were you annoying a puma on its way home from hunting?"

One of the coyotes suddenly rose on its hind legs, danced about and took off running. The other ran too, chasing its friend. They vanished into the shadows beyond the rim.

The morning air was chilly and odors of dry grass and sage drifted in the gently moving flow of wind. Behele grinned; he felt almost like shouting, like singing. The whole, vast earth seemed laid out at his feet, emerging from the shadows of night at peace with itself. The lone human being who observed it all felt at peace also.

Then from the low rise beyond the encampment came the distinctive crack and echo of a buffalo rifle.

Voices and shouts rang from the camp.

Behele, his rifle held tight to his side, began to run downslope, leaping small boulders and plunging into the shadows of the little basin through which the stream flowed.

Horses whinnied and stamped with excitement.

*　　　*　　　*

Pitalesharo came awake in a moment, a numbness in his leg. He grabbed for his rifle and hobbled to the cover of a dwarf cedar.

"Man Chief," Two Boulders cried out, "are you wounded? Someone is shooting at us."

Pitalesharo felt a painful bruise just below his knee. The numbness was giving way to a sharp pain.

Several Red Lance rifles cracked now, ineffectual but at least letting the attacker know that the camp was awake and ready to defend itself.

Then another shot echoed from partway up the ridge crest.

"Behele," Pitalesharo said. "He's found the one who attacked us."

Buffalo Runner and Spotted Wolf were immediately on their way to assist Grey Bear. They found him alone.

"Just one man." Behele shook his rifle. "He must have left his pony in the aspen grove on the other side of the rise. I caught a glimpse of him as I was coming back down. I threw a shot at him, but the distance was too great. I missed him, I'm certain."

"No Comanche would have followed us this far alone. It doesn't make sense. Was he a white man, do you think?"

"The coyotes were yipping when Spotted Wolf returned in the middle of the night. Maybe someone followed him."

"Four hours later?" Pitalesharo asked, shaking his head. "Not unless the man followed and then waited for the first light. But that doesn't make sense either. No one would do that."

The Red Lances gathered about their leader, whose bruise was the only hurt of the singular and brief attack. The men of the warrior society talked in a confusion of voices, one suggesting this explanation, another that. But nothing could be deduced and eventually the warriors set to building up the fires from the preceding night.

When the sun rose, Behele reached for Pitalesharo's rifle and examined the barrel. A portion of the forestock of the J&S Hawken was splintered and the heavy hexagonal barrel bore a distinctive grey-black lead marking.

"What is this?" Behele asked. "What happened to the gun?"

Pitalesharo took hold of his prized flintlock and examined the damaged wood. "The shot must have been aimed at me as I slept. My rifle was lying on top of my robes, across my legs. The bullet struck the barrel of my weapon and gave me the bruise."

Behele stared at the Hawken and shook his head. "The enemy must have fired from over there, near that ledge," he remarked, pointing. "*Hunnert yards*, as Termite Joe would say. But how did he know—"

"It was I? My headdress hung from the branch, perhaps. You think it was I the man wished to kill?"

Behele shrugged. Two Boulders ran his fingers over the damaged stock of the rifle, then spoke. "Hawk Foot. He followed Spotted Wolf from the village and waited until it was almost light."

"Hawk Foot," the leader of the Red Lances whispered, glancing from one of his companions to the other. "Yes, or someone he sent to kill me as I slept. But you didn't recognize him, did you, Grey Bear?"

"Too dark. Only a glimpse."

"Hawk Foot alone would have had reason, and it would have been seen as a sign that I had brought the god's anger upon myself. We will say nothing of this when we reach the village. If it was Hawk Foot, he will give himself away at some point, and I will be watching. Antonio, you follow the trail of his pony. He will not have gone directly back to Wolf-Standing-in-Water Village. He will ride toward the mountains first, up through the rocky plateaus, and then come down to the village from the other side.''

Behele nodded, rolled up his robes, fastened the bundle behind the half-saddle Termite Joe had given him and mounted. ''See if Hawk Foot is in the village when you get there.'' He turned his spotted stallion and rode toward the ridge crest. It was full dawn and sunlight glinted from the smooth surfaces of sandstone beyond the little stream.

The Skidi welcomed the return of Pitalesharo and the Red Lances as if the warriors were returning from a successful war party. Pitalesharo led his braves into the common area near the main fire pit, raised his rifle and drew his roan to a halt.

Lachelesharo was waiting and embraced his son. He glanced at the damaged rifle and looked a question at Pitalesharo.

''We have done what we set out to do,'' his son replied. ''The Comanche were glad to have the daughter of Chief Fox Shirt back among her own people. He is one of their most powerful warriors, Father, and would soon have ridden the warpath against us. Now I do not think he will, not for a time, at least.''

''It is good,'' Lachelesharo answered. ''But where is Juan Antonio Grey Bear? Why is he not among your warriors, Pitalesharo?''

''He will be here soon, I think. Grey Bear has followed a different path home. I will speak of this when we are in the lodge. Have you seen Hawk Foot this morning? There is something that I would like to tell him.''

Lachelesharo shrugged his big shoulders. ''He is with his uncle, I think. I saw the two of them together just before you entered the village.''

The people were crowding about now, as they invariably did whenever a party returned from hunting or the warpath.

Pitalesharo and his father walked quickly to the head chief's lodge and entered. Termite Joe Hollingback and Pierre Didier Papin were seated inside, eating from baskets of parched corn and venison that Raven Quill had served them.

"Ah, lad," Hollingback said, trying to swallow and speak at the same time, "it's good to have you back. Me and Pierre was afraid the catamounts might have et you."

"Man Chief, *mon ami*," Papin laughed, "did you deliver the pretty one back to her people, then? *Enfant de Dieu*, you have made the long ride quickly. Soon you will be trapping the beavers for M. Papin."

"What in blazes you done to your Hawken, Juan Pete? Looks to this nigger like you shot her with your pistol or something."

Pitalesharo nodded. "Or something."

"Where's Antonio? Ain't nothing happened to the nigger, is there?"

"He'll be here soon, Juan Termite," Pitalesharo answered. "Does either of you happen to know if Hawk Foot has been away from the village this morning?"

"Saw him with Wounded Man a leetle while back," Termite Joe answered.

"Yes," Papin said, "he was here somewhere. I saw his horse tethered beside Wounded Man's lodge. The animal, she was very sweaty, had been run hard. I notice these things."

"They some connection between your gun and Hawk Foot's pony?" Hollingback asked, raising an eyebrow.

"Grey Bear will tell us when he arrives at the village," Pitalesharo answered.

*   *   *

Behele came in early that afternoon and Pitalesharo walked out to meet him. "Did the deer you were hunting get away from you, my brother?"

"Not exactly. The one who shot at you was a Skidi. The trail I followed led back to the village, just as we thought it would."

Chapter 6

The following day Hawk Foot led his Thunderbird Lance warriors out of the village on a warpath against the Ute. Within four days the Pawnee had returned, making a victorious entry into camp. Several of the braves held up scalps as they yipped and gestured dramatically. Others were wearing various garments obviously not of Indian manufacture.

"Some whites were leading a supply caravan along Smoky Hill River," Hawk Foot said. "We approached these men and asked for presents in exchange for crossing our lands. Perhaps they misunderstood my words; I do not know. When they began shooting at us, we surrounded them, just as we do the buffalo. After that we waited for a while.

"When the Thunderbird Lances grew restless, someone shot a fire arrow into the whites' big wagon. In a little while it all blew up. Those men must have been taking gunpowder to our enemies, the Comanche or the Kiowa.

But then the other white men began to ride away, everyone in a different direction. Some of them we killed. After that we found a crate of rifles they had left behind and nearly twenty handguns, the kind Pitalesharo has. Now my warriors will be as well armed as his and the Skidi will not have to fear an attack from anyone.''

Lachelesharo nodded, accepting the result of the war party, for there was little else he could do. The whites, after all, had made the first offer of battle. But word of the attack would find its way back to St. Louis, and Red-haired Chief, Governor Clark, would not be pleased.

Wounded Man praised the victory and declared that the honor of the Skidi had been preserved. ''But more must be done,'' the shaman declared. ''Morning Star and the other sky spirits are still not happy with this people. The voices I hear sometimes tell me this is so. This night the Skidi will celebrate by having a scalp dance and the brave young men will recount their victories and enact them for all to see. We are a fighting people; it is from war that we gain our strength. This is good. But while you dance and celebrate, I shall climb to the pointed boulders high above the village of Wolf-Standing-in-Water and pray for guidance. Perhaps this will give me the vision I seek.'' With that Wounded Man turned and strode away into his own lodge.

Termite Joe Hollingback watched the shaman disappear and then glared at the strutting Hawk Foot. ''Them scalps might be the hair of some old compañeros of ours, for all we know,'' he said to Papin. ''This here's one victory dance I don't aim to watch. Wagh!''

Papin nodded. *''C'est vrai.* Better we should not know who these *hommes* were.''

On the night following the scalp dance Wounded Man appeared suddenly before the great fire at the center of the village. The scar across his face was painted with ocher and white clay and the blind eye was completely encircled with vermilion. Hawk Foot and most of his Thunderbird Lances were also present.

The shaman called out that he had seen a vision. He began to chant and gyrate slowly. Word of the incipient announcement spread quickly, and before Wounded Man had finished his dance, nearly half of the village had assembled in anticipation.

The medicine man stopped dancing, closed his one good eye and seemed to fall into a trance. The throng grew hushed. Several minutes passed in a silence marred only by the occasional yelp of a camp dog and the hooting of a horned owl.

Wounded Man twisted slowly, raised his hands high above his head and groaned. Blood rushed from his mouth, a vomit of blood that was taken in basins by two of Hawk Foot's men who immediately came forward as though the event had been planned in advance. The spectacle was stunning, and the women present began to cry and scream with fright.

"I have spoken to Morning Star," Wounded Man cried out, his voice high and frenzied. "I lay unclothed beneath the light of the heavens and took the voice of the god into my body. Hear me, Skidi Pawnee! Hear what Morning Star commands of you. For countless winters the Pawnee have made human sacrifice, cutting out the heart of the victim and burning the body. And because we were faithful in doing this, Morning Star favored us and allowed us to win victory after victory over our enemies. But now we have ceased to do as the god wishes, and so we are being punished and tested.

"White men come into our lands. They divert the young men from the warpath and encourage them to hunt for furs along the streams instead of pursuing those who hate us. And what do these white men give us in return? The stale urine that makes us into fools, that makes us drunk. The white men give us foolish trinkets for our women, and the women spend all their time admiring themselves in little hand mirrors. They demand the white man's colored cloth instead of weaving their own, instead of fashioning their clothing from the hides of deer and elk in the way of their mothers. This is what happens, Pawnee!

"And yet the traders themselves are not our true enemies. That is what Morning Star has told me. No, Skidi, we are our own enemies. We have grown weak from adopting the ways of the white men. Perhaps some of you actually wish to become like the whites, but that is not what Morning Star wishes."

The shaman paused, turned in a circle and then stepped quickly toward the crowd, which fell back with shrieks of terror. "We must grow strong once again," he cried. "We must regain our strength if we are to withstand the white men who have come into our lands. I tell you, there are many whites, not just the few that we have seen. No, far to the east where the sun rises there are great villages of whites. When Lachelesharo makes peace with these white men—and that is what he intends—then more whites will come into our lands, always more and more. They will turn us into drunken fools and take our lands away from us.

"The chief has seen these villages of the whites, and he knows what they have done to the tribes who once hunted on the lands where lie the great villages of the whites. Lachelesharo, do I see you? Do you dare to deny my words? No, because you cannot. And yet these are the people you would have us make peace with."

Many of the Pawnee now turned to stare at the chief, who stood beside Pitalesharo, Antonio Grey Bear Behele and the two white traders.

"Morning Star has caused me to vomit the sacred

blood,'' Wounded Man screamed. ''He is angry because the Comanche was taken away from him, and now he demands another sacrifice. My nephew Hawk Foot wishes to marry the Cheyenne slave I keep in my lodge, even though I do not wish him to.

''But now she must be sacrificed. Hawk Foot knows that my words are the words of Morning Star and he agrees with me. He has given his consent to the death by fire of the Cheyenne called Hummingbird. He will cut out her living heart while all of you watch, even though it will be like cutting out his own heart. He will do this because he knows that the god has spoken through me.

''Pawnee women! Go now and gather what fuel you can find, even though it is already dark. Hawk Foot will go to my lodge, for I have told the Cheyenne to remain there this night. He will bring her to the elder tree and bind her to it. This night we will finish the sacrifice that was begun before. I have spoken. But the words are not mine. They are the words of Morning Star!''

Pitalesharo was stunned by the dramatic effect of the shaman's words on the people. And Lachelesharo could only shake his head in silence.

''Crazy as a shithouse rat,'' Termite Joe muttered. ''That blood-spitting bastard is goddamned determined to butcher some female. Wagh! For a good chaw of tobacco this child would put a couple ounces of lead in him.''

''*Sacré bleu!*'' Pierre Papin gasped in agreement. It took no great visionary powers for the two traders to perceive that they themselves might find themselves bound to a burning tree if Wounded Man gained ascendancy in the village.

Pitalesharo turned to say something to Behele, but Grey Bear had disappeared.

*   *   *

A single warrior stood guard before the entry to Wounded Man's lodge. Behele crept close. He pitched a stone at a sleeping dog and the animal yipped and tore into one of his fellows, resulting in a noisy dog fight.

When the guard turned to kick at the struggling dogs, Behele was on him. He clubbed him senseless with a war axe, then entered the darkened lodge. He called out to the Cheyenne.

"Grey Bear?" she whispered. "You must not come in here. Go now! Wounded Man will be furious; he will have me whipped."

"No time to argue, little one. Grab your extra moccasins and come with me. The shaman just finished a big speech. Big medicine. He intends to burn you alive."

"No, he would never do such a thing."

"No time to argue. You come and no screaming. If you make noise, I'll cut your throat myself. Even that would be better than what they've got planned for you."

Behele stepped forward, groped in the darkness for her hair and dragged her to him. With another motion he clapped his big hand over her mouth and was pushing her out of the shaman's lodge.

Someone was coming! Two pitch-pine torches lit the darkness.

"If you wish to live, make no sound." Behele twisted Hummingbird about and flopped her over his shoulder. She gasped but said nothing and he hurried away.

Two horses stamped in the darkness. Two Boulders had them in hand. "Have you got her? Hawk Foot will be very angry when he finds the lodge empty. But perhaps he will think Hummingbird has run off to meet with a lover."

"Not when he finds the guard unconscious by the doorway."

Shouts came from the village. The light from several pine-pitch torches moved about.

"Is it true, what Grey Bear has told me?" Humming-bird stared up at Two Boulders.

"It is true. Go now. Ride far away, Juan Antonio. Do not return for many days. We will think of something. Man Chief will think of something. It is well known that you have had eyes for this woman. The Thunderbird Lances will come to search for you, for they will say you have stolen the shaman's slave. Not even Knife Chief will be able to prevent them. Where will you go?"

"Far away, just as you have said. Remember, Two Boulders, you know nothing of this. You must not speak of it even to Pitalesharo. It will be better for him if he does not know. Better for you, too. Then he will be able to speak the truth when he denies any knowledge."

"I have not seen you this night, Juan Antonio."

Behele and Hummingbird mounted and rode away from the village, heading west for the badlands and then the high prairies that lay at the foot of the great front range of the Shining Mountains.

Before dawn Behele glanced back to where the morning star hung above the eastern horizon, gritted his teeth and urged his grey stallion ahead.

"Will we never be able to stop?" Hummingbird asked. "I'm afraid I will fall asleep."

"We will rest only when it is safe to do so," Behele answered. "Do you wish to ride with me so that you can hang on?"

"Yes—no. I will not fall asleep. I will do what you tell me, Grey Bear. Why would the medicine man wish to kill me? I have served him well; I have not complained. Even though I was a slave, I have been a good slave to him."

"He has lain under the stars too many times. Part of him has become like a wolf with rabies, one that spits foam and bites at everything around him. But what it really is, he wants to see to it that Hawk Foot becomes the new chief. Wounded Man hates Lachelesharo so much that he can see nothing else. He will do anything to destroy Knife Chief. How could you live with him and not know that? He is willing to destroy our people if he can bring down Lachelesharo at the same time. Hatred like that obliterates everything that is good in a man.''

They rode on in silence after that. Later the sun rose, flooding the barren, ragged canyon with its light.

Ever upward they pressed and by midday had passed beyond the uppermost reaches of the tributary, a series of marshy meadows nearly encircled by grotesque benches of weathered sandstone. Behele filled a leather flask with water from the dripping ooze of a clay bank, urged Hummingbird to hurry when she sought the privacy of the willows to attend to the needs of her body. Then they remounted to continue the grueling ride.

The late summer sun, huge and white, bore down upon them like some malign presence, but Hummingbird did not complain now. She grimly clung to the back of her mount, her mind dull and empty and her eyes closed nearly to slits, following the tall man on the big horse.

"We must keep going," he said after they had ridden in leaden silence for a long while. "Hawk Foot and the Thunderbird Lances are behind us somewhere." His voice sounded cracked, like mud that had dried in the sun.

Hawk Foot? He wishes me to marry him, I am certain of that. Have I been taken for a fool? Is this Grey Bear's way of having me for himself? I do not understand.

"We must keep going, Hummingbird," he repeated.

From a rise in the plateau they could see the high mountains, still far to the west. The peaks seemed to hang like a great metal curtain above the blue-purple haze, portions still snow-streaked even this late in the year. The

high wall where the ice never melted beckoned them on
with a subjective but powerful force.

"Three days' ride from here—perhaps only two; I am
not certain—is a place where we will be safe, Hummingbird."

*Does he suppose he had to do all this to make me
want him? He is the one I have wanted all along. I will
follow him. I do not know what will happen next, but I will
follow him. I wonder if he will allow me to sleep tonight?
How can he keep going? No one can live without sleeping,
not even Antonio Grey Bear. I have always heard that the
white men lack endurance. Grey Bear is white. How can
he keep going?*

Wolf-Standing-in-Water Village was still in an uproar. It was supposed that the Cheyenne had somehow
become aware of what was about to happen to her and
knocked out the guard, the Thunderbird Lance named Mad
Crow, with a staff. Hawk Foot had ordered his soldiers to
spread out in a widening circle around the village, thor-
oughly searching the willow thickets. Another group, the
Dog Soldiers, in their role as village police went from
lodge to lodge seeking her. All the dwellings were searched,
save only that of Lachelesharo, for Pitalesharo's Red Lances
stood before the entry and refused to allow the Dog Soldiers to enter.

Reporting with this information to Wounded Man
and Hawk Foot, the police soldiers suggested strongly
that the slave must surely be inside. A great deal of
angry muttering went up against Knife Chief and his son.
Wounded Man directed the Dog Soldiers to encircle the
Red Lances to make certain that the Cheyenne was not able
to flee.

When morning came, Wounded Man chose to visit

the chief. Lacheleshareo welcomed the shaman inside, motioned for him to be seated and called to Raven Quill to bring food.

The shaman declined. He stared into the head chief's eyes. "Do you have my slave hidden somewhere?"

"No. When I heard she had vanished, I supposed Morning Star had grown impatient and taken her with him into the spirit world."

"May I search?"

"Of course," Lacheleshareo gestured with an open hand. "You may look as long as you wish. Perhaps I have put her into the little box over there, or in the basket on the shelf. If I had your magic, Wounded Man, I might be able to do such a thing. But as it is, I have no medicine of that kind. And you can see quite plainly that she is not here. What was her name again?"

Wounded Man stood up, glanced disdainfully about the lodge, nodded and left.

Shortly after that word came to Hawk Foot that no one had seen Grey Bear all morning. The warrior chief flew into a rage and sought out his uncle. "The Spaniard has taken Hummingbird. He is gone from the village. No one has seen him. He is the one who followed her about as though she were a bitch in heat. He has taken her away."

Again Wounded Man visited Lacheleshareo. This time the medicine man was sputtering with half-restrained rage.

"What can I do?" Lacheleshareo asked. "Even if what you say is true, I am helpless in the matter. Grey Bear is as a son to me, but I cannot control his actions. I was there when you addressed the people. Pitalesharo was there also. Neither of us is responsible for what has happened.

"Perhaps you should have agreed to give the Cheyenne to Grey Bear when he first approached you with an offer of five ponies and several pairs of moccasins. So now he has taken without payment what he had earlier been willing to buy. When men are in love, Wounded Man, they do desperate things. Now if he returns with her in two weeks, she will be his wife, and you will have to name the bride price that he first offered you. That is our way, given to us by Saynday and Morning Star and Tirawa Atius the creator himself.''

"This man has stolen my slave," Wounded Man insisted. "She is not like the other young women. She is a Cheyenne and she belongs to me."

Lachelesharo made the gesture of helplessness.

By noon the Red Lances and the Thunderbird Lances were facing off against one another, on the verge of breaking the most sacred of taboos, violence within the tribe. Pitalesharo and Hawk Foot glared at one another, neither speaking, each ready to leap at the other.

At this point Lachelesharo and Wounded Man found it convenient to act in accord. Together they stepped forward bearing the pipe, signifying that friendly relations would have to be restored and that the truce so effected would be enforced by the Dog Soldiers, the Brave Ravens and the Two Lances.

Pierre Papin also sought to intervene, offering the would-be combatants whiskey, gunpowder, coffee beans and various mirrors, beads and trinkets for their women. After that it did not take long for the sullen faces to clear. The Red Lances and Thunderbird Lances alike found their way to the post and took possession of the gifts.

"*Merde alors*," Papin moaned when the bribes had been distributed. "The company, it will take my job away. And yet Pilcher himself has told me that I must keep the peace. But what will he say when I am required to report what has happened? These savages will now have plenty of trouble every day."

"Ain't no goddamned way to run a trading post, that's for sure," Termite Joe agreed. "Think this child could do us all a leetle favor by putting a couple rounds of lead into old Scar Face and his nephew? Longer I think upon it, the more sense she makes, sure as buffalo dung."

"How does one keep the peace with such people?" Papin demanded. "Perhaps it would be better to poison all of them, mon ami."

Chapter 7

For two days more they rode westward over level prairie.
Great numbers of antelope drifted across the dry grasslands
and Behele was able to find water by following their trails.
The buffalo herds were moving south, the great animals in
no apparent hurry and yet all seemingly of one mind.
Behele and Hummingbird drew up their ponies to wait
while one huge herd passed before them.

"So many of them, so many," Hummingbird said.
"No number is large enough to count them all."

Behele nodded and gazed away toward the north.
The herd, perhaps as much as a mile in width, flowed
like a huge brown river of hoof and flesh and fur,
filling the horizon before them. "The tribes will never
be hungry so long as the buffalo people are among us,"
he said.

The strong stench of the animals carried to them on
the wind. "Why would the buffalo ever go away?" Hummingbird asked. "Where would they go? There are so

many that we will always be able to find them again. They cannot hide like the deer or the elk.''

"Soon it will be time for the Skidi to make their fall hunt," Behele mused, "and we will not be there. We will have to make our own hunt, dry our own meat. We will not be able to rely upon the others any more, little bird.''

"We will draw out the *recki* and cook it over the coals of our fire," Hummingbird said. "The small intestine—*boudin* the French call it. That is a strange word.''

"We are wanderers now," Behele agreed. "We will have to be our own tribe.''

"Perhaps we could go to live among the Cheyenne," Hummingbird suggested. "It has been four years, but my people will still remember me. If you are my husband, they will accept you, Grey Bear.''

Behele stared at the vast numbers of buffalo and considered Hummingbird's suggestion. There were several possibilities. Going to the Cheyenne was one. Far to the south lay the Spanish settlements of Santa Fe and Taos— but too much time had passed. He would be regarded as an Indian now. In fact, that was precisely what he was—a Skidi Pawnee.

And of course to the northeast lay the village of St. Louis and the world of the Americans. Could he and Hummingbird be accepted there? He considered the possibility of hiring on as a trapper or hunter with Pilcher and the Missouri Fur Company. His connections with such men as Papin and Hollingback might put him in good stead with the company. They might be willing to give him a chance.

He felt a great emptiness. In truth he wished for nothing more than to continue living among his friends in the village of Wolf-Standing-in-Water. In his own lodge with Hummingbird as his wife. Was there any possible way of going back? Even as the adopted son of the chief, was it conceivable?

"Do you wish to be my wife?" he asked suddenly.

"I have wanted that for a long while," Hummingbird answered. "Always I have been most happy when I knew that you were near me. Often I would think of errands for Wounded Man so that I might go where I thought you were. And when you offered a bride price to the shaman, my heart soared like the birds of the air. I thought he would allow me to marry you instead of Hawk Foot. I do not wish to lie with him, Grey Bear. I wish only to lie with you."

"But Wounded Man turned me away. And after that I learned that he refused to allow Hawk Foot to marry you either. Some of the men thought then that he wished you for himself—not as a slave but as a woman."

"I thought that too for a while, but he never approached my sleeping place. I used to think I would stab him with one of the steel knives if he ever tried to force me. I would have hated that."

Behele continued to gaze out at the moving buffalo. The end of the herd was in sight. Soon they would have to push on.

Behele thought about the fall hunt. Sometimes the great animals were driven by men on horseback onto a bench or plateau and then over the cliffs, the beasts falling to death on the boulders below. But most often a portion of a herd would be worked into a surround. Then the warriors would ride in or run in on foot to kill the animals with the short bow and wide-headed arrows or the white man's rifle.

But now, with the demands of the white fur traders, more buffalo were being killed than the people needed for meat. A single skilled hunter could take enough buffalo to keep several women occupied preparing the skins, particularly if he had a fine buffalo-running horse. Such an animal was valued as much as a good war pony. Because of the hide-taking good hunters had taken more than one wife, some as many as six, seven, even more. The more hides he took, the more wives he could buy. Such a man grew very powerful. The hides purchased guns, ammunition, tobacco, trinkets for the women, magic chants, medicine bundles. One man among the Pitahauerats Pawnee was reputed to have acquired more than twenty wives in this fashion and was consequently far more powerful than even the head chief, the warrior White Cougar.

The herd finally passed and Behele nudged his big paint. They resumed their westward ride.

Before them rose the highest of the peaks in the front range of the Shining Mountains. Pike's Peak, as Termite Joe called it, named for an American officer who tried unsuccessfully to climb it. But to the Skidi it was *Karitkucu,* the Big Rock.

High above the plain on the great mountain's south side was a cave whose mouth opened at the head of a lush meadow surrounded by spruces. Behele remembered it from several years earlier when he and Pitalesharo and Two Boulders crossed the mountains to steal ponies from the Ute on their first real warpath. Game would be plentiful there and they would be safe from pursuit.

Almost certainly Pitalesharo would follow them when he was free to do so, but would he remember the cave and conclude that his blood brother had gone there?

Shortly before they reached the big stream that came down from the mountain, Behele noted that a buffalo skull had been placed atop a small cairn of stones, a medicine skull, to ensure good luck at hunting.

Behele dismounted and scribed the sign for cave on the white bone of the skull. "Pitalesharo will find this mark when he searches for us," Behele told Hummingbird. "It will not be difficult to follow our trail this far."

It was much cooler high above the plains, and the stream running along the edge of the meadow provided an abundance of fish. Hummingbird reached under the bank where the trout hid during daylight and flipped several out of the water.

Behele was amazed at her dexterity. "I'll never have to hunt again," he laughed.

"Fish are smart too," Hummingbird replied. "Soon the word will spread among them, and then it will not be so easy to catch our dinner. Then we will have to find another stream."

The horses, happy for the long journey to be over, sported in the thick green grass of the meadow, snorting and whinnying with delight, nipping at each other and sloshing through the damper areas where clouds of gnats hovered in the thin late afternoon light.

"Mosquitoes," Behele complained as he encamped at the mouth of the cave. The opening looked out over the long, narrow meadow in a way that provided visibility in all directions while allowing protection for the new tenants.

At one side of the cave mouth was an old fire pit. The rocky face above it was stained black from many fires. Inside, faintly revealed in the dim reflected light were paintings on the rock in red, yellow, and white—scenes of hunting, of battle, of serpents that ate their own tails, buffalo and strange animals that neither Behele nor Hummingbird recognized.

"The Ancient Ones must have lived here," she reflected. "Perhaps that was long ago, when Coyote Man caused the world to be covered with water. Perhaps the Ancient Ones came up here when the waters were deep over the plains. Do you think there could ever have been that much water in the world, Grey Bear?''

Behele shrugged. He got a campfire to blazing and ran a willow whip through the gills of the trout.

''No,'' Hummingbird cried out when she saw what he was doing. ''We must wrap the fish in leaves and mud and put them on the coals when the flames die down. Otherwise they will not cook right.''

''Women know nothing of cooking,'' Behele scoffed, setting the string of fish over the flames.

''All right, then. Tomorrow I will cook the fish my way. Then we will judge which way is better.''

When they had eaten and laid out their robes over cushions of springy juniper and spruce boughs, Antonio Grey Bear and Hummingbird walked back down to the stream together. They bathed separately, dressed once more and returned to the cave.

They had no need to speak of what would come next. This was to be the night of their joining as man and woman. They had pledged themselves and this would seal the pledge.

Neither was innocent, and yet now both were. They lay beside one another and were silent as if uncertain what to do next. They could not even think of anything to say.

''*Pi-raski* and *cu-raki*,'' Behele whispered at last. ''Boy and girl. We are like children, Hummingbird. Why is this so?''

''Are you frightened, Grey Bear?''

''No, not that.''

''Will you undress me? I am ashamed to do it myself.''

He did as his woman requested, his fingers feeling large and clumsy. But then she lay naked among the folds of the buffalo robes. She drew one edge of the blanket up to cover her breasts, but left her lower body exposed in the reflected firelight.

Behele took off his deerskin shirt and his leggings and stood above her in his loincloth.

She stared up at him, smiled. "Your *kari* rises." But as he finished undressing, the kari wilted. He could feel it going away from him.

"Kneel above me," she commanded. "There is something that will bring him back. . . ."

He was soon aroused again by her gentle ministrations. Eagerly, gently, they explored one another, and where they touched lines of fire seemed to linger. Their lovemaking proceeded slowly, carefully, mounting to a crescendo of passion that was like a disturbance of nature itself.

Indeed, it merged with a sudden wind, flashes of lightning and thunder that rocked the earth beyond the cave. They moaned and cried out in pleasure as their climax blended with the storm that raged with increasing fury in the world outside.

They lay back and listened to the hiss of the rain flooding the dry land, the slam of thunder, the wind that brought the scents of wet grass and pine into their sleeping chamber. They felt transported beyond harm to a realm of pure joy and peace where it seemed they might dwell forever.

Chapter 8

Pitalesharo waited two days after the desperate elopement of Grey Bear and Hummingbird before setting off to find them. Hawk Foot and his Thunderbird Lance warriors had completed a careful sweep of the area surrounding the village, combing the region for twenty miles around without success. Or if they had found any traces, they had kept it from the Red Lances and anyone else whose loyalties still lay with Lachelesharo.

During this two-day interval Pitalesharo went on as usual, tending to small matters, engaging in shooting matches with Two Boulders and Spotted Wolf, playing handball with the village children.

From time to time he was aware of Mad Crow's presence close by. The guard who had been knocked unconscious on the night of the escape, he had now apparently been given the responsibility of keeping surveillance on the son of the chief.

Mad Crow will take his duties more seriously this

time, Pitalesharo thought. But he has to sleep some-time. I wonder if Hawk Foot has placed watchmen to observe my father's lodge at night.

It was nearly sundown when Termite Joe and Thin Cloud came in from hunting, all four pack mules heavily laden with antelope meat.

"Thin Cloud here's going to be a marksman yet, by the blue beard of Jesus," the mountain man said when everyone had gathered in Lachelesharo's lodge.

Raven Quill nodded. "That one learns faster than the others," she remarked as she served up woven baskets heaped with beans, squash, wild potatoes and roasted strips of the fresh-killed antelope. "I have always said that. It was from following Man Chief and Grey Bear when they were younger."

Lachelesharo nodded and shrugged as if to indicate to the men that Raven Quill talked too much. But Thin Cloud accepted the praise with a grin.

"Were you followed this day?" Lachelesharo asked.

"Didn't think so at first," Termite Joe responded. "But just after we come on the antelopes, this child caught sight of a pair of them damned Thunderbirds just over the rim. Ain't no one leaves the village without a couple of Wounded Man's mockingbirds following 'em. Seems like they'd get tired of it before long now."

"The shaman has been frustrated twice now," Lachelesharo said. "He will not give up easily."

"I think I will be able to slip away this night, Father," Pitalesharo suggested. "They may follow if they wish. But I think Mad Crow is getting tired of following me. This afternoon he spent more of his time flirting with the young women as they were pounding the beans for flour. I could have walked away then and he would not have known it for an hour or more."

"If your roan is missing in the morning, Wounded Man and Hawk Foot will know at once."

"My war pony will be picketed just outside the lodge for everyone to see. Two Boulders has taken three of his ponies to his grandfather's lodge and everyone will suppose they are gifts. I will take one of those. Two Boulders will tell his wife that I am sick with dysentery. Before the sun is half up, that one will have told anyone who is willing to listen. Wounded Man will think I am still in the lodge asleep. Mother, if you are asked, that is what you must say also."

Raven Quill nodded, pleased to be included in the scheme.

Morning found Pitalesharo well to the north of Wolf-Standing-in-Water Village. He was following the usual trail toward the Pitahauerats Pawnee villages, White Cougar's people, and yet he did not really believe he would find his blood brother and the Cheyenne there. Hawk Foot or one of his men would almost certainly have been there already. Even if the Pitahauerats chief had given sanctuary to Lachelesharo's adopted son, a messenger would have been sent back to determine what the head chief of the Skidi wished to have done. And that had not happened.

Along Arikaree Creek, as Termite Joe called that branch of the Republican, Pitalesharo discovered three white men camped, trappers, apparently. There were plenty of beaver ponds along the stream, and upon investigation Pitalesharo found one of the sets. Without having any real reason to do so, he dropped a stone into the water and set off the steel trap. But he avoided contact with the white men and decided to turn back upstream along the Arikaree.

If Hawk Foot's men were following, Pitalesharo reasoned, they would suppose the abrupt change of direction indicated that he really had no idea as to Behele's where-

abouts, was merely engaged in random search. But in truth
Pitalesharo's wanderings thus far had been little more than
that. Two Boulders, under questioning, had repeated what
Behele had said when he left: "Far away." And yet Two
Boulders, in the moment of recounting his final conversation with Antonio Grey Bear, had made a face gesture
toward the west. At the time Pitalesharo had attributed no
significance to this action. But now he began to wonder if
Behele himself had made a similar, half-conscious gesture.

Far away, he mused, far away westward. To what?
Only the short-grass highlands and areas of little water and
scattered boulders and grotesque sandstone forms. Not a
likely place to find safety.

Then an image of Big Rock Mountain flashed into his
mind, and with that came the associated image of a cave
and a meadow far up on the mountain's flank, a place
where he and his blood brother had gone many years past.
Without any further evidence than this, Pitalesharo knew
where he would go.

Near the headwaters of the south branch of the Arikaree
he began to suspect that he was being followed. In direct-
line distance he was no more than fifty miles from the
Skidi village, a day's ride, no more, although it had taken
him three days to reach that point. One of Hawk Foot's
men might well have picked up signs of his passage, might
even have caught sight of him from the long sandstone
ridge above.

An hour earlier a large band of wild turkeys, which
the Pawnee did not kill and which hence had little fear of
men, had begun to follow him. A large flock, perhaps as
many as a hundred or more of the creatures, had chosen to
trail along behind him, pecking at his horse's droppings
and searching for insects.

When Pitalesharo stopped and drew his pony about,

the turkeys halted their advance. Two or three large toms began to strut about, puffing themselves up to twice their normal size. When he whistled, the toms began to bugle and the hens and their half-grown chicks scurried for cover.

Then as he rode on the birds began once again to leg it along behind him. Now, with a sudden rattle of wings and a confusion of running and flying, they scattered.

Coyote close, Pitalesharo thought at first. But in the heat of the day it was far more likely that any sensible song dog would be dreaming in its den. Turkey-hunting coyotes waited until just before sundown, when the big birds could not see well and had not yet taken to roost in a cottonwood, scrub cedar or bush.

He crossed the nearly dry stream and directed his pony upslope toward the southern rim of the little canyon. He did not hurry. He made no sign whatsoever that he thought someone was behind him.

Along the top were a series of wind-sculpted sandstone formations. Behind one of these pillars Pitalesharo tethered his pony to some low-growing brush and slipped back where he could observe the entire canyon below. After a time a rider appeared near the stream, pulled his mount to a halt, examined the ground and then urged his animal ahead once more, upslope toward the rim where Pitalesharo waited.

Hawk Foot himself.

Pitalesharo crouched none too comfortably in a niche in the stone face of the rim rocks. When the leader of the Thunderbird Lances was fairly close and directly below, Pitalesharo called out, "*Tu-ra-heh.* It is good."

Hawk Foot wheeled his horse, his rifle ready, only to see the glinting barrel of a Hawken on him.

"Man Chief, I did not know it was you that I followed."

"Yes, old friend. But why have you come to disturb my vision quest? I have not yet found the right spot to dream. Perhaps we should take a midday meal together and go our separate ways." Pitalesharo climbed down from the rocks and formally embraced Hawk Foot, who had dismounted and was standing before his horse.

"I am surprised to find the chief's son here," Hawk Foot said after a moment. "But I am suspicious of your vision quest. Pitalesharo, I think you are going to meet with Grey Bear. Your brother has stolen my uncle's slave, and that is something that must not be allowed."

Pitalesharo grinned. "Saynday has called me here. But I have not come to find Grey Bear. I think he has eloped with the Cheyenne. Probably he did not know what plans Wounded Man had for her. Well, when the proper time has elapsed, they will return to our village as man and wife. Your uncle will be paid for his property; you do not have to worry about that. He will make a good profit from that which he was about to destroy. A few new ponies and some buffalo robes that he can trade to Papin; he'll be happy enough."

Pitalesharo nudged Hawk Foot. "Or do you feel the jealousy of a rejected lover, Hawk Foot? Since you could not have her, do you not wish anyone else to have her either? I think Hummingbird made her own choice, and just in time, I would say. If Grey Bear had not eloped with her when he did, it would have been a great waste. She will make my blood brother a fine wife. You should be happy for him, Hawk Foot."

Hawk Foot glared at Pitalesharo. "What do you have for us to eat, Man Chief?"

The two studied each other for a moment, and then Pitalesharo turned to unfasten his parfleche to withdraw some ball-shaped pemmican.

"*Tuhu ra-ka-kawa ac,*" he laughed. "Let's eat now."

But at that moment Hawk Foot lunged forward and grabbed Pitalesharo about the throat. The two warrior chiefs were instantly engaged in a desperate wrestling match, not in sport now, as they often had as young boys, but as enemies.

Pitalesharo twisted and threw himself down backward against some rocks, breaking his rival's grip. They grappled furiously, each struggling for advantage, squirming away, hurling their weight at one another, armed only with the strength of muscle and sinew.

Hawk Foot landed a kick to the side of Pitalesharo's head, sending him reeling back toward the rim of the sandstone cliff, where some gnarled and exposed cedar roots checked his course. He was able to rise only to his knees to set himself for Hawk Foot's charge.

But Hawk Foot picked up a ragged chunk of rock and hurled it down at Pitalesharo.

Man Chief dodged the stone and drove his head into Hawk Foot's belly. Taken by surprise, Hawk Foot was propelled backward and tumbled heels in the air over the sandstone rim.

Pitalesharo staggered to the edge and looked down at the rock and sand below. Hawk Foot's body lay crumpled, motionless.

Mortal combat between members of the same village. The violation of a strong taboo.

"Hawk Foot," Pitalesharo called out. "Are you sleeping now? Why do you not come back up so we can finish our game? Why do you ignore me, Hawk Foot?" But there was no motion, no movement in the human form below.

"I am sorry, old friend," Pitalesharo called out. "Why did you jump on me when my back was turned? Why did you attempt to kill me with the rock? I did not wish to kill you. Why did you die so easily, Hawk Foot?''

Pitalesharo did not climb down to examine the body. He did not wish to be the one who brought the dead man back to the village. Perhaps he would tell Spotted Wolf where to find the body. His mind was spinning in confusion as he turned away.

Southwest of the head of the Arikaree Branch, Pitalesharo came upon sign of the passage of a huge herd of buffalo from north to south. He rode in the direction the herd had gone, toward the distant mountain that Termite Joe and Papin called Pike's Peak, the Karitku-cu, still two days away unless he drove his pony harder. But there was little need for hurry now, for somewhere behind him at the foot of a rocky embankment lay the body of his pursuer.

Better if I had not set out, he thought. It would have been better if I had never begun to search for Grey Bear and the Cheyenne. Now I will have to speak of what has happened, and probably the Thunderbird Lances and all who are loyal to Wounded Man will depart from the village. Or else our clan and those who wish to be led by my father will have to go. We will be two peoples now instead of one. How did all of this happen? Only last year we were at peace with ourselves and powerful. Our enemies feared us, and none was hungry. The Skidi were happy last year.

Midmorning of the second day brought Pitalesharo to the lower end of the meadow. He had detected no smoke, neither seen nor smelled any. And he had begun to doubt the intuition that had told him Grey Bear would be here.

He sat his pony, listened intently, heard nothing. He urged his mount forward a few more steps, stopped once again, smelled the faint smell of horses.

He raised his Hawken, fired the weapon into the air and waited. There was no response.

He reloaded and rode into the meadow. He could see the peculiar formation of grey stone that marked the opening to the cave where the Ancient Ones had left their paintings.

"Pitalesharo," came a voice from the slope above him. He recognized it immediately.

"Juan Grey Bear!" he called out. "I have ridden into the spirit world to find you."

"No spirit world yet, my friend," Behele called out. "Welcome to our honeymoon lodge."

The tall Spaniard plunged down the slope to greet his brother.

That night they built a large fire at the cave's mouth and ate fish and roast elk. When the meal was finished, Pitalesharo asked the question whose answer he dreaded hearing.

"Will you and Hummingbird return to the village of Wolf-Standing-in-Water? But maybe I have made it more difficult than it was before."

"What do you mean, Man Chief?" Hummingbird asked.

"I have killed Hawk Foot," he answered.

"How did it happen? Did he follow you or were you still in the village where everyone could see? He is better off dead, amigo, but this is still not good news. Tell me how it happened."

"He followed me, or else he was out searching for you and Hummingbird. He attacked me. We struggled and he fell over a bluff. That is where I left him, even though I should have carried him back to the village. It all happened very fast and I was not thinking well. Grandmother Moon caused me to think like a guilty child. I—"

"It was not your fault, then," Behele insisted. "Look,

Pitalesharo. You must return to our people, but Hummingbird and I cannot do that. She is mine now and I will not give her up. Wounded Man is crazy. He planned to murder her once and he would certainly try again. He would find some way, even if the other medicine men and the counselors decided that we are properly married now.''

"Perhaps we will go to live with my people, the Cheyenne,'' Hummingbird said, edging closer to Behele and putting her arm about his waist.

"We have discovered something,'' Behele continued. "When two people become everything to one another, they cannot go back to being the way they were before, not even if it were possible to do so. Do you understand me, my brother?''

Pitalesharo stared into the fire and remembered the extreme pain of his own parting with Little Green Frog. Then he studied Grey Bear and Hummingbird sitting there together, like one being with two heads and four arms and four legs.

He grinned and nodded. "I understand.''

"So we will not return to the village,'' Behele continued. "No, when we leave this meadow, we will travel where we must because that is the price of our being together. It would be too dangerous for us to return. For all you know, Wounded Man has again used his speech medicine to make the people act crazy. And when he learns that his nephew is dead, he will be even worse. He will tell everyone that Morning Star has caused this misfortune. He will drive the warriors crazy with his screaming and they will do whatever he wishes. He will cause them to attack the whites and sacrifice the prisoners. He will not be happy until he has burned many people in the fire.''

"Yet those who love us live in the village,'' Pitalesharo said. "Lachelesharo and Raven Quill, Two Boulders, Thin Cloud, even Termite Joe.''

"It is true that Lachelesharo and Raven Quill love me," Behele said, "but I am not truly their son. I will always love them and be grateful to them, for they saved my life when I was a child and helpless. But now I have to go away from them. I do not do this out of choice, brother. I do it because I have no choice. But you must return. Explain what I have said to Lachelesharo and the others. I cannot give up Hummingbird. That would be a worse death than any other."

Pitalesharo stood up and faced away from the cave's mouth and into the darkness.

When he turned to his blood brother again, he said simply, "I have also made up my mind, Juan Antonio Grey Bear. The people will be divided now and I will be seen as the cause of it. It is better that I not go back either. No, I am going to ride south to the lands of the Comanche. I will fight Six Feathers to the death. I am the son of a great chief and the Comanche will have to honor my challenge. I will even be a slave to Fox Shirt in order to marry Little Green Frog. If you are riding south, back to where the Spanish live, then I will ride with you. That is what I have decided to do."

Behele shook his head. "If you kill Six Feathers, the Comanche will kill you anyway. It would not be wise to make such a challenge, my brother. If you are determined, though, we will ride with you. Perhaps we can think of some way to kidnap Little Green Frog. Then we can escape into the mountains and begin our own tribe. Do you like my words?"

Hummingbird began to laugh and shake her head. "From the beginning I knew that Grey Bear was crazy. Now I see that Man Chief also has a very soft brain. If I suggested such a thing, you would both tell me that women talk too much or that women look at the snow and say that it is black. Perhaps that is why I love Grey Bear, because he has a mind like a woman's. Pitalesharo, why don't you call your Red Lances to you and defeat those who back Wounded Man? Hawk Foot is dead now, and if the shaman were also dead, then all our problems would be solved. You see, even a Cheyenne woman can think better than the two of you.''

Pitalesharo and Grey Bear stared at the girl in astonishment. Then they began to roar with laughter and pound each other on the back.

Nearly a week passed and still Pitalesharo and Antonio Grey Bear had been unable to decide on a proper course of action. In fact, they preferred to put such considerations out of mind. Instead they swam in the beaver pond at the meadow's upper margin, admired Hummingbird's ability to catch fish with her hands and even made pitch-pine torches and explored the recesses of the cave, discovering a new set of pictures in the process—a single scene that covered an entire wall of the cave, huge buffalo and men with spears and bows and arrows.

"The Ancient Ones must have been just like us," Hummingbird mused, touching her fingertips to the still-brilliant lines and bands of color.

"The world was always the same until the Spanish people came," Pitalesharo said. "Then things changed. It was from the Spanish, long ago, that the Pawnee acquired medicine dogs, the horses. Grey Bear has heard the story; perhaps you have also, Hummingbird. And it was after that everything began to change."

"My people got horses from the Pawnee," Hummingbird mused. "Our tribes were not at war with each other then. That is what I think. My grandfather tells a story of how the Pawnee gave horses to the Morning Star People, the Cheyenne. And then they told us where the medicine dogs had come from. After that the Pawnee and the Cheyenne went together to the pueblo villages where the Spanish were, and we all stole many horses from them. The Spanish would not come out to fight, not even to protect their horses.''

Behele grinned, at the same time mildly annoyed with the woman he loved. ''That is not the way I heard the story. I heard the real version when I was just a boy, before my parents died. The old-time Spanish were searching for cities made of gold and the Hopi people told them to go north. But all the Spanish found were the mud lodges of the Pawnee. So they felt sorry for the Indians and gave them some horses and taught them how to ride. That way they could hunt the buffalo more easily and not be hungry so often.''

Pitalesharo glanced at Behele and shook his head. ''That is not a true story. My brother forgets that he is Pawnee now and not Spanish. I think he has just made up that story.''

''None of us is a Skidi now.'' Behele suddenly sounded forlorn.

Their week of indecision and sport ended one day when they stepped from the cave and confronted a ghost. Hawk Foot stood there, a half-smile on his face, and behind him were Mad Crow, Sits Alone, Bad Ankle, Laughing Dog, Hairy Leggings and half a dozen more.

''Are you surprised to see me again, Man Chief?'' Hawk Foot asked. His face was bruised and swollen, but otherwise he showed no sign of injury.

Pitalesharo was so stunned he couldn't utter a sound. Behind him Grey Bear and Hummingbird held each other tightly.

''I was not even badly hurt when my men found me. Wounded Man sent them out to search for me, and now we have found what we have all been searching for, the coward Grey Bear and the slave that he has stolen.

"Now I claim what was stolen from Wounded Man. She will be mine now. Wounded Man has said that she would be mine if I could find her. I have wanted you all along, Hummingbird the Cheyenne. And now you will be my wife. I will marry you even though I do not have to. You will be proud to have a great warrior for your husband. Perhaps I will even be the chief one day, who knows? If it is Morning Star's will, then it will happen."

Chapter 9

There was little the two Red Lances could do, encircled as they were by Hawk Foot's warriors. Most of the Thunderbird Lances were still on horseback, although two had dismounted to assist the shaman's nephew in subduing Hummingbird, who struggled when Hawk Foot grabbed her. Behele sprang to help Hummingbird, but he was stopped by the cocking of the rifles on him.

"Go easy, amigo," Pitalesharo murmured in Spanish. "If we live, we'll have a better chance of winning your woman back."

Grey Bear seemed not to have heard his friend's advice at all. "Hummingbird is my wife, Hawk Foot," he said quietly. "If you wish to take her from me, you will have to kill me."

Hawk Foot grinned. "Should that be necessary, Spaniard, I would not mind so much."

"So," Behele continued, "you think you will shoot me here with all your friends around you? I know that you are a coward, but perhaps these men haven't figured it out yet."

A murmur ran among the warriors. Mad Crow, who had not forgotten Behele's ambush the night he took Hummingbird away, called out, "Let me kill him for you, Hawk Foot. There was no fair fight when he hit me over the head and pushed me down with the dogs."

"This Spaniard may die any way he wishes," Hawk Foot snarled. "Do you wish to die with my knife in your guts, white man? I will be very gentle, very slow."

Behele replied by stripping to his breechcloth, kicking his clothing to one side and tossing his knife to the ground between himself and the Thunderbird Lance leader.

"This is foolish," Pitalesharo insisted, struggling to speak in a tone of authority. "Skidi warriors do not fight over a woman. If the woman has chosen one man, another does not lower himself to take notice of her. All the people will laugh at such a man."

"What the chief's son says is true," remarked the giant Hairy Leggings. "Let the Spanish and the Cheyenne go. We will kill them only if they come back to Wolf-Standing-in-Water."

Several of the warriors nodded agreement, but Hawk Foot was not moved by the argument. "This is not a Pawnee woman. She has no right to choose a husband. I could agree to have her burned alive if I chose to do so. She belonged to my uncle and she is mine because he gave her to me. This man has stolen my property. I will kill him for that. Let us fight, bastard of the Spanish."

Behele gritted his teeth. "First we must come to terms. If I kill you, Hummingbird is mine. Your warriors must agree not to interfere with us again."

"We do not need to worry about such a thing," Hawk Foot laughed. "Let it be any way you wish, Grey Bear. It will not matter when you are dead. Pitalesharo will have to pile rocks over your body here on the mountain, but perhaps the coyotes and wolves would not wish to eat your remains."

"You talk too much, old woman," Behele remarked calmly. "Let us begin."

A flat space in the meadow below the cave entrance was cleared for combat. Pitalesharo and Hummingbird were placed under guard, with Mad Crow and the sullen Sits Alone standing to either side of them, rifles at the ready.

"What will happen now, Man Chief?" Hummingbird whispered.

"Grey Bear will kill Hawk Foot and then the Thunderbird Lances will kill the three of us. When I give the signal, you must run to the cave and hide. Get back into a hole somewhere and do not make any noise at all."

"Silence," Mad Crow grunted, striking the side of Pitalesharo's head with his rifle barrel so hard that the chief's son had to struggle against oblivion.

In that same instant Hummingbird leaped forward and placed herself between Antonio Grey Bear and Hawk Foot. "Stop! I have chosen."

She glanced at Behele, her face pale and tense, her eyes large. Then she turned to Hawk Foot. "I will be your wife if you want me so much. I will not be a good wife to you because I hate you, Hawk Foot. But I will marry you. Let us go home now."

Pitalesharo, his vision clearing, saw the color drain from Grey Bear's face as if he had indeed been impaled on Hawk Foot's knife.

Antonio stared at Hummingbird, but she wouldn't

turn to face him again. He glanced at Pitalesharo and then at the rest of the Skidi, all of them struck silent. He studied the back of Hummingbird's head again and then nodded. He gathered up his belongings and strode from the circle of warriors. He mounted his spotted horse and rode away without turning, his back very straight.

The Cheyenne looked after the departing warrior, tears welling openly in her eyes now. But when Hawk Foot spoke to her, she obediently mounted her own pony and waited for the rest of the party to get under way.

Pitalesharo also stared after his blood brother, considering at first that he should follow and then rejecting the idea. *Grey Bear needs to be alone right now*, he decided, recalling vividly the terrible pain he had felt at the loss of Little Green Frog. *And it is best that I remain with these Thunderbird Lances so that Hawk Foot will be less inclined to mistreat Hummingbird.*

During the following days, as the party descended from the mountains and crossed the high plains, it became clear to Pitalesharo that his concern for Hummingbird's welfare had been unnecessary. Indeed, before the group reached Wolf-Standing-in-Water Village, he was almost feeling sorry for his enemy, for it became evident that she did not intend to make her future husband's life easy. She was the very model of obedience and proper gravity, but she would not speak one unnecessary word to her fiancé. Very politely but decidedly she rebuffed all his gestures of affection.

Hawk Foot for his part was patiently attentive, perhaps trying to atone for his complicity in Wounded Man's attempt to sacrifice her. During the first day's travel he rode close beside her, talking earnestly. Pitalesharo was not near enough to hear what the brave was saying, but he could see that Hummingbird did not turn her head toward

Hawk Foot at all, and when the warrior reached out to touch her arm, she kicked at her horse and pulled ahead.

Hairy Leggings, who rode beside Pitalesharo, also observed the little drama. "It could be," he remarked, "that our leader has captured a prize he will wish he had lost."

"Hah!" snorted Mad Crow. "He'll take a willow whip to her soon enough and make a good wife of her."

"He probably won't do that while I'm around." Pitalesharo stared coldly at the one who had just spoken.

"Tu-ra-heh," replied Mad Crow. "Who knows? Maybe your pony will stumble and you will fall off a cliff."

Hairy Leggings grunted. "Not a good way for two Skidi to speak to one another. We have had bad blood between us because of the sacrifices that never happened, but now it is time for our tribe to heal its wounds. We cannot go on hating each other."

The three rode in silence again, and Pitalesharo saw that Hawk Foot had resumed his one-sided conversation.

That night they camped in a grove of aspens near a little stream that tumbled down from a steep arroyo.

Hummingbird, after tending to her own horse, sat on her buffalo robe some distance from the campfire, making no offer to help with camp chores and paying no notice to any of the warriors. And since Hawk Foot did not order his woman to gather wood or cook the meat, none of the other men dared to intervene. Pitalesharo tried to maneuver himself near enough to Hummingbird to talk to her, but whenever Hawk Foot was not by her side, Mad Crow or Sits Alone would materialize close by, holding a lance and watching him.

"One thing we know," Laughing Dog called out to

Hawk Foot, "is that this one keeps her word. She said she would be a bad wife to you."

Several of the warriors chuckled, but Hawk Foot was not amused. "Perhaps Laughing Dog wishes to be called Howling Dog, unless he learns to keep his long nose out of the way when another man deals with his woman."

For a time the leader of the Thunderbird Lances made a great point of ignoring his prize, standing a distance away and gossiping with the other men, bragging loudly about his various war exploits; but when the meat was roasted, he slipped as unobtrusively as he could with a choice portion of fat over to Hummingbird.

"The great warrior is very kind," she said in ringing tones so that all might hear, "but a woman should not eat it. This is the best piece. I give it to you. I will go cut myself a little portion when the men are finished eating."

She pushed the gift back at Hawk Foot and refused to touch it. She rose and went to stand by the fire. None of the Thunderbird Lances ventured even to smile, but Pitalesharo laughed aloud, rising to meet Hawk Foot's glaring challenge. The two stood facing one another for a tense moment, and then Hawk Foot turned and stalked off toward the aspen tangle.

They made their way northeast, continuing through a landscape that changed little—gently rolling land, scattered clumps of sage, whitened bunches of buffalo grass that glared in the oppressive heat of the late summer sun, dominant short grasses, areas nearly devoid of any vegetation at all, sand, dust and scattered boulders.

Pitalesharo spoke little with his companions, though some of them were men with whom he had been close since childhood. He was not precisely a prisoner, but he was aware that all his moves were watched, and he was given no opportunity to speak with Hummingbird. Of the

Thunderbird Lances, only huge Hairy Leggings made any attempt to be friendly. Mad Crow and Sits Alone were openly hostile, while the remainder preferred to ignore him.

Oddly enough, Hawk Foot showed almost no hostility and in fact seemed all but oblivious to his existence. The frustrating obsession with Hummingbird, Pitalesharo supposed, was the reason.

With her Hawk Foot remained patient, although it was apparent that his patience was getting to be a strain. He could hardly speak to his warriors without snapping at them, and he frequently challenged one or another to fight over some small insult. Occasionally even his courtliness would wear thin and he would order Hummingbird about for a time. When he did this, she carried out the letter of his commands without comment but would do no more. And always after a while Hawk Foot would return to pampering her and whispering his entreaties.

Pitalesharo had forced himself to sleep very lightly during the journey back to the village, so he was aware that each night after the fire died down and the other warriors were settled, Hawk Foot crept to Hummingbird's robes and whispered to her, unquestionably trying to persuade her to go out of the camp with him. But each night Hawk Foot returned disappointed to his own sleeping robes.

Man Chief finally had an opportunity to speak to her on the evening that Laughing Dog and Bad Ankle decided to have a wrestling match. The other warriors were so caught up in watching and gambling on the outcome that they didn't notice the Red Lance edging toward the woman.

"Take care, little one," the chief's son whispered. "You are driving Hawk Foot to madness. There is no way of knowing what he may do."

She turned to look at him and Pitalesharo was shocked by her expression. It was not so much the lines of pain around the mouth and eyes as it was the strange emptiness, as if whoever lived behind the eyes had pulled a door shut. "Do you think I care what he does to me?"

Pitalesharo turned to watch the contest. There was nothing more to say.

When the fire had died down that night, Hawk Foot again made his visit to Hummingbird's robes, and sounds of a brief struggle ensued. Pitalesharo heard the slap of a hand striking flesh. He was halfway to his feet when he heard Hummingbird, speaking in a hiss loud enough to carry to anyone who was still awake.

"Get away from me, Hawk Foot. When we are married, you may order me to lie with you and I will have to obey. But if you try to force me now, I will scream and all your warriors will know what has happened. Go back to your own bed and let me be." The chief's son saw the shadowy form of the warrior rise and slink away.

In the morning Man Chief noted that it was not Hummingbird but Hawk Foot who had a new bruise below one eye.

It was very good, he thought, that the group would soon be back to the village, for he was certain that Hawk Foot's continued humiliation would lead the man to violence. Perhaps in the village among relatives and friends Hawk Foot would come to his senses and realize that Hummingbird was not the wife he wanted. Or if they were married, the presence of others in the lodge, particularly the influence of other women, might lead Hummingbird to temper her siege on his pride. At the very least the chances of the warrior's doing her a genuine injury would be lessened once they were in view of the community.

During the following day Hawk Foot spoke little to his captive and he did not visit her sleeping place that night. Pitalesharo began to hope the warrior had realized that marriage to Hummingbird would be a very hollow triumph. And yet Hawk Foot continued to follow her with his eyes.

The next night the group camped a short distance away from the village, and in the morning the Thunderbird Lances prepared themselves for their return, dressing in the ceremonial finery they had brought with them for this occasion and carefully painting their faces. Only Pitalesharo and Hummingbird refrained from such preparation.

Hawk Foot's finery was the most resplendent of all. His face was painted in concentric circles of red and yellow with broad streaks of black running from nose to ear. The ears jingled with shell ornaments and a tuft of feathers as well as the dried body of a woodpecker adorned his roach of hair. He strutted back and forth in front of Hummingbird, being very careful to pretend that he took no notice of her; once again Pitalesharo felt something close to pity for his old enemy.

When all were ready they rode toward the village, crossing two low ridges and pausing atop the one over-looking the mound lodges. They fired their weapons into the air.

A party of Dog Soldiers and Red Lances rode out to meet them, and when the two groups met on the slope above the village, the Red Lances encircled Pitalesharo, cutting him away from their rival society.

Two Boulders leaped from the back of his horse onto Pitalesharo, playfully pulling him to the ground and pinning him. The broad-shouldered man with the wide mouth sprang up and embraced his friend, pounding him on the back. "I was not sure we would see you again, Man Chief." Scanning the group of returned warriors and seeing

Hummingbird, he asked, "Where is Antonio Grey Bear? I think we may need to kill these Thunderbird Lances."

"No, my friend," Pitalesharo replied. He realized that a note of weariness and depression had come into his voice. "Grey Bear is alive. I will explain it all later. How are things in the village?"

"Better, I think. Isn't that true, Spotted Wolf?"

"Yes. It is soon time for the buffalo hunt, and the chiefs and the priests must work together to make certain the ceremony is carried out properly. Your father will wish to tell you all these things."

"One bad thing happened," Two Boulders admitted. "The Wolf Lances went off on a horse-stealing against the Kiowa, and they returned with many ponies, well over a hundred in all."

"That doesn't sound like a bad thing to me," Pitalesharo shrugged.

"It is good that we have the Kiowa horses. But the Wolf Lances found three white men on Arikaree Creek and killed and scalped them. Papin and Hollingback are not very happy about it. They say the soldiers may come to visit us."

The warriors rode down into the village. Lachelesharo was standing outside his lodge with Termite Joe Hollingback. The chief gravely greeted his son and the mountain man scrutinized the returned men. He saw Hawk Foot leading Hummingbird on her pony in the direction of Wounded Man's lodge.

"Tarnation, it's good to see you, coon," Hollingback said after a moment. "But what the devil have you done with Juan Antonio?"

"I will explain. Don't worry, he's alive and well. Let's go inside, Brother Termite."

Inside the lodge Raven Quill embraced her son warmly and insisted that he eat a large bowl of elk stew and several slices of corn cake before he began his story. Pitalesharo gladly complied, leaning luxuriously against his own headrest and spooning up the savory broth of meat and vegetables. As he ate his father and Termite Joe filled him in on what had happened in the village since his departure.

"Wounded Man was like a crazy person for days over the loss of his second sacrifice. He kept wandering through the village with his hair in tatters and his clothing torn like one in mourning. He would stand outside this lodge and prophesy horrible things.

"At last it became necessary for me to give him presents for Morning Star in order to ease his grief, for the village was very uneasy over the way he was acting and the other shamans were stirring up trouble. I gave him much meat and three good hides, a dozen pairs of fine beaded moccasins and some other things. Our friend Termite Joe helped too."

"Give the old fraud every danged bit of powder and tobacco I had in the world. Now I'm going to have to go in the hole with Papin before I take a single plew this fall," the trapper grumbled.

"Perhaps that is not quite true," continued Lachelesharo, "but our friend was very generous. We presented these gifts in the center of the village so everyone would see. Wounded Man burned everything in honor of Morning Star."

"Even sprinkled the gunpowder all over and burned that too," Joe said. "Whooee! She looked like the goddamned Fourth of July, I tell you."

"Yes." Lachelesharo nodded, "whatever this *Fourajuly* is. After that Wounded Man said Morning Star felt better, although he was still sad about not having a human sacrifice. But probably the great star would not kill us all. And Wounded Man stopped acting like a crazy person. Pitalesharo, soon it will be time for the fall hunt, and it would not be good if the chiefs and the shamans did not act as one in our prayers for the buffalo. Wounded Man knows this. I think he will not do anything to spoil the hunt.''

Pitalesharo nodded, considering the import of his father's account. He had finished his meal, and now Lachelesharo asked Raven Quill to bring his pipe. Termite Joe sighed and pulled out his tobacco pouch.

"Here she is. This is all I managed to save, coons, and it ain't going to get us through the last days of summer, no sir.''

"When we go on the hunt, I will make a present of two buffalo hides to my friend the Termite," Pitalesharo comforted him. "Perhaps then the good Frenchman will give you some more tobacco.''

"Someone is coming to visit," called a voice from the entry, and after a polite interval Two Boulders entered the room.

"I have come to tell Man Chief that I sent my little brother to take care of his horse. He has taken it down to the river. I did not think you would want to worry about this, since you must have a great deal to tell your father.''

"It is good of you to do this," Lachelesharo smiled. "My son has just finished telling us that story. He is too weary to talk any more right now, but you are welcome to share this pipe of tobacco with us.''

Two Boulders' wide mouth drooped in disappointment.

"I thought—did Pitalesharo not wish to rest and perhaps eat something before he began his tale?" he asked.

Lachelesharo chuckled. "One cannot always believe even the chief. Now I may as well wait a little longer, for there will probably be other visitors soon, and then my son will have to tell the story only once.''

Within a few minutes indeed most of the Red Lances had managed to crowd into the lodge, and Pitalesharo told them of his adventures since he had left the village. When he reached the part concerning Behele's departure from the high meadow and Hummingbird's promise to marry Hawk Foot, Termite Joe snorted.

"Ain't nothing but a pair of dungheads, the both of you. How could you go and let that two-headed rattlesnake take hold of that innocent leetle critter? By the Great Blue Jesus, no telling what devilish things he'll up and do to her. Coon, you made your mistake when you didn't cut Hawk Foot's throat after he fell off that there cliff. Hell, ain't no point in doing a job halfway."

"I am not certain, Juan Termite," Pitalesharo answered, "but I think you may be feeling sorry for the wrong critter."

"What is my friend talking about?" Two Boulders asked, squinting and pursing his mouth.

Pitalesharo told the story of the ride back to Wolf-Standing-in-Water Village and of Hummingbird's relentless campaign against Hawk Foot's pride. By the end of the tale Two Boulders was sputtering with merriment.

"Oh, that is very good," he cried. "Perhaps if I put on a woman's dress, the great warrior will let me boss him around."

"You must not make fun of him, Two Boulders," Pitalesharo cautioned him. "My father says the village is at peace now. We must keep it so. Besides, Hawk Foot is not so patient. I am afraid he will take his shame out on Hummingbird after they are married."

"Wal then, let's go get her, you ignorant nigger," shouted Termite Joe. "Just like I said in the first place, you cain't let him have the leetle gal. What's to keep him and old Scar Face from sacrificing her all over again?"

"No," said Lachelesharo, "that will not happen. Wounded Man also wishes to keep the peace for right now, at least until after the fall hunt. But perhaps our friend Termite is right. Perhaps we should try to keep this marriage from happening. Since we gave Wounded Man presents for her, she should belong to us. I will think on this thing."

In the silence that followed Lachelesharo's statement, Wounded Man himself entered the lodge. "Speak of the devil's own grandmammy," Termite Joe muttered softly.

The shaman stood just inside the doorway, staring coldly at the assembled warriors for a moment before he turned and gestured to someone behind him. Hummingbird entered, her hands folded before her and her eyes lowered.

"I have brought you your slave, the one you bought from me, Knife Chief," the shaman said without other greeting.

"Tu-ra-heh," Lachelesharo replied, nodding. "It is good, Wounded Man. Will you smoke a pipe of tobacco with us?"

"No," replied the shaman. "I have something else to do. I came only to give you your property." He turned, stooped to go out the door and then turned back. "My nephew will probably bring you some horses this evening. I leave it to you whether you choose to accept them. I have nothing to do with this affair."

With that he was gone.

The men sat in stunned silence for a long moment, but Raven Quill hurried over to Hummingbird, embraced her and found her a place to sit. She brought food to the newcomer and fussed about her a great deal.

Pitalesharo rose and walked to Hummingbird. He bent over to look into her face. "Little one, you do not need to marry Hawk Foot. We will not let him take you, even if it means war between the Red Lances and the Thunderbird Lances. I will take you with me and we will find Grey Bear."

"I will marry him. I gave my word, Man Chief."

"That does not matter, child," said Lachelesharo. "What my son has said is true. You are safe with us. I will make you my daughter and Hawk Foot will not be able to do anything. Why would I wish to have such a man as my son-in-law?"

"No," she cried, looking scared. "I made a promise to Morning Star that I would marry Hawk Foot so that Grey Bear might live. I do not dare break that promise."

Termite Joe shook his head. "Danged foolish notion, if you ask me. Making promises to the blasted, bloody god what wanted your poor leetle body all cut up and burned. Ain't no god anyhow, only a plain, simple old star."

"I am sure that Morning Star did not wish for my death," Hummingbird said quietly. "I am Cheyenne. My people are the Morning Star People. Why would he wish my death? Only Wounded Man wanted that. Besides, perhaps Hawk Foot will grow tired of me and divorce me. I am not allowed to hope for such a thing, but perhaps it will happen anyway. When will Grey Bear come back to the village?"

Two Boulders burst out laughing again but lapsed into silence when Pitalesharo glared at him.

That evening Hawk Foot did indeed come to the lodge. He was leading two ponies loaded with a buffalo robe, a few cooking utensils, a good quantity of dried meat and a pouch of tobacco. The war chief tied the ponies near Lachelesharo's lodge and sat down by the entrance to wait for someone to invite him in.

Chapter 10

Termite Joe, who had been looking out through the doorway, turned to report the arrival of the leader of the Thunderbird Lances. "Ought to make him set out there all night at least."

"No," Lachelesharo replied. "We will not shame this warrior anymore. I will ask him in."

Hummingbird rose. "No, Knife Chief, I will go out to him. It is not right that you invite your enemy into your lodge on my account. I will go to his lodge. You have been kind to me." She glanced at the chief and his wife, then at Pitalesharo. "I . . . will go now," she concluded, her voice threatening to crack.

"It is still not necessary for you to do this thing," said Lachelesharo. "It is bad medicine when a woman marries a man she does not love. If the woman dislikes her man, how can they ever manage to share the same lodge?"

"I must do it. I have given my word."

Raven Quill embraced Hummingbird once more,

watched her leave the lodge. There were tears in the eyes of the chief's wife. "It is a terrible thing for a woman to marry a man she does not love. My husband is right. When we were young, we were very much in love and neither of us wished to be with anyone else. And that is why Lachelesharo has never wished to take a second wife, though perhaps he will soon, now that I am growing older. It will not be bad to have a younger woman in the lodge with us."

The chief shook his head. "For twenty winters and more she has been saying the same thing," he muttered.

"Poor leetle dumb brave mite," sighed Termite Joe. "She thinks she be saving Juan Antonio, and he's probably off fucking a she-bear somewheres. I hope the dunghead nigger gets hisself home all right. This child surely hopes so."

The following day Raven Quill went to Hawk Foot's lodge, choosing a time when he was not at home. She took one of the horses the warrior had brought as part of the bride price as well as the robe and the cooking utensils. In addition she brought some other articles useful in setting up housekeeping: a few baskets and wooden bowls and some well-tanned elk and deer hide as well as awls and sinews for the manufacture of clothing. These things she gave to Hummingbird as a dowry.

The Cheyenne expressed her gratitude, and although she still seemed sad and distant and the new husband's sisters and mother did not seem overly friendly, Raven Quill was able to report to her own family with some relief that she showed no signs of physical abuse.

The marriage was thus completed, with honor if with little show. But Hawk Foot had scant time to enjoy his honeymoon, for within a few days the chiefs and the

shamans had decided that it was time to begin the final
stages of preparation for the autumn hunt.

These leaders, including Lachelesharo and Wounded
Man, disappeared from Wolf-Standing-in-Water Village.
They went to various lonely places to fast and to purify
themselves for the solemn ceremonies to follow. The young
men who would be the hunters and would participate in the
buffalo dance were also expected to fast and to sweat
themselves and to abstain from sex in order to ensure a
good take of the great shaggy beasts.

The rest of the village was in a state of subdued
excitement, each family making its own preparations for
the trek. Women packed food for the journey and stowed
household utensils in the pack saddles. They checked the
hide covers of the traveling lodges and loaded them onto
travois rigs so that when departure time came, all that
would be necessary would be the loading and tying of the
cargo.

The medicine lodge was ritually purified with sweet-
grass smoke. Prayers were chanted for the buffalo ceremony and the twelve sacred buffalo skulls were reverently
arranged in a circle.

At last came the time for the blessing of the buffalo
staves and the bows and arrows to be used in the hunt.

Pitalesharo quietly entered the medicine lodge, made
his way through the crowd to the rear of the sacred circle.
His own bow and arrows lay with the rest, inside the ring
of buffalo skulls. The lodge was packed with silent, solemn men.

When the chiefs and priests arrived, it was the first
time anyone had seen them since they left the village to
fast. Now they came forward out of the crowd and stood in
silence about the skulls. After a time Wounded Man and
then some of the other shamans began to pray aloud. The
chiefs added their voices in turn, each man speaking his

own prayers, calling upon Tirawa Atius and Morning Star and the various animal spirits to have pity upon the people and to grant them a successful hunt.

The prayers increased in intensity and volume and some of the priests began tearing at their hair and clothing. Wounded Man went into a frenzy of twitching, at last falling to the ground in convulsions.

He rose to his knees shrieking. "We know of your anger with your people, Great Star, and yet we hope that you may have pity on us and grant us food for our poor children. Perhaps we will learn to love you then and realize we must punish those who are your enemies."

Lachelesharo's face remained impassive as he continued with his own prayers.

Pitalesharo felt his anger rise like a red tide despite his efforts to fight it down. He knew that anger was inappropriate at such a sacred time, that such bad feelings might spoil the hunt. Wounded Man did this thing so that my father and I would be angry, he thought.

The ritual seemed suddenly devoid of meaning to the son of the head chief, although he remained quietly in his place and watched his arrows blessed by Wounded Man. When the ritual was over he sprang forward with the other young men, all of them draped in the hide and horns of a bull buffalo, and danced the buffalo dance.

The ceremonies continued for three days. Some of the young men dropped out of the dance from time to time to sleep while others took their places. At last, on the morning of the fourth day, the dance was finished. The people dispersed to their own lodges to load their belongings on the ponies for the trek.

Raven Quill gave her husband and her son some corn cakes and jerky, for the men were now permitted to end their fasting. But there was no time to rest. The chief's family was expected to ride at the head of the village, following only the Wolf Society leaders, who would serve as the police for the duration of the hunt. These men bore buffalo staves fluttering with bright feathers and dyed cloth as the ensign of their office.

Behind the Wolves and Lachelesharo's family, the entire village stretched for a mile or more. Only those too ill to travel or too old had chosen to stay behind. The mood of the people was festive. Many of the young men raced their ponies among the marchers, performing breathtaking feats of horsemanship. The unmarried girls rode or walked in clusters, giggling and watching the young men. Mothers rode along on travois-burdened ponies or walked beside them chatting with one another. The children scampered about under everyone's feet, except for those who bounced along on horseback, as many as three or four to a mount.

It was a time of year that Pitalesharo had always loved. Since he was a young boy, he had looked forward with building excitement to the great fall and spring hunts. But this year he found that he had little enthusiasm. He felt in some ways as if he had become a different person, someone he himself only half recognized.

"My heart is not good for this hunt, my father," he confessed.

Lachelesharo glanced briefly at his son. "It is best not to talk of this thing yet."

"They's some as would spile anybody's Christmas," muttered Termite Joe Hollingback as he rode up alongside. "They's some as would do the world a favor by not being in her." He glanced darkly toward the figure of Wounded Man, riding some distance away, silver hair fluttering about his shoulders and his back very straight as he sat his splendid white stallion.

"This is not a good way to talk on the journey to hunt the buffalo," Lachelesharo insisted.

"What my father says is true," Pitalesharo agreed.

They rode in silence for a time. Then Lachelesharo turned his pony and moved back along the line of march to speak with one of the camp soldiers.

"Wagh," Hollingback snorted. "Seems to this child like the chief's walking on eggs. And you too, lad."

"It is not only that one of whom we will not speak, Termite Joe," Pitalesharo said. "It is that everything is changing. The world is not as it was when I was a child. I thought things would always be the same. Now Grey Bear is gone. Many things are wrong. Sometimes I think the world is falling apart. Even I do not seem the same to myself. Is there something wrong with me, Juan Termite?"

Hollingback shrugged and then broke into a whistle. "Couldn't have anything to do with a certain leetle Comanch, now could it?" He smiled faintly.

"If so, there is no point in worrying about it." Pitalesharo gazed toward the distant line of mountains to the west. "I will never see that one again."

"Maybe it's time for you to settle down with a woman or two of your own. You'll forget the other one in a while."

"I don't want any other women, Joe. It would be much better if I did, I think."

"Some folks is peculiar that way." The mountain man shrugged. "Now me, I've been married half a dozen times. This nigger's got children all over the damn place. Never could stay in one lodge very long, that's for sure."

"But it's not just that, either," Pitalesharo continued. "I fear my people are coming apart. This has never happened before."

Joe snorted. "Ain't nothing a leetle ball of lead lodged in the right place couldn't cure."

They marched on for five days, heading southeast, for there had been reports of a large herd somewhere on the

Smoky River. Toward evening of the fifth day the scouts brought back word of a huge mass of buffalo perhaps ten miles distant.

The hunters set out the next dawn, riding at a fast trot and leading their buffalo ponies. The women followed more slowly, but they would set up camp close by for the butchering.

As the hunters neared the herd, they proceeded carefully, scouts riding ahead. The leaders moved forward to the top of the last rise, motioning the others forward. The party mounted fresh horses and topped the crest. The valley below was black with buffalo, the great beasts grazing in bunches of thirty and more.

Pitalesharo waited tensely for the signal. At last he was alive with the spirit of the hunt, his mind emptied of all other concerns.

The chief bearer of the buffalo staves turned back toward the waiting men and shrilly shouted, *"Loo-ah!"* The long line of horsemen hurled itself forward at full gallop, the ends of the line sweeping out wide to form the surround.

Pitalesharo rode hard for the far side of the valley. The buffalo had sensed the danger and had already begun to stampede toward the distant rise. His roan pony surged beneath him and the wind roared in his ears. Pitalesharo shrieked both to drive the buffalo and in pure, wild exultation.

The herd was a thundering mass to his right. He kicked his horse hard, racing to get ahead of the lead cows. If these creatures could be turned, the bulls and the younger animals would follow blindly.

Other warriors were close behind him. Pitalesharo lashed a rawhide whip against his horse's flanks.

He had caught up with the lead cows now. He drove close in against them, shrieking and howling to turn them. The foremost cow rolled a small red eye at him and veered aside. Pitalesharo nocked an arrow and pulled back the bowstring, holding steady despite the wild movement of his pony. The horse crowded the cow, driving her against the flanks of the other buffalo. Pitalesharo let go the shaft, saw it plunge deep into her side just behind the front shoulder. The cow's forelegs crumpled and she skidded heavily.

He drove another of the bison back into the herd. Pressing on, he got ahead of the herd, turning the panicked animals back on themselves. He was aware of other shouts and the herd began to mill, blindly seeking a route of escape, trampling each other.

He was in the midst of the milling brown mass of flesh and fur and hooves, the great creatures all about him. He trusted his pony to find its own way and to avoid being trampled. He nocked and let fly arrow after arrow. He breathed dust and the rank odor of buffalo for what seemed an eternity, the eternity of the hunt. He had no idea how many of the creatures he shot in the turmoil and confusion.

At one point the roan stumbled, and for a heart-stopping instant Pitalesharo was certain he would be thrown beneath the frantic hooves. But the pony recovered and took him to the side of yet another cow, and the long slaughter continued.

At last it was over. The thunder grew quiet as the last of the huge herd escaped over the ridges and up the gullies.

Termite Joe galloped beside the chief's son as he pursued a group of stragglers up a dry creek bed.

"Yee-haw," the trapper yelled. "You sure know fat cow from stringy bull, and that's for certain. Thought you was a goner there for a minute, though."

Pitalesharo grinned and pulled his pony to a walk. The buffalo were too far away for a shot and the horse was tired.

"It's been a good hunt, Juan Termite. Where were you?"

"Right there behind you, lad, but I reckon you was so busy you didn't even hear my old buffalo gun. Likely most of them fat cows you thought you had your name on'll turn out to have a speck of galena in 'em." Pitalesharo threw his head back and laughed.

The women had moved the camp to the scene of the hunt and were about the business of butchering the inert brown masses. Knives flashed in the early afternoon sunlight and the adept hands worked.

One Broken Feather, sister to Spotted Eagle, had taken it upon herself to look for Pitalesharo's arrows and count his kill. Time and again she ran to where the son of the chief and the mountain man lay back in the shade of a hide lean-to, resting.

"This makes fourteen," she giggled excitedly. "That already makes three more than Hawk Foot killed and one more than Brave Bull. I think when all the buffalo are counted, you will be judged the greatest hunter of all, Man Chief."

She ran off to continue her counting and Termite Joe chuckled to himself. "Looks like they's one of us ain't going to sleep alone tonight," he remarked. "Best cure in the world for what ails you. Trust me on that, coon."

"The young women compete for the favors of the best hunter," Pitalesharo nodded. "I should have thought of that ahead of time."

"Hope they counts the ones with lead in 'em," Joe chuckled.

That evening when the hump ribs and the other choice parts of the fresh-killed buffalo were roasting in great slabs over the fires, the tales of the day's hunt were recounted.

The official tally of individual kills confirmed that Pitalesharo had slain more than any of the other hunters.

Broken Feather and two other girls squeezed up close beside him, giggling and suggestively rubbing against him.

For a moment he felt the familiar tightening in his loins as his flesh began to rise. But then he remembered Little Green Frog, her soft moans as they lay together, her warm body curled against his in sleep. The great, cold emptiness inside seemed to open out into a void again, and his desire for the laughing, plump-bosomed girls next to him vanished.

He rose abruptly and gently pushed the trio toward the grinning Termite Joe Hollingback. "These women are in heat. They will not be satisfied until they have been made love to. Juan Termite, you must take care of this matter for your friend."

With that he turned and walked off into the night. He went down to the nearly dry river, where he sat alone. He stared at the half-visible surface of the dark water trying not to think, searching the blackness of the stream as if for some answer.

Chapter 11

In the mornings there was frost on the grass and along the edges of the little river. Soon the geese would be flying south and the ground would begin to freeze at night, taking even longer to thaw by day as the light grew shorter and shorter. The leaves of cottonwood and elder had already begun turning to a pale yellow. Funnel clouds would touch the earth and hurl things about and hail would sing through the air and hammer the roofs of the village of Wolf-Standing-in-Water.

The Skidi had returned from the buffalo hunt to their permanent village. The women were busy drying long strips of meat, making pemmican, gathering the last squashes and gourds and digging the potatoes out of the crumbling black earth.

Many of the men, at the urging of Pierre Papin and Termite Joe, cleaned their traps with handfuls of gritty sand, repaired chain and made other preparations for a fall beaver hunt along the branches of the Republican River. It was not work that the men enjoyed; most declined it altogether, considering that they had taken a sufficient number of buffalo robes to allow them to trade at Papin's post for whatever they might need this winter.

For Wounded Man the coming of autumn signaled no need to trap or to hunt. Instead, working in conjunction with several other medicine men, he prepared a ritual celebration in honor of Tirawa Atius, the creating power, and all the other spirits and deities. Morning Star and Old Man Coyote, Evening Star and all of those who dwelt on the face of Earth Mother or in Awahokshu, the spirit world, were to be feted. Among them were the *chixu*, the ghosts; Hotoru, the wind god; H-uraru, the earth spirit; Shakuru, Grandmother Moon; Uti Hiata, the spirit of the sun. They also honored the Corn Mother; White Bear; Dawn; male and female spirits; Delgeth, the flesh-eating Antelope; the Protectors and the various lesser animal spirits.

It was a time of harvest and of thanksgiving for the bounty of the land. The flesh of buffalo, antelope and deer was roasted in great fire pits. Hide tables were set up at the center of the village and piled high with woven baskets of roots and tubers, dried berries, steamed squashes, yellow melons and roasted ears of corn as well as fish and flour cakes, baked fowl and pots of honey.

The people feasted and danced and told stories. The older men in particular regaled bands of wide-eyed children, delectably terrified. The various societies performed their stylized dances and the warriors recounted and acted out their most prized coups. Older women scurried about happily gossiping, and groups of children chased through the village, played games and tossed sticks and stuffed balls of laced hide for the yapping camp dogs to fetch. Young men and women wandered away from the village to meet in the wooded area downstream, returning after a time wearing looks of happy guilt.

Young wives dressed up in their finest deerskins, their faces carefully painted by those husbands who had won the right to do so. And young husbands and unattached swains affected elaborate and gaudy fashions with intricate designs painted on arms and chests and faces. Some wore animal skins—bear and cougar and wolf. A few wore the clothing of the white men, garments received as gifts or taken in battle or purchased from the supply room of Pierre Didier Papin.

In particular, Papin noted, blue jackets with yellow braid were much in demand.

On the third and final night of the celebration Wounded Man appeared in full shaman's regalia, the long scar across his face and through his bad eye brightly painted, as was his custom at such times.

The medicine man walked slowly to the opening between the main fire pit and the crooked box-elder tree. He had the undivided attention of all present. He stood in the firelight, his hands held high above his head, and began to croon. His voice rose in pitch and his head was thrown back.

Some of the men in the audience began to moan loudly. Pitalesharo shook his head and wondered if the audience response had been arranged in advance.

Then Wounded Man was silent. His body quivered as though some terrible power had taken control of him. And when he opened his good eye, only the white was visible in the irregular firelight. He spoke in a voice that did not sound like his.

"Skidi Pawnee, hear my words. I speak through the lips of Wounded Man, your shaman. This is Morning Star who addresses you."

The Pawnee were horrified and yet fascinated. Many cried out in wonder.

"You are my people, but I am angry with you nonetheless. I have asked for sacrifices, but they have been taken from me. In the spirit world your fathers and grandfathers cry for you and pray that you will yet return to the true way. Sacrifice is required, Skidi!

"The white men come into your lands and only a few of the warriors are brave enough to fight them, even though the Pawnee are strong enough to kill all of these invaders. I thirst for their blood, Skidi!

"But you are weak now because you have no one to lead you. That is why I speak through the lips of Wounded Man, so that all may hear me and know my will. Now hear me well. I say it is time for the council to select another chief, for the man called Lachelesharo has lost the will to fight. His medicine pouch is full of dust and the dung of dogs. Once he was a brave warrior, but he is so no longer. It is time for you to choose another."

With this Wounded Man fell to the ground and began to writhe as though in great agony. When the spasm had passed, he rose to his hands and knees and began to disgorge great quantities of what appeared to be blood.

The people screamed and shouts of fear, horror, outrage and anger went up.

The shaman lay as if dead. The other medicine men rushed to his assistance. They gestured over him and sprinkled him with water and pollen. They chanted words that no one could understand. At last they assisted Wounded

Man to his feet and the Thunderbird Lances came forward and surrounded the great shaman and those who assisted him.

.''What am I to do?'' Lachelesharo cried out as he sat in his lodge staring into the flames of the cook fire. ''He is more powerful than any other medicine man in this village or in any of the others. Could White Cougar stand up to this man? Could any of the head chiefs?''

''The son of a bitch puts on one hell of a good show, don't he?'' Termite Joe remarked as he carved at a stick of firewood. ''That blood-vomiting gets it every time, sure as buffalo shit. I swear, he's good enough so's even a civilized white nigger like me half thinks it's goddamned real.''

''I do not believe in the shaman's medicine,'' Pitalesharo asserted. ''Is he the one who heals us when we are sick or wounded? No, the other medicine men do that. This one believes he *is* Morning Star or whatever god he wishes to be. He is a fraud, a man who uses tricks and strange words to get what he wants.''

''Could be, could be,'' Termite Joe agreed, ''but whatever she is, she damned well works. I figger half the village must have shat their pants, by God.''

''Perhaps I should resign,'' Lachelesharo said. ''What good is a leader if the people do not wish to follow him? And it is true that I have forsaken the warpath. Long ago I listened to Red-haired Chief, and his words sounded very good to me. I believed that he was right. I came to believe that there is some other way than constant war. Was I deceived in this? Now the warrior societies do as they wish. They kill whites who come only to trap in our streams and the people applaud them. And yet if the whites truly attempted to take our lands from us, I would fight them until I died. I love my people, but I fear that they no longer have any respect for me.''

"If you tell the council you no longer wish to lead the people," Pitalesharo said, "they will surely remember Wounded Man's words. And they will most likely choose Hawk Foot, for all believe that his medicine for war is powerful.''

"You belong to the council, my son," Lachelesharo said. "If you spoke what you know of Hawk Foot, the other members of the council would listen to you.''

"No, Father, they would not listen to me. Nor would they choose me to lead in your place, even though I am the chief of the Red Lances. They would think only that I resented Hawk Foot, that there was bad blood between us.''

"Well," the chief asked, "what can I say now that will counteract the words of Wounded Man? I cannot vomit blood or pretend to speak with the voice of Morning Star. Could I say that Tirawa Atius has come to me in a vision and told me Wounded Man is hateful in his eyes? Not all believe in the shaman's trickery, but even fewer would believe in mine.''

Pitalesharo and Termite Joe glanced at one another and turned their eyes to Lachelesharo.

"I think I must call the council together and tell it that I no longer wish to be head chief, that they must choose another.''

"Has my husband grown old and weak, then?" Raven Quill asked. "I am only a woman, so it is possible that I should not speak at all. Yet Lachelesharo trusts my judgment in many things, even though he does not tell the people. So now I will speak what I think.''

Lachelesharo pretended to glare at his wife, but his eyes were soft.

Termite Joe slapped his leg and snorted.

"Wagh! Knife Chief, you'd best listen to her. She ain't never been wrong as I know of, and that's a fact."

"Yes. This is what Knife Chief must do. Many of the warriors are still loyal to him. All the Red Lances are loyal, and I think the same is true of the Two Lances and the Brave Ravens. Who knows about the others? But most of these men will still follow the chief.

"My husband, you must announce a warpath. We are still unavenged upon the Ute, and our pastures are large enough for many more horses than we have now. Often we have had twice as many. That way the people will see that you have accepted Wounded Man's challenge, and they will do nothing until they see whether your medicine for war is still strong. That is what Raven Quill thinks."

"Bravo," Hollingback cried out. "Coons, she's right again, sure as fucking causes kids. By God, she is. Lachelesharo, that's exactly what you got to do. Ain't that right, Juan Pete?"

"My men will all ride with you, Father, and many of the others also. I agree with Mother."

The chief stood up and paced back and forth. Then he turned, placed his hands on Raven Quill's shoulders and touched his forehead to hers.

"I will do it. This night I will climb to the high rock and ask for guidance. I will ask Old Coyote Man and Morning Star and all the others to strengthen my medicine. I do not believe that the great star speaks through the shaman. Have I grown old? Am I weak now? No, neither of those things is true. I will lead my warriors again, just as I have led them many times before. This shaman has never been stronger than I am, and he is not stronger now."

*   *   *

He lay naked on the medicine rocks and allowed the cold moonlight to bathe his body. The Fire People slowly revolved about the pole star, and somewhere out in the rolling prairie a cougar screamed twice.

Lachelesharo lay with his eyes open staring upward. No vision came.

At length he withdrew his skinning knife and slashed himself across the chest, laved his hands in the welling blood and smeared it over his face and into his hair.

"Lachelesharo of the Skidi Pawnee calls to you for help," he said softly. After that he closed his eyes and remained quiet for a long while.

When he looked again, the stars had all vanished. The night had turned intensely black, so dark that he could not even see his own hands when he lifted them over his face.

He heard distant thunder and there was a smell of rain in the air. A moist, gentle wind moved about him. Then a blue-green light appeared above him and gained in intensity.

A face formed out of the light. "Knife Chief, why do you seek me? I was hunting and unable to come sooner."

Beads of sweat stood out on the postulant's face. He could feel them like little points of fire. "I need a vision. I seek the guidance of the spirit people."

"Do you wish to lead the warriors, Knife Chief? You have only to tell them so."

"My people live in pain. They do not know which way to go. They do not know whom to follow."

"Then why do you cease to lead them, Knife Chief? Your son is a powerful warrior, but is the son greater than the father? Is he the chief of the Skidi? Perhaps this happened while I was wandering."

"He leads the Red Lances."

"The young dog runs faster than the old dog, but the young dog is not so wise. That is why there are several lesser chiefs and only one head chief. It is foolish to talk this way. I am hungry and must leave you very soon. You have taken many coups during the past years, but now you must take more. Is this what you wish me to tell you? Shall I tell you to go into the great mountains and bring back many horses, Knife Chief? You do not need my help.''

''Morning Star is angry with my people. He demands death by fire, and yet I believe it is wrong to do such a thing.''

The blue-green light pulsed and the face inside the light contorted with mirth.

''Then you have no need for me at all. Look, Knife Chief. This is how it was. Once Morning Star came close to earth itself and destroyed everything. Water covered the prairies and the mountains burst into flame. Rocks fell from the heavens and the earth groaned and screamed. That was long ago. Perhaps someday it will all happen again. But why should a god wish to see a helpless human being burned to death? Seek your own wisdom, Knife Chief. Now I must go.''

Great tongues of fire went up before Lachelesharo's eyes and a warm rain began to fall.

It was raining when he awoke. The eastern horizon glowed silver grey, and mingled odors of wet stone and moist, dead grass filled his nostrils.

He rose and touched at the wound on his chest, but no wound was there, not even a scratch. There were no bloodstains on his hands.

Lachelesharo grinned and looked up into the greyness of the sky and felt the rain touch his face. ''I have heard a voice from the spirit world, a voice from Awahokshu. My medicine is still powerful; my strength is still my own.''

He dressed without hurrying and began his descent to the village.

Pitalesharo and Termite Joe were still asleep when the chief entered his lodge, but Raven Quill was awake. The cook fire was dancing and a kettle of broth was steaming and giving off a most delicious odor.

"My husband?"

Lachelesharo nodded. "My medicine is good. This day I will call the chiefs and their warriors to the war lodge. Soon we will have so many horses we will not know what to do with them, my wife. I will be so wealthy that I will wish to buy five new wives. Will that please you?"

"Knife Chief needs something to put in his belly," Raven Quill said. "The night air has scrambled his brains."

Lachelesharo laughed softly and accepted the bowl of broth his wife handed him. He drank the hot liquid slowly, placed the empty container beside the fire and strode across the room to where his medicine shield and crossed lances hung on the wall.

At noon he spoke to the warriors and advised them of his plan to go on a revenge-taking against the Ute. His war medicine, he said, was very strong, and he could not resist its call any longer.

The men studied the chief's face, and then many of them began to grin and to slap their thighs in rhythm. Only Hawk Foot and the Thunderbird Lances remained silent, making no sign of approval.

Pitalesharo and all of the Red Lances were eager to ride, and with them came warriors from the Brave Ravens, the Two Lances, the Horse Society and the Knife Lances. The latter in particular were well represented, for this was the group that Lachelesharo himself had led in his youth, and many of the warriors had accompanied the chief on various warpaths.

"Tu-ra-heh, it is good," said Buffalo, the leader of the Knife Lances. "It will be like old times, Lachelesharo. When we two ride together, no one can withstand us. We will once more darken our lodges with the scalps of our enemies."

"Perhaps our enemies will see us coming and run so fast that we will not be able to scalp them," Lachelesharo laughed, pleased with Buffalo's words.

"We will catch them," Buffalo insisted.

Word rapidly spread through the village, and by afternoon the Pawnee men were consulting their medicine bundles, preparing their shields and weapons and purchasing lead and powder from Papin's trading post. The Frenchman and Termite Joe were kept busy, and a number of buffalo robes were taken in trade.

"Mon ami," Papin asked after the needs of the warriors had been taken care of, "will you too ride with Lachelesharo? It is time to begin trapping, Joe. Everything goes bad, friend of me. I do not think Pilcher will send us here again next year."

"The boys don't need no white nigger following 'em," Termite Joe said. "I'm fixing to mosey up to the headwaters of the Platte. Nobody working that country, I figger. I'll take some mules and be gone a spell. Should be beavers climbing the trees over there."

"Good, good. Something will come of it. But I think you will be looking for our friend Antonio, no?"

"That crossed my mind," Termite Joe grinned. "Maybe the whole thing'll work out."

At day's end Joe filled his whiskey flask from Papin's big keg of undiluted alcohol, noted his purchase in the company log and strode across the village toward the lodge he shared with the head chief's family.

A dark strange figure crouched in the shadows to one

side of the entry, hands moving overhead as though weaving something out of strands of air.

Termite Joe dropped back into the shadows, and moving silently, came up and loomed over the squatting form. When he set the hammer of his horse pistol, the man shot to his feet.

"Wounded Man, is it?" Hollingback asked. "Pizening the well, was you? Coon could get shot sneaking around like that, Chief Big Scar."

The shaman, taken by surprise, was furious and all but speechless.

"You are not wanted here, white man," he growled.

"One of us ain't, anyhow. Why don't you just head on home and skin one of your dogs alive? Lachelesharo don't need no more bad luck than he's got."

The shaman disappeared into the shadows.

Joe knelt down and ran his fingertips over the area where Wounded Man had been crouched. "Goddamned design of some sort." Standing up, he scrubbed the area smooth with the sole of his moccasin.

Inside the lodge, Lachelesharo, Pitalesharo, Two Boulders and the old warrior named Buffalo were discussing the upcoming warpath.

Joe went straight to Raven Quill, who dished him out a bowl of boiled antelope and cornmeal. The mountain man sat down and began to eat. He said nothing of the shaman's little performance outside the lodge.

Chapter 12

Two days later just at dawn Lachelesharo led his band of more than a hundred warriors out of the village and up-stream along the little river. The morning was hushed and intensely cold, with heavy frost over the grass and even along the edges of the slow-moving water.

Their objective lay some two hundred fifty miles to the west, six days of riding, more if early snowfall made the going difficult through the mountains and even more if the wandering Ute were not in their usual encampment at the fork of the Tomichi and the Cochetopa. If the Ute had not already gone into winter camp there, probably they would be even farther west, perhaps on the Cebolla.

If the warpath were kept on schedule, Lachelesharo reflected, he and his men might well be back at Wolf-Standing-in-Water Village within two weeks.

The day moon was a thin crescent. If Old Coyote Man favored them, it would be nearly full when the Pawnee undertook to borrow horses from the Ute.

*   *   *

In late afternoon of the second day of their ride Lachelesharo and his warriors passed over into the drainage of the Big Sandy and were surprised to find a small encampment of Pawnee already there. Lachelesharo, Pitalesharo and Buffalo rode forward and immediately recognized a group of warriors from Pitahauerats Village. White Cougar's people.

The two head chiefs embraced formally and then pounded one another on the back. "I heard that my brother was going to steal horses, so I decided to come along," White Cougar grinned. "Those Ute ponies, they are very difficult to capture."

"You are welcome to join us, old friend. Now between us we have a very large war party. Our enemies will think we have come to destroy them and to burn their hide lodges. But instead we will only take their horses. They can always borrow more from the Shoshone or the Crow. Besides, those people spend too much time riding anyway."

"Pitalesharo rides with you, I see. It is good for a father and son to spend time together. Too often they compete with one another."

"I wished only to go trapping so that I could catch beavers for the white men," Pitalesharo joked, "but the head chief insisted that I come."

"All of my son's Red Lances are with me," Lachelesharo declared. "Every one of them. Man Chief's warriors are very loyal and all of them wish to have a Ute pony or two."

White Cougar nodded. "Tu-ra-heh. We will take our Ute friends by surprise, I think."

The weather held and the Pawnee were able to make good time. They had to take cover only for an hour or two one afternoon when pebble-sized hailstones from thunderclouds piled high above the mountains near Poncha Pass beat down upon them. They waited under a heavy stand of young spruces for Old Coyote Man to tire of this particular whim.

The following morning a wolf scout came in with good news. The Ute village was precisely where the Pawnee had hoped it would be, at the confluence of the Tomichi and the Cochetopa. And furthermore, a huge herd of horses was grazing peacefully in the meadows upstream along the Tomichi. They were guarded by half a dozen young warriors, but these were posted between the herd and the village.

"These Ute are not expecting visitors from across the mountains," Pitalesharo grinned as enthusiasm for the horse-thieving grew within him.

"We must approach carefully," Lachelesharo cautioned him. "Even if we are able to take them by surprise, the Ute outnumber us at least three to one. We must strike quickly and drive the animals back into the mountains. Then if the Ute follow us, we will have a much easier time of it."

White Cougar shrugged, his expression suggesting that it did not concern him whether the Ute chose to fight or not.

"Loo-ah," he laughed. "It is a good day to die, my friends. There is nothing to fear. We are all going to go to the place we came from."

Pitalesharo clucked his tongue. "Let's stop talking and go steal horses. If we don't hurry, the Pun-nak or the Absaroka will have taken all the ponies and there will be none left for us."

Pine and spruce woods shimmered with silver moonlight. The air was intensely cold. A great horned owl called. It was hunting somewhere up on the rocky ridge to the north.

The horses stood close to one another against the cold in the broad meadow, their breath rising in filaments of steam. Yellow-white grasses glistened with frost. The smell of lodge fires from the Ute village hung in the air.

The Pawnee raiders tethered their own ponies half a mile away. Spread out, they crossed the last ridge on foot and approached the horses from all sides.

"It is better if we kill these guards," Two Boulders whispered as he, Pitalesharo and Thin Cloud approached the lean-to and the dying campfire of the Ute warriors stationed with the herd.

"But they are only boys," Thin Cloud objected. "Look at them. They are much younger than I am. Is there no other way?"

"Only three guards for all these horses," Pitalesharo mused. "But I can see no one else. The others must have returned to the village. Perhaps they held some ritual this night."

"They were not expecting company," Two Boulders said, licking his tongue along the flat of his knife blade.

"Some colder night you will do that and get your tongue stuck to the steel," Pitalesharo warned him. "Then it will stay that way until spring comes."

Two Boulders grinned, his square white teeth glinting with moonlight.

"Can we not bind them and gag them?" Thin Cloud asked.

Pitalesharo considered the matter. Already the Pawnee were moving out among the horses and beginning to lead the best of them away toward the pine woods. "Can we do such a thing quietly enough?"

"Perhaps we do not even need to worry about these three," Two Boulders said. "They are busy talking to each other and have forgotten all about the horses. Look,

Lachelesharo and White Cougar are getting all the best ponies. We must hurry or there will be none left for us."

"Can you whimper like a wolf that has been injured, Thin Cloud?" Pitalesharo asked. "I have heard you do that before. You do it very well."

"Now?" Thin Cloud asked. "But the Ute will hear me."

"Yes, exactly. Crawl over by that clump of choke-cherry brush and whimper. But have your knife ready. Let's see what happens."

Thin Cloud crawled to the tangle of leafless choke-cherry and began to moan. Within moments two of the Ute had risen from their nearly extinguished fire and begun sneaking toward what they supposed to be a wolf in pain. As they approached where Thin Cloud lay hidden, the two Ute became more cautious and one stopped to fashion a noose-halter.

Pitalesharo and Two Boulders rose up out of the shadows and deftly knocked the boys senseless with the flat of a war axe.

"Bind these two, Thin Cloud. Stuff grass into their mouths. Two Boulders and I will attend to their friend—"

But the third Ute had already heard the scuffle and come running. Two Boulders grabbed him from behind and slit his throat. The Ute sagged forward, sputtered out a foam of blood and dropped to his knees. He made a last desperate attempt to retrieve the pistol he had dropped and then sprawled face down in the frozen grass.

Two Boulders picked up the pistol, examined it per-functorily and knelt to take the dead man's scalp. "He has gone to the spirit world, Pitalesharo. It could not be helped."

"Yes. Come, Thin Cloud. Let's pick out some ponies."

Driving an uncounted number of horses before them, five hundred or more, the Pawnee rode through the night and into the following day. How long would it take the Ute to discover what had happened? Would new sentries have been sent in the middle of the night, or would the theft go undetected until morning?

It was difficult going up through the pass, and several times the borrowed horses attempted to drift away. Others simply came to a standstill and had to be goaded forward.

They had still not reached the pass when the nearly full moon disappeared beyond the long, black ranges to the west. But the Pawnee warriors, dead tired though they were, managed to keep pushing their newly acquired animals over the pass.

By noon they had reached a small tributary of the Arkansas River, and there they allowed the horses to take water and grass. The Pawnee ate a quick meal of dried meat and cakes of cornmeal and then at a signal from Lachelesharo took to their ponies once more and continued the drive.

Late afternoon found them across the Arkansas and on their way up the low pass that separated this drainage from that of the upper reaches of the South Platte. At this point a trailing wolf scout came in with word that a very angry band of Ute warriors was close behind.

"We cannot fight them and still protect the horses, Father," Pitalesharo said. "What must we do?"

"Your son is right," White Cougar agreed.

"Spotted Wolf, Two Boulders, Thin Cloud and some of the others must go on ahead," Lachelesharo declared. "They will go with some of the Pitahauerats warriors. They must drive the horses as fast as they can. The rest of us will split into two groups. White Cougar's men go with him, the Skidi with me. When the Ute reach that notch up ahead of us, we will be waiting for them."

"I like your words," White Cougar said. He called out the names of a dozen of his men.

The drovers, most of them disappointed at not being able to participate in the skirmish, moved ahead with their hard-won herd of Ute ponies.

"Now, Buffalo, old friend," Lachelesharo called out, "we will go into battle once again, just as we have done many times before. White Cougar, you take the north rim. Pitalesharo and I will take the south. Position your men so that they cannot be easily seen. I think we will have some Ute scalps to take home with us."

"Tu-ra-heh," White Cougar agreed.

The Pawnee warriors rode into the narrow defile and took their positions. Within an hour the scout atop the pinnacle rocks signaled down to Lachelesharo and White Cougar. The Ute were coming, riding hard, a hundred warriors or more.

Lachelesharo nodded, spoke a few words and waved his otter-tail lance three times. Across the way White Cougar waved back and the ambush was set.

The Ute came through the defile two abreast, angry and heedless of danger. When gunfire and arrows began to sing down from the rocks above, they were thrown into confusion. Horses tossed their riders as a withering hail of crossfire took its toll. The Ute leaped from their horses and sought cover or turned their ponies and ran headlong into their fellows coming up from behind.

Lachelesharo signaled those of his men who were still on horseback, and from both sides of the defile the Pawnee poured down, their cries of "Loo-ah" echoing from the rocks.

Hand-to-hand combat raged. Pistols and rifles discharged at close range, war axes crushed skulls, horses fell and stumbled to their feet again minus their riders, men rolled together on the earth locked in mortal combat.

The Red Lance warrior Buffalo Runner was down, and Pitalesharo drove his roan forward to protect his friend, hurling his lance and taking a Ute brave full in the stomach. The man fell backward, grasped at the shaft, groaned and died.

Lacheleshshro and Buffalo raged through the melee like men possessed, striking out to every side with their battle axes. But it was all over in a few minutes. Demoralized by the carnage and believing themselves badly outnumbered, the Ute fled on horseback and on foot, leaving many war ponies and weapons behind in the haste of their flight.

The Pawnee, however, chose not to pursue. Three warriors from the Pitahauerats village were dead and several more were wounded, though not seriously. None of the Skidi had been killed, but Buffalo Runner had broken a wrist when his pony threw him and had taken a pistol ball through the shoulder for good measure.

Pitalesharo took the scalp of the Ute he had slain with his lance, rose and looked about him. In all, sixteen of the Ute were dead and the Pawnee had acquired an additional twenty-three ponies as well as pistols, axes, bows, shields and two buffalo rifles of recent vintage.

Lacheleshshro also surveyed the results of the conflict, clicked his teeth together and smiled.

Had Termite Joe been present he might have said, "Coon, for a chief what prefers the way of peace, you've done yourself proud. Look at you setting there, a big victory over your enemies and four scalps dangling from your saddle. Wagh!"

So Pawnee honor had been avenged at last, but now a new round of battles was inevitable. Those of White Cougar's men who were related to the slain would be obliged to take revenge on the Ute or upon some other enemy so that the wives and sisters of the dead warriors would be able to wash the paint of mourning from their faces. The wounded Skidi would waste little time in mounting another venture if only their wounds healed properly.

And of course the Ute, who would have to return to their village in disgrace, would be able to think of little else until they had evened the score with their enemies. But the warpath they mounted might well be against the Wind River Shoshone to the north or the Cheyenne or the Arapaho. And so it would continue, and so it had always been among peoples who were seldom at peace.

"Our medicine is still strong, Chief of the Skidi Pawnee," Buffalo grinned. "These younger men will think twice now before they dare to claim again that our medicine has grown weak. You will give all your new ponies away as gifts to the others, Knife Chief. But Buffalo will buy a new young wife. There's a girl in the village I have been watching for some time now. Twice she has met with me down by the willows and we have lain together. Now I will offer her father three of the best ponies and some buffalo robes as well. He will be pleased for his daughter to marry me. Then I will have four women in my lodge. You should do that too, Lachelesharo. It would make things easier for Raven Quill."

The Pawnee, bearing their dead with them, caught up with their drovers the following day at Oily Creek. They proceeded south to the Arkansas and thence out onto the High Plains. They turned north toward Many-Streams-Start Plateau, through undulating lands cut by sharp arroyos and covered with sage and short grass and strewn rocks.

Pitalesharo remained with the victorious war party until White Cougar and his men separated from the Skidi to travel on to the Pitahauerats village on Arikaree Creek. Then he told Lachelesharo that he wished to leave the others and ride back to the mountains.

"You will enter the village as a hero, Father," he said. "It will be the way it was when I was a boy. Always I dreaded that you would not return, but my fears were foolish. Now you will call for the scalp dance and Raven Quill will be proud when you recount the coups you have taken. You will have many horses to give as presents and the people will praise your medicine. Old Wounded Man will gnash his teeth."

"Why do you wish to return to the mountains, Pitalesharo? Do you believe you will be able to find Antonio Grey Bear and persuade him to return to Wolf-Standing-in-Water Village?"

"Perhaps that will happen. But even so, it is time for me to seek a powerful vision. My mind is very confused, Father, and I need to be by myself."

Lachelesharo stared at his son. "Your medicine tells you to do this thing?"

"Yes."

"Go well, then, Man Chief."

With no further explanation to anyone Pitalesharo turned his roan pony and began to ride toward the great white peak of Karitku-cu, the Big Rock.

Two days after Lachelesharo and his warriors left the village to undertake their war party against the Ute, Termite Joe Hollingback loaded his pack horse, said so long to Pierre Papin, Raven Quill and a young woman named Broken Feather, gathered together an additional four mules and rode westward. His destination was the area around the headwaters of the South Platte and his primary purpose was to trap beaver, invading the lodges of M. Castor, as Papin referred to it. But he also had in mind to discover the whereabouts of Antonio Behele.

"Just ain't the same without old Juan Antonio about," Hollingback mused. "Didn't never figger I'd miss that gangly Spanish renegade so much, but this child does. Wagh! Why's life always getting so godawful complicated?"

He rode due west along the tributary stream that

emptied into the Republican at the village. He used his Virginia rifle to shoot three beavers at various points along the way. He missed a fourth in the attempt to nail the big rodent in the head so as not to spoil the pelt.

On the second day he detected a slip of smoke issuing from a bench high up on a grotesquely eroded sandstone formation. His curiosity got the better of him.

"Some Indian poking holes in his red hide and trying to get old Tirawa to give him a medicine vision, I expect. Or maybe some poor devil as don't have anything better to do. Well, let's take a look-see."

He tethered his stock in a secluded glade of cotton-woods and worked his way up to the rim. He studied the castle rocks and decided to approach them from the far side.

He saw that a horse had been picketed next to a brush hedge beyond a pile of tumbled red-brown boulders of broken sandstone. He stared for a moment, then shook his head and grinned.

"Don't go jumping to conclusions, Joseph," he cautioned himself. Checking the load in his buffalo rifle and tapping the pan to guard against misfire, Hollingback cautiously made his way up through the big rocks. The path, he noted, had been used quite a bit of late.

He reached the bench, stepped behind a stone wall and cautiously peered around it. A tall man, his clothing nearly in shreds, was stooping beside a little fire.

"Grey Bear," Termite Joe called out, "what on God's green earth are you doing here?"

Chapter 13

She awoke in stages, feeling as if she were pushing her way up through depths of dark water, but she realized that she had not really been sleeping. Something was dreadfully wrong. Her cheek was damp and cold from lying against something wet, and there was an odd salty taste in her mouth.

The taste of blood.

She began to hear small sounds, the cheerful single notes of birds, small rustlings as they hopped among the branches of trees. And a gurgling, rushing sound meant she was near water. The thought of water brought with it a terrible thirst, and she tried to move, then moaned as pain like fire shot through her head and her limbs. She lay still, waiting for the onslaught to subside.

What has happened? Hummingbird. My name is Hummingbird. Have I fallen from my pony? Perhaps my mother will come find me.

She tried to open her eyes but found that she could raise only one lid, and that not all the way. She could see light, something deep brown, a few green splotches. The effort or perhaps the intrusion of light intensified the ache inside her skull and she closed the eye.

Memories returned in fragments, like sharp-edged bits of broken pottery.

Hawk Foot. My husband.

He was shouting at her, his face red and contorted; he did not look human at all. She could not understand the cause of his anger. She was fleeing frightened from the lodge, running wildly, brush tearing at her ankles, branches whipping her face, and all the time hearing the thrashing and cursing of pursuit. Then she fell by the river. She clung to the forlorn hope that if she lay quietly enough among the willow tangle where she had fallen, he wouldn't find her.

Then came the shock of blows and a dim amazement that their force did not break her neck, that she was still alive through it all. She put up her arms to shield her face, but he continued to strike her, hitting her arms and breasts with something that she knew was not his fists. He was using a club on her and kicking her in his fury.

She drifted into semi-consciousness, a place warm with the promise of sleep, and she no longer felt the beating.

Then cold air touched her thighs, her buttocks. Hawk Foot was grunting as he turned her over, pulled her dress up and pushed her knees apart.

"No," she cried out, seeing the dark form crouched over her. "Why are you doing this, Hawk Foot? I never denied you that."

"You have denied me everything, Hummingbird," he hissed. "You have opened your thighs for me, but you have denied me even then. Now we will see if you can deny me."

At last she felt a pain worse than the rest as he forced the dry passage, ripping at the delicate tissues. His hand was clamped over her mouth and she couldn't scream. The pain went on for a long while, but she forced it away from her, lost interest and drifted back to the dark, warm place, to sleep.

The memories brought with them a flood of desolation.

"I am not a little girl any longer. It has been four summers since I saw my mother. I will never see my mother again. I will never see Grey Bear again. I said that I did not care what Hawk Foot might do, but I didn't know what I was talking about."

She lay for a time in darkness of spirit, far worse than the oblivion she had just emerged from. She tried to return to unconsciousness again but found that she could not.

The need for water became overwhelming. She raised her head a little, gritted her teeth against the agony of movement and crawled blindly toward the sound of the stream. Feeling cold liquid on her hand, she rolled into the shallows, put her face into the water and sucked it through her swollen lips.

The chill of the stream eased some of her agony, and she let the slow current wash around her. She rested with her cheek against a stone, not thinking of what she might do next.

My body will not let me die. My body must be stronger than my spirit.

She became aware of voices and thought in terror that Hawk Foot might be returning. She tried to get out of the water, but then she realized that the voices belonged to a group of women laughing and talking gaily.

Then one of them shrieked, "Come here, Broken Feather, Quail, there is someone dead, I think."

Hummingbird tried to speak but couldn't. She moved one hand over the sand beneath the water.

"No," Broken Feather shouted, "look, she moved. I think it is Hummingbird."

"What could have happened to her?" Quail asked in hushed tones.

"I don't know, but we've got to get her out of the stream. Here, Dancing Girl, you help me. We'll try to raise her up."

Broken Feather knelt in the water and called loudly, "Hummingbird, can you hear me? Can you get up if we help you?"

Hummingbird opened the puffed slit of her one good eye but could see only the darkness of the other form against the intolerable light of the sky. She forced her lips to move, struggled to make words.

"I can't understand what she's saying." Quail was leaning over Broken Feather's shoulder. "Can you understand her?"

Broken Feather shook her head. "We're going to help you, Hummingbird," she called again. "We're going to turn you over onto your back and help you to sit up. Do you hear what I'm saying?"

Hummingbird could only nod as the three women pushed and tugged at her to get her to her feet. Hummingbird endured it, whimpering faintly but not crying out. They managed to get her up, but it was obvious that she would not be able to walk.

"I will go home and make a small travois from my buffalo robes. When I come back, we can pull her on that," Quail said.

While they waited by the stream for Quail to return, Broken Feather and Dancing Girl ministered to Hummingbird as best they could, washing her face with water from the river and speaking to her in words of soft encouragement.

"We'll take care of you, Hummingbird," Broken Feather said. "I don't think you have any broken bones. Someone beat you, didn't he?"

Hummingbird muttered, "Yes."

"Who did this thing? It is shameful that anyone would do such a thing. But you will be fine in a few days, I promise. I will come to your lodge and stay with you if you wish. I am very good at caring for people. I know many good herbs and I can sing very well and make you feel better. Your husband will kill whoever did this thing to you," Broken Feather went on, mixing tenderness and indignation.

Hummingbird struggled wildly at these words, moving her hands and trying to shake her head. "No," she managed to mumble. "Not home. Don't take me to Hawk Foot, please. . . ."

Broken Feather and Dancing Girl exchanged glances.

"Was it your husband who did this thing to you? Was it Hawk Foot?"

Once again Hummingbird whispered, "Yes."

"Hah," cried Broken Feather. "I knew he was no good. But everyone thought he loved you. Many people even thought he had changed completely since he married you. Well, it is a husband's right to beat his own wife, they say, but if my husband ever beat me, I would kill him. *If* I had a husband. No, you will come to my lodge.

Hawk Foot will not come there to beat you. My father is Wolf Chief. He will not let Hawk Foot come into the lodge. And I will stick a knife into him if he does come in.''

Broken Feather put her arm around the injured woman's shoulder as she spoke and Hummingbird lay against her, gradually sliding down with exhaustion until she was stretched out with her head in Broken Feather's lap.

When Quail returned with her makeshift travois, the three women lashed Hummingbird to it, covered her with another buffalo robe and piled a few sticks of driftwood on top, hoping thus to conceal their burden from casual notice. Broken Feather dragged the rig from the front, and her two friends lifted it at the sides to ease the painful jouncing as much as possible. Several boys laughed at them for being too lazy to carry their firewood, but no one else paid them any particular notice.

They dragged Hummingbird into the lodge that Broken Feather shared with her mother and father, her brother Spotted Wolf, his wife and several other relatives. There they agreed that Hummingbird's arrival had gone unnoticed.

Wolf Chief sat by the flickering lodge fire, listening to his wife Puma Child's account of their daughter's adventure that day. Broken Feather herself crouched in the sleeping alcove that had been given to Hummingbird.

The injured Cheyenne slept fitfully, moaning and speaking unintelligibly from time to time without waking. Broken Feather, with a patience neither of her parents had ever expected of her, would rouse out of her half-doze to murmur to the patient or to bathe her face with an herbal ointment.

"This is not a good thing," Wolf Chief said gravely.

"We have no right to interfere in what may happen between a man and his wife."

"Would you send her back to her brute of a husband so he can kill her next time?" Puma Child interrupted, her voice rising.

Wolf Chief sighed. "You never hear what I have to say to the end. You must let me finish, wife. What I was going to say is this. A woman also has the right to go back to her parents if she wishes, and they may decide to return the dowry."

"But Hummingbird has no parents among our people," cried Puma Child. "Who will protect her?"

Wolf Chief glanced at his other wife, Good Beadwork, in mute appeal. "I was going to tell you that. This Cheyenne was married to Hawk Foot out of Lachelesharo's lodge. Spotted Wolf was there when Wounded Man brought her over. Lachelesharo made gifts to Wounded Man after she escaped from the shaman—at the time of the sacrifice that never happened. Spotted Wolf told me that the chief offered to make the Cheyenne his daughter and told her several times she didn't need to marry Hawk Foot. I am sure that Knife Chief will let her come back to his lodge. It is not wise for us to stand between the shaman's nephew and the head chief."

"But Lachelesharo isn't here," Puma Child persisted. "He has gone with his men to steal horses."

"That is true, wife," Wolf Chief replied patiently. "What I was going to say is that perhaps it would be best after all to keep her here until Lachelesharo returns."

Puma Child jumped up from her side of the fire and ran over to hug her husband. "I knew you would say that. You are such a good husband. I will always listen to everything you say from now on."

Good Beadwork burst out laughing. "Why did you

bring this one into our lodge, Wolf Chief? Anyway, it is good that you two understand each other so well. I will go over to tell Raven Quill what has happened. I will do that in the morning. That way if Hawk Foot comes to take Hummingbird, we can say that we are keeping her until Lachelesharo returns because that is what Raven Quill wishes. It is better that the Cheyenne stay here for now, since there is no man in Raven Quill's lodge. Even that white man has left, the one called Joe.

"It will also be best if no one from this lodge tells anyone else in the village what is going on. I am not certain we can keep the children and the old ones from gossiping, but I will warn them. I will threaten the children with the cannibal women. Maybe that will keep at least the little ones quiet. Do you think Broken Feather's friends can hold their tongues?"

"Both of my women talk too much," laughed Wolf Chief. He held out his hand to Good Beadwork and drew both her and Puma Child into his embrace. "Yes, I am blessed with women who talk too much."

At that moment Hummingbird stirred and moaned from her couch again. Broken Feather roused and began to sing softly. Wolf Chief and his two wives glanced in her direction and smiled at one another.

"I am indeed blessed with women," said the pater-familias. "I think it is time to sleep now."

In the morning Hummingbird seemed much better. She was able to talk without too much difficulty, and Broken Feather persuaded her to drink a little warm broth laced with soothing and pain-killing herbs. She could open her swollen eye enough to determine that it still had vision in it. Her whole body ached, but the pain was tolerable. The atmosphere of warmth, the good-natured quarreling and cheerful frankness of Wolf Chief's lodge eased the hopelessness that had oppressed her since she agreed to marry Hawk Foot and Grey Bear rode off.

Both Good Beadwork and Puma Child went to speak with Raven Quill, but it was late in the afternoon before they set out. The two had young children to care for and Puma Child was nursing an infant.

Hummingbird dozed under the influence of the herbal medicine Broken Feather had given her, but then some disturbance, some presence she was but dimly aware of caused her to stir and then to sit up suddenly.

Antonio Grey Bear Behele was sitting next to her on the hide cot where Broken Feather usually sat.

She closed her eyes and lay back down. "I am still dreaming," she murmured.

But the dream persisted. Grey Bear stroked the hair back from her forehead, touched his lips to her skin in the manner of the whites.

"I was a great fool to let you do this thing," he said softly. "You aren't dreaming, little Hummingbird. Please wake up and speak to me again."

Hummingbird opened both her eyes, stared, then closed them again.

"It is you," she whispered. "I am too ugly for you to see me now, Grey Bear."

"It is the medicine that I have given her," Broken Feather explained. "She will probably sleep for a long time yet."

"Jist like I'd have told you, you dunghead, if you'd been anyplace around to listen," added Termite Joe.

"I will sleep some more, a little longer," Hummingbird whispered.

When she awoke next, it was to the sound of Hawk Foot's angry voice. "Where is my wife? I have heard that she is here and come to take her home."

Hummingbird involuntarily pulled herself back into the shadows, but Grey Bear, who was still sitting beside her, stood up.

"She's not your wife, Hawk Foot," he said quietly.

Chapter 14

Hawk Foot glanced disdainfully at Behele and strode toward Hummingbird's sleeping alcove. As he approached, Grey Bear lashed out with his right fist so quickly that Hummingbird hardly saw the blow. It caught Hawk Foot on the jaw and he toppled backward to land heavily on the earthen floor.

"Go to her, Antonio," shouted Termite Joe. He stood up from his place by the lodge fire and pulled Broken Feather back against the wall with him.

Hawk Foot rose and Behele advanced on him again. He swung hard and Hummingbird saw her husband pitch back once more, this time rolling through the smoldering fire. He leaped to his feet, the flash of a knife in his hand. She cried out a warning as Hawk Foot crouched grinning and made slicing motions in the air.

Grey Bear moved toward his antagonist, erect and confident. He lashed out with his foot, pivoting and twisting. The knife spun from the Pawnee's hand and thudded against the dried mud wall and fell to the floor. Termite Joe retrieved it.

Grey Bear struck again, and this time his enemy staggered, recovered and fought back. Hawk Foot landed a solid blow to Grey Bear's jaw and aimed a kick at his groin. But Grey Bear caught the raised foot and hurled his opponent heavily to the ground. He leaped on top of him and rained blow after blow on Hawk Foot's face. He continued to pound his foe until Wolf Chief pulled him off.

"This is enough," said the older man. "I will not allow one Skidi to kill another in my lodge."

"Aw, Wolf," groaned Termite Joe. "Why'd you want to go and spile things, jist when they's starting to go right?"

Grey Bear shook his head and looked around him as if he were waking out of a dream. Hawk Foot lay without moving. "Is he dead?" Antonio Grey Bear asked between heaving breaths.

Good Beadwork came forward, squatted by the inert warrior and watched him critically. "No, he breathes. I guess Tirawa Atius does not want him in the spirit world yet. I think I understand the will of the creator in this one matter."

She turned her head and looked up at Grey Bear. "We will take this one back to his home. I think Grey Bear will be wise to leave the village now."

"She's got a point there, Juan Antonio," Termite Joe nodded. "I was fixing to set out for the high country after beavers when I stumbled across you. Think maybe I'll head on back. Be glad for a spot of company, this child would."

"I cannot leave Hummingbird here," Grey Bear Behele protested.

"I can ride," Hummingbird called out. The next

moment she had risen from her bed and was standing unsteadily beside it.

"It is wonderful what love can do, is it not, Termite Chief?" suggested Broken Feather. She smiled innocently up at the trapper so that the dimple in her right cheek was prominently displayed.

"That's got to be it, ma'am," Joe replied.

Broken Feather continued to look at him and smile.

The mountain man raised an eyebrow and scowled. "God no," he said, now squinting at her, "this white nigger cain't be packing no female women with him out to the Shining Mountains. But I'll be back with you when the creeks get froze, I guarantee her."

"I would be very good to have along, Termite Chief. I can cook very good things. I can take care of you if you get a fever or if a rattlesnake bites you."

"Ain't no rattlesnakes this time of the year," Joe interrupted.

"And there are other things I do as well," she whispered, her eyes sparkling. "Or has Hollingback forgotten the night of the buffalo hunt?"

"Now, shit, leetle gal, it ain't no place for a woman out there."

"What if Hawk Foot decides to take revenge on me?"

Termite Joe turned to Wolf Chief, hoping the father would provide him with salvation. But Wolf Chief's eyes were smiling. Joe cast a desperate glance at Puma Child, but the minx's mother was grinning broadly.

"By the beard of Christ's Mama," Joe groaned, "I think I've been cotched. Aw, all right, hang it. But this coon warns you—"

Broken Feather interrupted him with a shriek of delight and threw her arms around his neck.

"I knew you loved me, Termite Chief," she cried.

Joe looked around him, much embarrassed. Every eye in the lodge was on him. Even Hummingbird, standing supported by Grey Bear's arm around her waist, was trying to smile with her swollen lips.

"So, Termite Chief, how many ponies are you going to leave behind for Wolf Chief and his family?" called Antonio Behele.

Termite Joe was at a loss for words. "Well, dang it," he finally spluttered, "cain't a man have some privacy to discuss matters with his father-in-law?"

The trapper now removed his battered felt hat, which so far as anyone there could remember had never been off his head before. He approached Wolf Chief, who was by now politely looking away from the afflicted man.

"Father," said Joe, "you know we ain't got much time for proper ceremonies and all, but I'd be honored if you'd take my three ponies what are out with Lacheleshar's herd and my two buffalo robes and—well, whatever else I got that you might take a fancy to. If you say so, then I'll be taking your daughter along with me right now. And mighty pleased to have been hornswoggled into it, sir," he added, throwing a malign glance at Behele.

Wolf Chief inclined his head gravely. "I understand that Hollingback's heart is good. I am pleased that you wish to marry my daughter—"

"You must not keep him here any longer, my husband," Puma Child interrupted.

"I was not going to say any more," Wolf Chief continued, "except that it would be good if we could smoke a pipe of tobacco together. Well, we will do that when you return, Termite Joe Hollingback."

Joe replaced his hat, and with Broken Feather helping Behele to support Hummingbird, the two men and the two women left the lodge.

It was obvious that Hummingbird was having trouble

walking. "Are you sure you can ride, pretty bird?" Grey Bear asked. "Perhaps this is not wise."

"I can do anything, my husband," she whispered. "But there is one particular place I wish to go."

Antonio Grey Bear watched her a moment longer and then nodded. "I think I know the place."

Broken Feather reached out a sly hand and squeezed Termite Joe's crotch. She giggled when he jumped.

"You leetle heathen devil," he hissed. "Just wait till later, when I get you off in the willow brush."

"Do I have to wait, Termite Husband?" she hissed back, showing the dimple again.

Pitalesharo lay in the cave as he had lain for two days, with no fire, no food, no water. He had gashed his chest and arms and cried aloud to the spirits to send him a vision, but nothing had come. He had dozed from time to time and had dreamed, but they had been ordinary dreams, images of Little Green Frog, images from the horse-stealing raid and the battle with the Ute.

In one dream Two Boulders pulled back the head of the boy guarding the horses and slit his throat, but Pitalesharo had seen at the last moment that the Ute boy was actually Little Green Frog. He had cried out for his friend to stop, but already the knife had slashed across the neck and the blood gushed out. Man Chief had awakened screaming, tears streaming down his face. It had taken a long time to lose the feeling of desolation that followed.

There had been others. In one Wounded Man became a cannibal head and devoured the entire village; in another Hawk Foot wrestled Pitalesharo to the ground and then began to tear pieces of flesh off his body with his teeth. All the while Pitalesharo was laughing.

In yet another he and Little Green Frog were sitting in

front of a lodge, watching children that he knew were their own playing with a hoop.

But these were not medicine dreams, only the ordinary kind. It was night outside the cave. He knew this only because the very faint light that filtered its way to the interior chamber where he was lying had disappeared. He lay with his eyes open, staring into the blackness.

He heard voices, voices of many people coming closer. He could not understand what they were saying because they were speaking in a foreign language. And then he saw them even though it was dark. They looked like ordinary people, although they were dressed differently from the Pawnee. They walked past Pitalesharo as if he weren't there.

More and more people came out of the back of the cave, all filing past and speaking in ordinary tones of voice. After the first group had passed more came, and these he recognized as Comanche, Cheyenne, Ute, even Pawnee. After a time the Indian people were gone, followed by white people, men and women.

And then these too disappeared and the cave was dark and silent once more, nothing but blackness, blackness that seemed to extend forever.

A very large man walked out and stood looking down at Pitalesharo. The giant was quite handsome and light appeared to pour out of his body. He turned away and seemed to be dressing, pulling on some kind of clothing. When he turned back, he had transformed himself into a grizzly bear.

"Are you satisfied now that you have waked me up?" the bear asked. "What is it that you want? Tell me so I can go back and finish my nap."

"I do not know what I want," Pitalesharo whispered. "I want you to tell me what to do."

"You are the only one who can decide what to do." The bear seemed annoyed. "If that is all you can ask, I'm going back to bed."

"Wait, please. I have been waiting for you here, with no food and no fire for all these days. Tell me something."

"I cannot tell you anything," the bear yawned. "You saw all those people leaving. Well, that must mean something."

"What? What should I know?"

"The first people were the ones who painted the pictures in this cave. They are gone now." The bear turned and began walking away.

"But what does it mean? Please don't leave yet."

"Only the mountains stay the same, as they say. Only that isn't true either. Follow your heart, Pitalesharo." The bear turned and disappeared into the recesses of the cave.

More people began to issue from the depths again, these like none Pitalesharo had ever seen. The procession went on and on, bizarre foreigners in different costumes and with different kinds of skin, until at last no one else came out. The cave was silent and empty for what seemed an eternity. Pitalesharo grew more and more afraid, and at last he cried out to fill the vast silence and emptiness.

He awakened sweating. He stood and stretched his cramped limbs. It was light outside again. He pondered the vision he had been given. It made little sense to him. Bear Spirit had said that he should follow his heart and the other part of the dream meant that things change.

He did not even give me a song, Pitalesharo said to himself. But that is the vision the spirits chose to give me. Perhaps it will make sense later on. He tried not to feel disappointed.

He stepped out of the cave, bewildered but certain the

time of dreaming was past. He walked to the stream that wound across the meadow.

The sky was heavy dull grey and a chill wind bent the yellow grasses. Pitalesharo knelt by the water to drink and found a small green frog sitting in front of him. The creature stared up at him, its eyes a beautiful golden color.

"What are you doing here, little sister?" he asked, surprised. "It is long past the time for the frog people to be out. You should be sleeping buried in the mud."

He reached a finger to push at the frog, but it didn't jump away from him. Instead it continued to sit, still staring at him. He picked the animal up and stood with it on his palm, examining it.

"You don't act much like a frog. I think you are a gift from Bear Person. What should I do with you? Perhaps I should kill you and dry out your body and keep it with my medicine, and yet I don't wish to harm you."

Follow your heart.

The words came from inside his head and suddenly he laughed. "I follow and what do I find but a little green frog?"

He laughed again. "All right, small messenger. Come, I'll take you into the cave. There's a little water in there, and perhaps you won't freeze to death when the snows come."

After he had deposited the frog in an inner room of the cave where a trickle of water formed a pool, Pitalesharo returned outside and whistled for his horse. The roan trotted up from the lower meadow.

"I wish I had something to give you, my friend," he whispered, stroking the pony's neck. "I have no corn cake, no dried fruit. I only called you because I was lonely.''

The horse fluttered its lips and nuzzled at his midsection. Pitalesharo laughed. He sat down on a boulder near the entrance to the cave and began to chew on a small piece of jerky that he had fetched from his bundle.

"I feel better, I guess, Red Medicine Dog," he said as he ate, "now that the spirit people have given me a vision. But I wish I knew what I am supposed to do about it. I have seen a time when the white people will replace the Pawnee—at least I think that is what it means. And Bear Person told me to follow my heart. Then I saw what must be the time when there will be no more human beings of any kind. I do not know if there will be horses."

The roan snaked out his head and snuffled at the piece of jerky his master was eating, then pulled back rolling his eyes.

"That made me feel very lonely," Pitalesharo continued, "a terrible kind of loneliness. And then I came out here and found the small green frog. That was a sign. Perhaps I am supposed to go to the Comanche and marry my own Frog, and yet I don't know how that can be. Well. I will stay here and sleep in the cave tonight and think about this vision. Maybe I will become a Comanche. My own people are coming apart. And yet my mother and father and the others who love me are there."

The horse had drifted off down the meadow, apparently losing interest in Pitalesharo's conversation. The chief's son sat on the big rock by the cave and chewed on the rest of his jerky, then went down to the stream to drink again. After that he picked up his Hawken and walked into the woods, thinking to kill a rabbit or a squirrel if he could find one. He still had a supply of dried meat, but the thought of something fresh made his mouth water. Now that his fast was over, his body began to send him urgent signals that it wished to be fed. But nothing moved except for a few small birds scratching among the fir needles and hopping from branch to branch in the trees.

He drifted up onto a bench that gave him a wide view of the mountain's flank and scanned the country below. He discerned four dark figures heading his way. At first he thought they might be elk, but as he watched he became convinced they were people on horseback.

Pitalesharo cut across a gorge and emerged above the cave. He climbed down to the meadow and called Red Medicine Dog again. He led the roan into the first large room of the cave, concealed himself near the entrance and sat down to wait. He placed his loaded and primed rifle across his knees and took out another strip of dried meat to chew on.

It was some time before the group reached the meadow near sundown, and although the heavy sky had never lightened, the clouds to the west glowed purple-red. In the dimming radiance he watched as the figures emerged from the trees below.

Near the stream the leading rider stopped, dismounted and examined something on the ground. Pitalesharo laughed aloud, for now he recognized the newcomers. He leaped out of the cave, shouting a bloodcurdling war cry, laughing wildly and leaping down the hillside even as the men crouched and raised their rifles.

"What is this?" Pitalesharo demanded. "Would you shoot your own brother?"

Termite Joe and Antonio Behele stood up startled, and Joe fired off a shot into the air, yelling back his own war whoop. Then the three men embraced, pounded each other on the back while the two women sat their mounts smiling.

Pitalesharo glanced at the women and recognized

Hummingbird and Broken Feather. "But what has happened, Grey Bear? Is Hawk Foot dead?"

His brother shrugged. "He was alive when we left the village. He is probably still alive."

"And a goddamned shame it be," added Termite Joe.

"I think that we must have a great deal to tell each other," Pitalesharo said. "Let us go make a fire inside the cave mouth. I hope you have brought me something good to eat. So, Juan Termite, is this what I think it is? You have committed matrimony again? Broken Feather, do you not know that white men aren't to be trusted?"

The bride laughed and shook her head.

"It's your fault, Man Chief. You are the one who made me discover how much the Termite Chief needed a woman to protect him."

"What's this you say about something good to eat?" asked Joe. "This coon figgered you'd have dinner cooking for us or I'd never have wanted to come visit you."

The group sat around a blazing fire that night. Pitalesharo was filled in on what had happened since he had left with Lachelesharo's war party and in turn told them of his vision.

It happened that the newcomers did indeed have a pair of haunches of relatively fresh venison, the remains of a buck that Grey Bear had killed the preceding day. And while the flesh roasted, Termite Joe brewed a pot of the coffee that he always carried with him. Pitalesharo carved off a chunk of meat when only the outside layer had begun to turn brown, ate it red and dripping, drank a tin cup of sweetened coffee and sighed.

"This is like a gift from Tirawa. I am still not sure that I am awake. But tell me, Juan Grey Bear, what is to keep Hawk Foot from following you here and killing you from ambush?"

"I reckon old Bird Droppings has got hisself a belly-ful of Juan Antonio," Termite Joe drawled. "Maybe of Hummingbird, too," he added, smiling at the Cheyenne.

"He is very stubborn, though," Pitalesharo mused. "Perhaps you are right. The time of snow will come soon, and then I don't think he will wish to follow. Only beaver catchers and other insane people go off to the mountains in this season."

The eating and the talking went on for some time. A cougar screamed high on the mountain and the coyotes sent up a chorus in response. Owls cried and the wind soughed through the pines.

Very late, after Hummingbird and Broken Feather had succumbed to exhaustion and lay sleeping curled against their mates, Pitalesharo asked the question that was on the minds of both himself and his blood brother.

"What are we going to do next, Grey Bear? My visions didn't tell me what to do. And now it seems like a very bad idea to return to Wolf-Standing-in-Water Village."

"I don't know, amigo. I thought maybe I would go and live with Hummingbird's people. She says they probably won't kill me." He stared disconsolately into the red embers of the fire.

"Wagh," Termite Joe grumbled. "Me and Broken Feather's going off to the headwaters of the Platte and spend our time at profitable work. A coon's got to keep working or the madness gets him. You boys is welcome to join up. I've got more goddamned traps than I know what to do with anyhow. Probably enough castors for all of us, though I'm not so sure now that I've got a new wife to provide for."

"I do not want you to go off with the Cheyenne, Grey Bear," Pitalesharo said. "I would never see my brother again. It is a bad thing to lose people."

Antonio nodded and looked down at the embers again. "You're right, my brother."

"Wal, coons, this nigger's going to pack her in for the night," Termite Joe yawned. "Think about what I said, now. Me and my young wife is going to spread our buffalo hides outside, I reckon, where there's a mite of privacy. I'll brew you up some coffee before I head out come morning. But if you don't rise early, you won't see me. If you decide to trail along with Joe Hollingback, then don't sleep in."

"*Vaya con dios*, Juan Termite," said Behele, "and many thanks for everything. When I needed you, you found me. You're a good man, Joe."

The Termite Chief gently roused Broken Feather and then looked up at Behele and Pitalesharo.

"Glad I don't savvy that heathen Mexican talk," he growled, " 'cause I never say good-bye. Brings goddamned bad luck, and that's a fact. Good-bye sounds like you ain't never going to see some coon again."

Joe and Broken Feather stumbled together outside the cave and Pitalesharo and Behele sat talking for a time longer. They still had not resolved their course of action when they went to sleep.

When they woke in the morning, they found that Termite Joe and Broken Feather had indeed vanished. But Joe had left them a tin kettle full of the thick black brew, as he had promised. The canister sat at the edge of the embers of a fire outside the cave.

"Pitalesharo," said Behele as the three young people sat about Joe's fire, drinking the coffee and eating cold roast meat, "I know now what we must do. I have had a very strong dream. Someone, it may have been Tirawa Atius himself, told me—"

"Tirawa never appears in dreams. You know that," interrupted Pitalesharo.

"Ah, yes," Behele nodded. "Then perhaps it was Jesus. That is not very important. He had a beard, so I guess it must have been Jesus. I should have asked to look at his hands—"

"Tell us what he said," Hummingbird cried impatiently.

"Ah. He suggested that we go on a horse-stealing raid. He thought it might be good for us to head toward Comanche country because those people still owe us horses. He told me that there may be someone among the Comanche we would be glad to see. I told him we probably wouldn't be able to accomplish anything, but he seemed to think that we would be more welcome among our own people if we brought back horses. Two warriors bringing back a large herd of ponies would be very important men. All would praise our medicine. Perhaps I would even be able to give Hawk Foot something to ease his grief over losing Hummingbird."

"And a couple extra for beating him half to death," Pitalesharo murmured.

"Anyway, I am not certain that it was Jesus because he had a furry tail and talked about chasing rabbits. Whoever it was, he promised that this venture would be a very happy one. Besides, what else is there to do?"

"Yes," Pitalesharo said slowly, "if only the two of us—"

"Three," interjected Hummingbird.

Pitalesharo smiled. "Three. If we bring back enough horses, Hawk Foot will not dare to oppose us openly, at least for a time. Let us think about this further. You say the Comanche?"

"I am told they have very fine horses."

"Let me consider this matter further."

· Chapter 15

The sunset flamed above the westward ranges and later, when the moon rose, it wore a great halo. Very few stars were visible. A steady wind blustered through the canyon.

By morning the sky was completely grey, clouds running in long wavy trails across the backs of the mountains. Clouds of steam drifted from the mouths of the ponies, and the spring where Pitalesharo, Grey Bear and Hummingbird got their drinking water was frozen. The earth was hard underfoot and the aspens that had blazed with such a brilliant display of gold and crimson only a few days earlier had now been stripped of nearly all their leaves.

Behele built up the fire and placed half a dozen strips of cold venison on the downwind side.

Hummingbird brought up an armful of wood from the tangle of drift next to the creek and set it down. "It will snow," she said. "I think we are going to have a blizzard, Grey Bear."

"These clouds are dry," he argued.

"It is going to snow a lot," Hummingbird insisted. "We will have to leave the mountains now."

Grey Bear turned and shouted into the cave. "Juan Pete, it is time to wake up and eat some breakfast. The storm god is getting ready to give birth."

Pitalesharo emerged and walked to where the other two were shivering by the fire. "Looks like it will snow. Even though we have not decided what to do, my friends, the mountain is telling us it is time to leave."

"You see, I was right," Hummingbird laughed.

"The meat is not really warming at all," Antonio growled. "We may as well eat it now." He lifted the spit and offered it first to Hummingbird and then to Pitalesharo.

"If deep snows come, we may end up spending the winter in our cave," he said. "I think it is time to go for a long ride. Perhaps we will find some unguarded horses to steal. The Kiowa Apache and the Comanche always have more horses than they know what to do with. If we don't take too many, they will never even miss them."

"I think we should return to the village," Pitalesharo argued. "I have a number of horses if my father hasn't given them all away. Among us we can put together a bride price that will satisfy Hawk Foot."

"When we were boys," Antonio said to Hummingbird, "Man Chief was always wanting to go on adventures. Now he is growing old too soon, like Termite Joe. Pitalesharo has been around the whites so much that he has begun to think like them."

Pitalesharo chewed on the barely warm deer meat and swallowed. "Trying to keep up with Juan Antonio is like trying to keep up with a coyote that has caught its tail on fire. All right, we'll do whatever you say. Let's get our things together and ride toward the high plains. Better to do that before the snow begins to fall."

"I said it was going to snow," Hummingbird insisted.

Pitalesharo glanced at her and then continued, "If my brother wishes to steal ponies, I will go with him. But the Cheyenne have many horses also, and it will not take us so long to reach their villages. I think that is where we should go."

"Cheyenne horses are very poor," Hummingbird laughed. "That is why my people steal theirs from the Pawnee and the Comanche. Everyone knows that."

La Ranita Verde. The Little Green Frog, daughter to Chief Fox Shirt. A village far away to the south, but where? That people are wanderers; they never stay in one place. This is not something to think of.

"We cannot take Hummingbird with us if we wish to steal horses," Pitalesharo said. "It is too dangerous."

"Not so dangerous as it is in the same village with Hawk Foot," Antonio insisted. "She might be safe for a while in Lachelesharo's lodge, but Hawk Foot would find a way."

"He would not dare to confront my father, not now. Lachelesharo has scored a great victory against the Ute, and not even Wounded Man can speak against that. Hummingbird could ride in after dark, and then my mother and father would be able to protect her. She would be safe. But perhaps it would be better if all of us returned to the village first. Then some of the Red Lances would wish to go with us."

A sudden burst of wind sent sparks streaming from the fire, and the first flakes of snow began to fall.

"Pack up your possibles, coons," Grey Bear shouted, "That's what Termite Chief would say. Let us be on our way. It's going to snow heavily, just as I've said all along."

*   *   *

By the time they had reached the Arkansas River and the High Plains, the wind had increased and was driving snow in long streamers nearly horizontal to the ground. Ahead of them stretched the vastness of the prairies, but they could see nothing. The world had been transformed into a featureless swirl of white without dimension or direction.

They managed to cross the river, its current still low and strangely warm. But when they emerged onto the southern bank, the wind against their wet leathers numbed them.

"We've got to hole in," Pitalesharo called out, his voice barely audible in the keening of the wind.

"We should have stayed in the cave, like I said," Grey Bear laughed, pounding at his wet leggings to bring some circulation back into his hands.

They moved downstream along the river for a time, taking advantage of the scant protection of cottonwoods, alders and hedges of willow brush. At length they came to an overhanging floodbank hemmed in by young cottonwoods. Pitalesharo dismounted and pointed to a tangle of deadwood the river had deposited against a fringe of willows.

Hummingbird led the horses back to the leeward side of the leafless cottonwoods and kicked the snow away from several clumps of long-stemmed grass, hardly a horse's favorite food but all that was immediately available. The ponies turned their rear ends to the wind, fluttered their nostrils and began halfheartedly to chew at the coarse grass while stamping their feet in apparent dissatisfaction.

"Perhaps we will all be sleeping together before this is over," she told the animals as she brushed the snow from her pony's mane. She then struggled back to where Grey Bear and Pitalesharo were attempting with no great success to kindle a fire.

"This night we sleep in one big pile," Behele complained.

"Some poles in the tangle," Pitalesharo said. "Maybe we can pry them loose. We'll need about four. Lean them up against the bank and tie one of the extra robes across them. That'll give us some shelter at least."

The mound of twigs, though fairly dry, refused to ignite despite repeated efforts.

"Let's get those poles," Behele said. "We'll have to hurry; the light's beginning to fail."

After an hour's work in cold, wet clothing they were able to extricate two somewhat crooked cottonwood branches and a young spruce branch.

Behele hacked off the remaining limbs. "These will have to do. We can't see what we're doing as it is. Get the hide stretched and maybe we'll be able to light the fire."

"If the whole thing doesn't blow away with us hanging on," Pitalesharo laughed. Hummingbird thrust her numbed hands under her clothes and against her breasts to warm them, but it didn't help much.

They laid the poles out in a row and tied down the flapping buffalo robe, then struggled to get the whole thing upright against the bank. The wind tore it from their hands and the two men grimly tried again. This time Pitalesharo fastened his horsehair lariat to an exposed root, banded it across the hide-covered poles and tied it off to the bole of a young cottonwood. The makeshift shelter, a loose end of the hide snapping, was in place.

With hands almost devoid of feeling, Grey Bear scooped up the snow-covered remnant of their first attempt at fire-building, carried the sticks in behind the lean-to, kicked the snow away and placed them in a mound.

Pitalesharo struggled with his flint and steel and the sparks sank into a chunk of punky pitch wood and glowed. When he knelt forward to blow on the little red seed,

Hummingbird burst out laughing. "There is not enough wind, so Man Chief makes more. Hurry, Firemaker, or we will all freeze to death."

Pitalesharo began to laugh also but forced himself to concentrate on what he was about. And then the fire was burning. With great care Pitalesharo placed twig after twig into place, nursing the little blaze. The flames stuttered, gained, fell back and then took hold.

"Bring more wood, Antonio."

The Spaniard dashed back to the tangle of driftwood for more fuel. Soon the fire, fanned by the occasional gusts of wind that curled around their lean-to, was blazing brightly.

The three stood close about the magic of heat, held out their hands and felt the first tinglings of returning sensation.

"Food," Pitalesharo bellowed. "Let's cook one of the horses."

"The pack sack is still on the pony," Hummingbird said. "I'll fetch something." She returned with half a leg of venison, and soon the meat was cooking, the droplets of fat flaring above the growing pile of orange-red embers.

They ate greedily, wiped their mouths, built up the fire and added a good-sized backlog. Then they huddled together with their robes drawn as tightly as possible about them.

"You know what would be good right now, my brother?" Pitalesharo asked.

"What's that?"

"To smoke the pipe, Grey Bear. It is a good time to smoke some tobacco. We are far from the village and no one will ever know. Even Hummingbird may smoke if she wishes."

Hummingbird glanced at Antonio, her eyes glinting with mischief.

"If she wishes. But the pipe and tobacco are also in the pack sack. You must bring them to me."

"I have spent my life waiting on this one," Pitalesharo said to Hummingbird as he untangled himself from the robes and strode out into the darkness of wind-whipped snow. He was back in a moment, pipe and tobacco in hand. With an ember-end from the fire he lit the pipe, made a sign to the four sacred directions, the earth and the sky, and puffed. Then he passed the pipe to Behele, who repeated the ritual.

"I would like to try," Hummingbird said, "but I do not know how to do it."

Antonio Grey Bear handed his woman the pipe and said, "Now offer the prayer sign."

"I know how to do *that*. How do I *smoke* it?"

"Suck in with your tongue, little one. But do not breathe the smoke or swallow it. You will get sick if you do that."

Hummingbird puffed, coughed, sneezed. "It burns my nose, Grey Bear. Perhaps I didn't do it right."

The men laughed and Pitalesharo took the pipe, smoked and passed it back to Behele. "About those Cheyenne horses, Juan Antonio. How many do you think we can get?"

"The Comanche horses? Oh, many of them. Far to the south where the Comanche villages are, there is probably not even any snow."

"Comanche horses? Such animals are buffalo dung. Why do you wish to take me into the lands of the Comanche?"

Behele puffed at the pipe and passed it to Hummingbird, who succeeded this time, even though the smoke brought tears to her eyes.

"If we are able to return to the village with many horses, the people will be glad in their hearts. You already have lots of horses, Pitalesharo, but I do not. I will be able to give many gifts and Hummingbird will move into Lachelesharo's lodge with me. Hawk Foot will never take Hummingbird back now, for there would be too much disgrace in that. I will give him twenty horses, maybe, and he will have to accept. And everyone will know what a great bride price was paid for Hummingbird. The other women will honor her and be friends with her."

"I understand all that," Pitalesharo persisted, "but why Comanche horses?"

"Is there not a certain Comanche woman that you love, Man Chief?" Hummingbird asked. "That is why Grey Bear wishes to travel to the south so that perhaps you will be able to find out about her. You are the son of a great chief. There must be some way for you to marry Little Green Frog. And I would like that very much also. She is one whom I have loved. Then perhaps we can all live in one lodge together, and later our children will have two sets of parents. Could this thing not happen?"

"Do you wish to ride south?" Behele asked. "If that is so, then I am willing to go wherever you wish."

"Little Green Frog," Pitalesharo mused. "It is true. She is still in my thoughts so that I can think of no other. But what you propose is very dangerous, Juan Antonio. Perhaps it would be better if I went alone. In my dreams she came to me. I saw her just as if she were right beside me. I do not think she has married anyone else. But the Comanche have always been our enemies, Grey Bear. It is possible to steal their horses, but they will not allow a horse thief to marry the daughter of Fox Shirt. Perhaps if I were to bring many presents and agree to live with them and to be one of them, Fox Shirt might allow it. But I cannot pay a bride price for Little Green Frog with ponies I have stolen from her own people."

"No," Antonio agreed, "that probably wouldn't work."

"Among my people," Hummingbird put in, "a stranger may sneak into the village and sit before one of the lodges. Then he must be given hospitality and will not be harmed. Even a Crow may do such a thing, even though the Cheyenne have always been at war with those people. Would such a thing not be possible among Little Green Frog's people? Why would they wish to kill you, Man Chief, when they know you are the one who saved Little Green Frog's life? She would tell her father to invite you into the tepee."

Pitalesharo tapped out the ashes from the bowl of the pipe and put the pipe back into its otterskin pouch. "Then I would show the Comanche all the horses we have stolen from them?"

"No," Hummingbird said, "you would not do that. Such a thing would be very foolish."

"Termite Joe would know what to do," Antonio mused. "He always has a plan for everything. Right now he and Broken Feather are probably lying together in a nice, warm hide lodge. They are probably very comfortable and are making love. And yet we are huddled here beside the river in the middle of a blizzard, and we shiver even beneath all these robes. Our clothing is still wet from crossing the river and our ponies will be dead and covered with snow by morning. Termite Joe is very intelligent for a white man."

"You are also a white man," Pitalesharo said, "even though you are a Skidi now, just as Hummingbird is a Cheyenne, though she is one of us."

"That is different," Antonio Grey Bear insisted.

Pitalesharo pushed the backlog farther into the fire and drew the robes about his shoulders once again.

"Let us ride south, then," he said.

* * *

By morning the sky was completely clear and the wind had ceased. The world was uniformly white in all directions, though not very much snow had fallen. In places it lay ankle deep, but elsewhere the wind had nearly swept the ground clear. The earth was frozen, but the morning sunlight was warm.

They rode southeast to the Huerfano and on to the Apishapa, just at the base of the Spanish Peaks, arriving there at sundown of the second day. They found numerous hoofprints heading due east from the stream. Antonio and Pitalesharo studied the signs and glanced at one another in surprise.

"Twenty riders perhaps, Antonio. Only a few of the tracks are those of pack animals, and none of them is shod in the white man's fashion."

"A war party," Antonio mused. "If the Comanche wished to visit the Kiowa or the Kiowa Apache, they would not come this way. It does not make sense."

"Do you suppose this is a group of Ute? Perhaps they came down onto the plains before the snow fell. That must be what it is. But this is a strange time of year to go horse-stealing. If more snow comes, they will never be able to take their animals back across the mountains."

"If Lachelesharo scored a great victory against those people," Hummingbird suggested, "then perhaps the warriors intend to turn north toward Wolf-Standing-in-Water Village."

Pitalesharo nodded. "It's possible. But why would they have come so far to the south? There would be no advantage to that."

"How long ago, do you think?" Behele asked, touching his fingers to the edges of a hoofmark.

"Midday, maybe even earlier. Tomorrow we must investigate. It is a mystery, Grey Bear."

They pitched camp a short distance from the river, taking shelter at the base of some slabs of sandstone. They built a small cook fire in against the rocks, roasted the three ducks Behele had shot earlier in the day and brewed some willow-bark and sage tea.

By first light they were already on the trail of the unidentified war party, a trail that led ever eastward across the Timpas and on to the Purgatoire.

On the morning of the second day they caught sight of their quarry several miles ahead on the prairie.

"Hold back," Pitalesharo cautioned his companions. "Whoever they are, we do not wish them to discover our presence."

Antonio Grey Bear shook his head. "It is still too far to see, but I think these are Ute."

"Perhaps they will cross over to Two Buttes Creek then. Sometimes the Kiowa Apache make winter camp there. But with a party so small, they would be fools to attack the Apache. Maybe they are desperate to regain their honor."

Behele laughed. "Whoever they are, they have a much larger party than we have, brother. And yet we are also looking for ponies to steal."

Pitalesharo squinted at the tall Spaniard and grinned. "I hadn't thought of it that way. You know, I think it may be possible to have these Indians do us a favor. If they should succeed in stealing horses from the Apache, they will be in a very great hurry when they ride back this way. They will not ride north. They will return as they went, and as quickly as possible. They will try to outride the Kiowa Apache. They will wish to get back into the mountains, for the Apache will not follow them that far. Do you see what I am thinking, Grey Bear?"

It was Behele's turn to grin. "We use these horse

thieves to bring the Kiowa Apache ponies to us so that we can take them just as they suppose they have made their escape.''

"Yes. When they have ridden as far and as fast as they can, they will wish to sleep. But they will have one or two of their wolf spies behind them, several miles from the ponies, to give warning in case the Apache have continued to pursue them.''

"Then we sneak in and steal what they have stolen,'' Behele laughed. "It will be very dangerous, but still better than taking on a whole village. The idea is such a fine one that we have to attempt it.''

Hummingbird was biting at her upper lip. "You two compete in craziness. You have spent too much time in the moonlight and it has gotten into your brains. And for such a man I left a perfectly good husband like Hawk Foot?''

"My brother,'' Behele asked, "who is this Hawk Foot? Any man with such a name should probably be killed.''

"Unless Termite Joe was exaggerating, Juan Antonio, that may be exactly what you did.''

"He will survive, but now I will have to pay the price.''

"What price?'' Hummingbird demanded.

"Price?'' Behele chuckled. "Oh, that. Well, now I must spend my life listening to a nagging woman who chatters all the time.''

"When do I ever complain?'' the Cheyenne girl insisted. "I don't. You are no good, Grey Bear. That is what I say.''

Behele grinned, made the hand sign for lying down together and turned back to Pitalesharo.

"Where shall we wait for our horses, Man Chief? I think these mystery raiders will be back in four days.''

Pitalesharo nodded. "If they come back at all.''

* * *

"They do not bring the horses as a gift to us,
Pitalesharo. Have you forgotten that? Do you know which
tribe these horse thieves belong to?"

"Of course," Pitalesharo grinned. "I got a good look
at them. A band of stupid Ute, just as we suspected."

"So how do you intend to get the horses?" Hummingbird asked.

"It's simple, my friends. We go in the direction they
are going, toward the big mountains, and we stay out of
their way. They are riding hard, so they must believe they
are being followed, whether they are or not. When they
think they are safe, they will slow down. When we see this
happen, then we will come in to where the horses are and
make a great deal of noise and drive the animals away.
The Ute will believe the Apache have taken their horses
back, and I do not think they will follow. They will be
afraid that there are many other Kiowa Apache nearby. I
think they will thank Old Man Coyote that they have been
able to stay in this world and not go to the spirit world just
yet."

"Amazingly simple," Behele nodded.

"Amazingly stupid," Hummingbird sniffed. "Only a
Pawnee and a Spanish could think of such a foolish idea.
Well, they will not kill me. They will only take me
captive, and then I will have to marry one of the Ute.
Perhaps they will allow me to marry a man who has not
walked in the moonlight too much."

"Señor y señora," Behele said, "I suggest that we
depart as quickly as possible. We have big medicine ahead
of us."

The Ute were pushing hard, as though they feared
the Kiowa Apache were right behind them. They rode on
into the night, camped only with a small cook fire that was

extinguished immediately after its purpose was served, slept for a few hours and were ready to go again at dawn.

Keeping well to the north of their line of travel, undetected, rode the two men and the reluctant woman.

The third day brought them abreast of the Wet Mountains. Around its southern extremity flowed the Huerfano. This river came out of a huge trench basin between the Wet Mountains and the northern Sangre de Cristos. From here the Ute would undoubtedly turn northwest toward Ouray and the headwaters of the Tomichi and on to their village.

Inside the gates of the mountains the Ute sent scouts back down the Huerfano, and apparently believing themselves safe from pursuit, made a leisurely camp early in the afternoon. They sent out some hunters and built up a roaring fire when these men returned with game.

Pitalesharo, Behele and Hummingbird watched it all. At nightfall the scouts returned from down the Huerfano and a round of delighted cheering went up from the Ute camp at the news that the Apache were nowhere in sight. The warriors began to pound one another on the back and engaged in an impromptu victory dance.

The weather had remained clear since the night of the snowstorm, and the moon had once more come round to full. "I do not think our luck is going to hold," Pitalesharo said, gesturing toward the south where heavy grey clouds formed a storm front running over the mountains and reaching from horizon to horizon.

"The clouds move quickly," Behele agreed. "It may be that we will not have any light to work by. We will have to stay close together, for otherwise we may lose each other in the darkness."

"The fire the Ute have built," Hummingbird noted, "its smoke hangs low to the ground. I think it is going to rain before long."

"Snow," Antonio Grey Bear argued, "snow, without a doubt."

"Tell him to be serious, Man Chief," the girl complained. "He is like a great child sometimes."

"Let's hope for rain if we're going to have anything at all," Pitalesharo said, his face serious as he studied the approaching wall of clouds.

"Cheyenne women have no sense of humor," Grey Bear snorted.

"If we use our heads," Pitalesharo said, clicking his tongue, "we can get along without much moonlight. We may not be able to see what we're doing, but the Ute won't be able to see us either. They won't be able to see anything. This is not going to be your usual horse raid, Antonio, but I have an idea how we can even the odds against us."

Occasionally the moon broke through the running clouds, but the darkness was nearly complete by the time the Ute fire had died down and the warriors perceived that the rain was about to begin and rolled into their robes under makeshift shelters.

The three Pawnee waited for another hour, until the first large drops of rain began to fall.

"At least it is warm," Hummingbird observed. "I have always said I do not wish to die in the cold."

"The rain is our friend tonight," Grey Bear whispered.

"Yes," Pitalesharo agreed, "and it is beginning to fall heavily now. Our new horses will be restless, even though I don't think they wish to travel any more tonight."

"Is it about time, then?"

"I think so." Pitalesharo reached out to press his brother's shoulder. The three mounted their ponies and urged them downslope into the wet darkness.

The stolen horses and the Ute war ponies were grazing disconsolately no more than fifty yards from the enemy camp.

"All weapons loaded and primed?" Pitalesharo whispered. "All right then. Start driving the horses downstream. When they begin to fuss and whinny, I will give the Ute their little present. Then we fire the rifles and the pistols."

"I don't think this is going to work," Hummingbird protested. "I think we should ride away and leave the Ute with their booty."

"This one loves to quarrel," Behele chuckled.

At the edge of the clearing Pitalesharo urged Red Medicine Dog toward the sleeping Ute. Antonio Grey Bear and Hummingbird moved in the opposite direction, toward the herd of horses.

The ponies were stamping their feet and snorting. One whinnied loudly.

Pitalesharo lit the fuse to the canister of gunpowder he had prepared and tossed it in the general direction of the smoking and sputtering remains of the fire. Then he took a commanding grip on his horse and held his breath.

The canister exploded with a roar and a burst of blue-white light. Embers scattered through the air, flaming out and bouncing wildly among the circle of startled warriors.

He fired his pistol at one of the hide shelters, fought to control his startled horse and then shot off his Hawken as well.

Rifle and pistol fire sounded from below the camp, where Behele and Hummingbird were driving the stampeding horses.

The Ute leaped from their robes in confusion and panic and scrambled for their weapons.

Pitalesharo reloaded his horse pistol, fired once more into the Ute camp, turned Red Medicine Dog and rode after his companions.

Dawn found them out on the plains once more, driving nearly two hundred Kiowa Apache horses and fifteen Ute war ponies in a great herd. A few had been lost during the frantic run down the Huerfano, but not many.

Pitalesharo, Antonio Grey Bear and Hummingbird were exhausted, soaked from the steady downpour of rain and consummately pleased with themselves.

"The Ute will have to walk back to their village," Pitalesharo laughed. "Perhaps they all ran away when the bomb went off, I do not know."

"I did not think the plan would work," Hummingbird conceded, "and yet it did. Now I am a warrior too. Later on I will become a very good horse thief."

"I am also a rich man now, hermano," Behele shouted. "I will be able to buy several more wives if I wish to."

"I will kill you while you sleep if you even think about it," Hummingbird threatened.

"Ah," laughed Pitalesharo, "you will not be a rich man for long, my brother. When we get back to the village, I think you will be poor once more. No matter what has happened, you will have to give Hawk Foot presents. He will have horses to ride then, and you will have only a few left. I tell you, Hummingbird's a skinny little thing to give up so many ponies for."

Chapter 16

"This is crazy, Juan Antonio," Pitalesharo remarked. "*Loco en la cabeza*. We will never find Little Green Frog's village, but one group of Comanche or another is certain to find us soon. It is too difficult to travel unobserved with a herd of more than two hundred horses. I think it is time for us to head back to Wolf-Standing-in-Water before we lose everything."

"Have faith, amigo," the big Spaniard said easily. "Look, here is a good stream. I don't even know what it is called, but if we follow it up, we will certainly come to a good place to rest the horses for a few days and you can go off to search for a time. Perhaps Hummingbird and I will find something to do while you are gone."

Pitalesharo was not convinced of the soundness of Antonio's reasoning, but he helped turn the herd up the stream that flowed south along the base of the mountains.

The three Pawnee, along with their stolen herd, had been drifting slowly south for several days, wandering sometimes out into the plains but keeping mainly to the base of the range. They tried to maintain an elevation with adequate cover and a good view of the desert below. When they found likely streams, they followed them until they discovered grazing grounds, where they would stay for a day or two. Pitalesharo would make forays onto the plains, following rivers and creeks downstream, searching for some sign of Comanche settlements. He found one encampment, but after watching it for an afternoon determined that it was not Fox Shirt's village.

The weather had so far favored them, but the chief's son had grown discouraged, confronted by the vastness of the land and the smallness of a single roving village. He realized too that as the days passed, their chances of being discovered by enemies increased.

One afternoon under a sky threatening snow they pushed their herd up still another stream to a meadow surrounded on three sides by steep walls. The creek fell over a sheer face of stone at the upper end.

"Look at this, hermano," Behele said cheerfully. "Coyote Jesus himself put this meadow here for us to find. There cannot be a better place. We will stay here as many days as it takes you to find your Ranita."

Pitalesharo shook his head. "It's too important that we get these horses back to the village," he said. "Maybe I will come back in the spring. I can travel more easily without two hundred ponies."

"I am afraid that by spring the semen will have backed up your spine and your head will explode," Grey Bear said.

Pitalesharo laughed in spite of his gloom. "I will try not to let that happen, amigo. Come, let us see what we can do about a shelter back among those rocks. I think it will snow tonight."

*   *   *

The snow did not come and in the morning Pitalesharo set out alone, promising himself and his companions that he would return the next day. He insisted that the three of them would have to return to their own village if he didn't find Fox Shirt's village this time. As he rode back down the canyon, following the stream out toward the plains, the sun topped the peaks behind him. The grass sparkled with frost and a thin skim of ice glistened along the edges of the creek.

The sun after days of heavy skies buoyed Man Chief's spirit and he felt unreasonably happy. As he rode along a rise near the stream, he saw vultures circling in the arroyo to the south. There were perhaps twenty of the big birds, and others coming in. He turned his pony in that direction, thinking perhaps they were attracted by the remains of an animal killed by Comanche hunters or an abandoned campsite that would contain some clue as to where the inhabitants might be. He found that the birds were over a drainage to the south of the one he followed, a stream that had cut a deep trench into the desert floor.

It took him some time to find a place where he could work his way down to the bottom of the ravine. He temporarily lost sight of the birds, but he was certain he would find them by merely continuing along the stream. Around two bends, he found the vultures again as well as their prey.

A mule lay sprawled in the stream bed, its head twisted at a sharp angle that suggested it had broken its neck in a fall from the narrow trail that led into the ravine from above. It still wore a bridle and a pack saddle.

"White man," Pitalesharo mused, "probably a trapper. I wonder where he is?"

At that moment he heard the faint click of a hammer being pulled back. He turned his pony, searching both for cover and for the source of the sound.

"Jist stand where you be, sonny, if you understand the white man's lingo. If you don't, you're a dead red devil."

The voice came from behind a tangle of brush along the stream; Pitalesharo now saw the glint of a rifle barrel poking through the shrubbery.

Pitalesharo's face remained impassive. For all its bluster, the voice was less than fear-inspiring.

"I speak English," Pitalesharo said to the rifle barrel. "Now I'd like to know why you're threatening to kill me."

A face appeared among the branches, a leathery countenance with sandy grey bristles of beard and small bright blue eyes. It studied him suspiciously before speaking again.

"Not planning to kill you especially. Jist don't trust strangers, be they red or white."

"You've had an accident, friend," Pitalesharo said. "Maybe I can help."

For a time the eyes peered intently at the Pawnee. Then the white man spoke again.

"I am a trifle stove up," he said. "Worthless cuss of a mule. Always was a worthless cuss. You done it to us this time, Jack Rabbit," he yelled at the dead animal. His voice was beginning to crack. He crawled out of the brush, dragging one leg behind him.

"Broken?" Pitalesharo asked, dismounting and approaching the injured man.

"Looks like, don't it? I set her myself, stuck my foot between some rocks and pulled her straight. But I figger it'll be a leetle time before she's good as new. You really be wanting to help me or is it my scalp you're coveting?"

Pitalesharo began to laugh. "Who'd want your scalp, white devil? It only has a little hair around the edges."

The man looked offended, then grinned. "Guess you're

right on that, too. You're pretty sharp for a red Indian. Name's Michael McCullogh. Folks call me Curly Mike. Used to, at least. Don't much anymore.''

"I am Pitalesharo of the Skidi Pawnee."

Curly Mike pushed and turned himself until he was sitting, his back partially propped against a boulder. He stuck his hand out, and Pitalesharo shook it.

"Reckon the best thing you could do for me is to head back down to the Comanch village. I was wintering with White Hoof's folks down on the Canadian. Was heading up to do a mite of trapping when old Jack Rabbit there done us in. Sure am going to miss the old cuss.''

"I cannot take you to the Comanche," Pitalesharo explained. "They have always been our enemies. But I will take you back to my friends and they will care for you. I'll splint your leg and then we will see about loading you on Red Medicine Dog."

It took the remainder of the day to get Curly Mike back to the box canyon. Pitalesharo walked and led the roan, the injured trapper strapped to the animal's back. When they had maneuvered up out of the wash and the traveling was easier, Pitalesharo put to the trapper the question that had been in his mind since the man had mentioned the Comanche.

"Do you know of a chief named Fox Shirt?"

"Sure do. He's mighty famous among the Comanch. Why? You got some special grudge against him?"

"No, I just wondered if you knew where his winter camp is."

"Now, this child cain't go telling Fox Shirt's enemies where he's living. That ain't no way to repay hospitality. I appreciate mightily what you're doing for me, Big Pete, but—"

"I have no grudge against this Comanche chief. I do

not wish to harm Fox Shirt. If that were true, wouldn't I have brought my warriors with me?''

"How do I know you didn't?" McCullogh asked.

"All right, Curly Mike, I'll tell you why I wish to find Fox Shirt's village. I'll tell you the whole story. . . .''

When he had finished, McCullogh was silent for so long that the chief's son turned back to see if the white man had fallen asleep. But Curly Mike was quite awake, peering at him and thinking hard.

"What is it now?" Pitalesharo asked. "Will you still not tell me where the village is?"

"Jist considering, is all. That's a whopping good story, Big Pete, but the Pawnee is famous for telling good lies. At least among the Comanch."

"I think I should have left you back there for the vultures. Vultures have to eat too," Pitalesharo growled.

"Truth to say, that's something this child has been worrying about."

"Vultures?"

"Nope, eating. You ain't hauling my ass back to your friends so's you can kill me and eat me, are you? I've heard one or two tales about the Pawnee being sort of cannibals."

"Your flesh would be too tough and stringy," Pitalesharo laughed.

"Figgered so," Mike nodded.

It was close to sundown when they reached the meadow where Hummingbird and Behele waited with the herd of horses. After checking Man Chief's story with the others, Curly Mike at last agreed to divulge the whereabouts of Fox Shirt's village.

"I know old Fox Shirt pretty well," Mike allowed. "His woman and White Hoof's squaw are sisters, and they do a good bit of visiting back and forth, trading young ones and such. You'd have come along a leetle sooner, you could have caught 'em where I was, with White Hoof. But now they're back down to the Pecos. Take you three, four days to get there, sonny. Yes sir, I seen that Little Frog gal. Sure is a purty number, that one. You really think she's sweet on you? I heard about how the Pawnee was going to burn her and then changed their minds. So you're the one what brought her back, huh?''

Hummingbird studied McCullogh's face and then nodded.

"There, you see, Man Chief," she said. "I told you this thing would turn out right. Now all you have to do is ride down to Fox Shirt's village and bring Little Green Frog back, and then we can take our horses and go home. If Hawk Foot doesn't wish to give me up, then we will kill him.''

Behele laughed. "Simple as greased buffalo dung, as Juan Termite would say.''

"You really compañeros with Joe Hollingback?'' Curly Mike asked. "Wal, I wouldn't trust that son of a bitch no way. Cheats at cards, he does. Played monte with him three years ago up at St. Louis, and that's where my bad luck started. Listen here, Pete. Here's how this child sees it. All you got to do is walk into a village full of coons what wants your Pawnee scalp and then waltz back out with the chief's daughter. Shit, nothing to her. You a betting man, Behele?''

Grey Bear thought the matter over. "I'd better go with you, Pitalesharo,'' he said.

"Good idea," chortled Mike. "That'll make the Comanch twice as happy.''

"You be quiet, Baldy Mike," Hummingbird ordered. "No such thing will happen. Fox Shirt will not kill the man who saved his daughter's life. No father would do that.''

"Jist wanting the boy to be careful is all. Likely he saved my hide, too. You do a lot of that sort of thing, Pete?"

Pitalesharo turned back to Behele.

"It is best that you stay here, mi amigo. If they kill me, I don't much care. If they killed you too then what would happen to Hummingbird? Besides, they are more likely to accept one man than two, is that not so?"

"Think the lad's got a point there, Behele," interjected Curly Mike. "Say, how long you knowed old Termite Joe, anyhow? Up with the Pawnee, is he?"

"Sí," said Antonio. "You know him well, amigo?"

"Hell, yes. Me and Joe was together up the Missouri a few years back. Truth is, he were a greenhorn at the time. Looked to be shaping up as a good one, though. Then old One Lung Charley taught him how to cheat at cards. Wal, we saw some wild times together, me and Joe. Yes, sir, some wild times. Why, they was once when—"

"You must tell us that story sometime, amigo," interrupted Behele, "but now you must tell my brother where to find Fox Shirt's village."

"Like I said, down to the Pecos, last I heard. Likely still there."

"How do I find this place on the Pecos?" Pitalesharo asked.

"Wal, if you head down south to where these here mountains gets small and peters out, and find a stream and follow her down, pretty soon you'll reach the Pecos. Ain't much of a river most times, kind of muddy and small. I reckon old Fox Shirt and his boys don't be too far downstream. That's how this child sees it."

Pitalesharo nodded. "I know that river. That is where my father found Grey Bear many winters ago. I have been on a horse-stealing in that area."

"Wal, the Comanch have some other name for it, but I forget a lot of them heathen monikers."

"How is your leg feeling, Baldy Mike?" Hummingbird asked.

"Dang it, leetle lady, I sure wish you wouldn't call me that, begging your pardon. A man don't like to be reminded all the time. Anyhow, it feels as comfortable as can be expected, I reckon.

"Listen, Pete, when you get down to Fox Shirt's, providing they don't scalp you right off, do you reckon you could nose around and see if there's somebody who might be hankering to go visit with White Hoof's gang? Usually is somebody just looking for an excuse to go visiting. I guess the best thing for my busted carcass is to get back with the Comanch. I been paying court to a widow woman and it often do impress the ladies mightily to let them take care of you when you're damaged some. Hate to pass up the opportunity."

Pitalesharo and Behele burst out laughing, and Hummingbird, whose English was sketchier, looked to her husband for a translation of Mike's long speech. When Behele complied, she looked indignant. "Ha. I would throw hot water on you and drive you out of the lodge."

"Now, you wouldn't do that, would you?" Mike asked, looking sideways at her. "A tender and lovely young critter like yourself and a poor old busted fellow like me?"

Hummingbird laughed then and shook her finger at him. "I think you are an old coyote. You slip in and take the meat from the wolves while they're laughing at you."

"Enough," cried Behele. "We must get back to business. I see that it would be foolish to go off and leave my woman with this man even if he can't run fast. Very well, Man Chief, I will stay here with the horses. Perhaps we should move the herd down toward the Pecos. I do not like to remain here, not knowing what has become of my brother. I could come and watch outside the village."

Pitalesharo shook his head. "No, it is best that you stay with the horses and Hummingbird. And the crazy bald one. If I do not come back in ten days, then you must take the horses and head back toward Wolf-Standing-in-Water."

Behele nodded but still looked less than completely convinced. "I do not see any other way, but I would feel better if I could come with you."

Pitalesharo stood up and walked about for a moment. "No, the Bear Person will help me. If it is his will that I die, then there is no way to escape my fate. Now I had better try to sleep."

Hummingbird embraced Man Chief warmly, tears glinting in her eyes. "It will be lucky for you, Pitalesharo. I know you will find her. Then you and Little Green Frog will be as happy as Grey Bear and I are. You must tell her that I love her and that I have missed her."

Pitalesharo slept little that night. He lay in his robes and gazed at the stars. He tried not to think, but his stomach was knotted with anticipation and his mind kept revolving uselessly on what was to come. The Comanche might simply kill him before he ever got into the village. Or they might kill him later, with his beloved watching. Perhaps Little Green Frog would no longer love him. Perhaps, perhaps. . . .

Chapter 17

He slept for a time, then awoke sweating. He sat up. The moon was down and the stars glittered intensely against the black sky.

Near dawn, he thought. He slipped out of the warm robes, made his silent preparations in the faint starshine, then led the big roan down the meadow and away from his companions. As he passed, Behele rose and walked beside him for a short way without speaking.

When they were some distance from the others, Behele turned and gripped both Pitalesharo's arms. "My friend, my brother," he began, and then stopped, at a loss for words.

Pitalesharo embraced his friend. "Gracias, Antonio. I know. I do not have the right words either. I will be back soon."

He mounted and set off down the canyon, glancing over his shoulder once to see his brother still standing where he had left him. The Spaniard raised his arm and waved it in a wide circle.

"Loo-ah!" Behele's voice reverberated from the rock walls of the gorge.

"Loco," Pitalesharo shouted back and kicked his horse into a trot, laughing and suddenly feeling fierce and strong. "Your lover is coming, Little Green Frog," he called. "Tell all your men to arm themselves well, for Pitalesharo will overpower them all. Coyote Jesus and the Great Bear have strengthened his arm, and he is as ten thousand."

The Sangre de Cristos gradually dissolved into a tangle of low hills, short grass, mesquite and a few trees along the sluggish streams. Pitalesharo followed the meandering course of an intermittent waterway. He camped after dark where the tiny trickle of water he was following merged with a slightly larger flow. As he sat near his small fire, he could see lightning flicker over the mountains to the north and hear the low mutter of thunder.

The storm came closer. Lightning bloomed in great, crazy stalks, the thunder roared and crashed and the wind howled.

Pitalesharo struggled with a buffalo robe, trying to tie it to the boles of two trees as a windbreak, but each time he held the robe up it was snatched out of his hands. And then the storm broke. Rain and hail bounced painfully off his body. He drew his robe up over his head.

Red Medicine Dog whinnied frantically, pounding his hooves as he tried to pull loose from his pickets. Pitalesharo fought his way through wind, hail and darkness to the horse, cradled the animal's head and pulled the robe over both of them.

As quickly as it had come, the storm receded, but then he heard a new sound, a deep rumbling that grew louder and made the earth tremble.

Flash flood, he thought. Got to get to high ground.

He fumbled for a moment at the rawhide rope tying the roan to a tree. The rumble was a roar and the ground shook beneath his feet. He couldn't loosen the knot. He drew his knife and cut through the lashing. He ran, pulling the frightened horse after him, stumbling up the creek bank.

He remembered his weapons and his other goods and plunged back toward the creek, uncertain he'd even be able to find them in the darkness. He smelled the drowned campfire and moved toward it against a great noise of surging water and a strange, raw odor in the air. Wind swirled about him. He heard the sounds of trees breaking and falling.

He sprawled on the wet earth, found the embers of the fire, touched the rifle, pistol, leather pouch.

He grabbed them and bolted uphill. Thick mud pulled at his legs as he plunged on in the darkness. The torrent of water and mud and boulders and fractured trees swept relentlessly toward him.

He heard Red Medicine Dog whinny. He plunged toward the faint sound and threw himself up the bank to where the horse was rearing and twisting.

The flood rolled past him with the noise of ten thousand buffalo in full stampede. For an hour or more it rushed onward before it gradually quieted and then receded.

Pitalesharo stood with his arms around Red Medicine Dog's neck. They were both trembling.

"I am not sure the gods of the country welcome us, horse," he whispered. "We may as well go on for a time. Neither of us will sleep well now. Perhaps morning will bring sunlight."

Stars began to emerge in the sky once again as the man and the horse felt their way downstream over stony ground, keeping to the low rim. After a time Pitalesharo stopped. He tethered his horse to a clump of mesquite, sat down and pulled his drenched buffalo robe about his shoulders. He fell into an exhausted sleep.

On the third day the sky was clear once again and the weather turned colder. A sharp wind blew from the north. Pitalesharo continued to follow the stream, not sure where it turned into the river Curly Mike had called the Pecos. He kept to what cover there was, but that wasn't much, for this was a country of dry grasslands broken only by low swells.

It was late afternoon when he first saw traces of smoke staining the sky.

Coyote Jesus is with me again, he thought. If the sky were not so blue today, I would not have seen the smoke, but perhaps the Comanche would have seen me.

He stopped, dismounted and led Red Medicine Dog to the scant cover of the bare cottonwoods along the river. He stopped frequently to walk up to the low ridges along the river and look. When he saw the first of the Comanche pony herd, he scrambled back to the river and picketed his own horse.

"I hope that when I come back for you, you are not a Comanche horse, Red Medicine Dog. Do not whinny even if you see other ponies. Your rope is long enough so that you may graze and drink. You must care for yourself for a time now."

The horse nudged the man, then fell to munching dry grass. Pitalesharo stroked the smooth neck for a moment and moved away downstream once more.

When he began to smell the smoke of the village, he stopped again, took cover in a tangle of brush and waited for dark.

There was no sound except the purling of the slow, muddy river. He was completely inside the tangle of dry brush, curled on his side. The thin, leafless branches made his skin itch and sting. But he was very glad that it was not the time of year for mosquitoes and flies.

He remembered Little Green Frog's words: "My father's lodge is the most beautiful in the village. It is not the largest, but it is very handsome. We have a big rainbow painted from the ground all the way up over the entrance and back to the ground again. Above the rainbow are four horses, one black, one brown, one yellow and one white. I do not know what they are supposed to signify. It is something from my father's medicine vision."

Did she know I would return one day? Pitalesharo wondered. Why else would she have described so many things?

At dusk he ventured out into the open. He made his way cautiously to high ground. He saw a few horses in the swale beyond. Three boys were moving them toward the village for the night.

The camp itself was hidden by the hills to the south. He wrapped himself in his buffalo robe and moved on to the next rise.

He had to make his way over two more low ridges and skirt two more swales before he came in view of the village, a collection of perhaps thirty lodges ranged along a gentle slope above the river.

Pitalesharo studied the village from above, lying flat on his belly in the grass. The camp was alive with evening activity. He could hear the shouts of children at play, the barking of dogs. A woman's voice called out. Men and women moved about the lodges, which glowed from lodge fires within. But in this light and from this distance he could not determine which lodge might be Fox Shirt's.

He knew what he would do. He was sure he had known all along.

With his robe pulled tight around him, he walked

down from the ridge toward the village, fighting to keep
his pace to that of a man casually re-entering his own
camp for the evening. He kept his head down as if he were
deep in thought and passed in among the outermost lodges.

Two children tumbling over one another fell against
his legs, nearly knocking him to the ground. The imps
looked guiltily up at him and one said something apologet-
ic. Man Chief grunted and moved on and the children
scurried away.

*Do they know I am not Comanche? Are they going to
call their parents and tell them there's a stranger in the
village?*

Pitalesharo forced the thought from his mind, continued walking toward the heart of the village. A man passing
him called a casual greeting and Pitalesharo raised one
hand in reply, keeping his head down.

This can't work much longer.

He took another deep breath and waved in response to
yet one more perfunctory greeting.

*I follow my heart. They cannot kill me more than
once. Little Green Frog. Mountain Lily. Ranita Verde,
your people can do no more than kill me.*

Now he recognized the lodge. He was sure it was the
right one, although the colors of the painting were not
discernible in the dusk. There was the high arch of the
rainbow, the forms of the two horses above. The light-
colored horses, Pitalesharo reasoned, would be nearly in-
visible until he drew very close. He strolled ahead, trying
not to be obvious in his inspection.

His heart pounded as he moved close enough to hear a voice from inside, an old man's voice telling a story. Pitalesharo knew enough Comanche so that he could understand much of what the old man was saying. It was, he was certain, the voice of Ranita's grandfather, old Whistling Bird. She had told him about the old man's passion for telling tales.

The activity outdoors had almost ceased now. Lodge flaps were being closed and only a few people moved about. He could hear from across the village the sound of a flute as some young warrior serenaded outside the tepee of a young woman he wished to impress.

Gradually Pitalesharo began to believe that his ruse had worked. He had gained his first object almost too easily.

He continued walking slowly here and there until he alone remained outdoors. Then he sat down near the doorflap to Fox Shirt's lodge. Now if anyone should notice him he would be taken for a lovesick young suitor for Little Green Frog's hand.

And so he was. He silently laughed, a little at himself.

Time passed with maddening slowness, but gradually the sounds within the village died out. Even the warrior with the flute had ceased his tunes. Pitalesharo saw him as he walked through the village, shoulders stooped slightly as if in dejection, and Man Chief felt a pang of sympathy for the suffering swain.

Inside Fox Shirt's lodge Whistling Bird had finished his story and a woman's voice called out a question. Then he heard Little Green Frog answer.

Her voice! Pitalesharo sucked in his breath. Her voice was like a sound from a dream, a reminder of a different world, impossibly distant.

Perhaps she would come out before going to sleep. Perhaps he could simply take her then, and they could run up the river to Red Medicine Dog and ride double back to the box canyon.

Or perhaps her father would come outside and discover him there. He remained where he was, barely breathing. The voices from inside ceased and the glow from the fire faded by degrees until it was no longer visible from outside. The only light remaining was the moonlight that touched everything. The horses picketed outside were standing like statues frozen in pale luminescence. A dog trotted by looking for something to eat. Another paused, sniffed at him and growled softly before going on.

After a long while, when Pitalesharo was certain that Little Green Frog would not be coming out and that everyone inside the lodge was asleep, he moved to the door flap and tugged one corner of it aside.

An explosive snore from within caused him to drop the flap immediately. He waited, listening to the snorer. He stifled with difficulty an hysterical urge to laugh. He raised the flap again.

He slid slowly forward on his belly, stopping often to listen to the regular breathing of the inhabitants. Once fully inside, he got to his hands and knees and moved toward his left along the circle of open space about the fire pit. His hand struck some object leaning against a lodgepole and it toppled, making a faint clatter.

Pitalesharo froze crouched against the wall. A man's voice called out softly and in a moment a woman replied sleepily. Man Chief waited, not breathing. He heard the robes rustling as the man rolled onto his side, mumbled something, and then returned to silence.

After a tense eternity he resumed his slow journey around the lodge. He came to the couch of the first sleeper—two small mounds. Children. He moved ahead to the next heap of robes. A woman, but the face was hidden. All he could see was one dark braid.

He bent closer.

The scent of her hair, the smell of her. Little Green Frog.

The sleeper turned then, as if aware of him, and pushed the robes away from her face. Her eyes opened and she saw him. She sat up and slapped both hands over her mouth as if to keep from crying out.

Little Green Frog sat rocking back and forth with her hands to her lips. They studied one another in the semi-darkness. After a time she reached out a bare arm and touched his shoulder, and he slipped into the warm bed next to her, pulling off his own robe and spreading it over hers.

"Man Chief," she whispered, "it is not possible. I was just dreaming about you. That is what woke me. I was dreaming that you were sitting by my bed." She stifled a giggle. "I am still dreaming, I know, but it is a good dream. Please, please put your arms around me. I do not wish to wake up ever again."

She snuggled against him, wrapping her arms about his neck. He felt the softness of her breasts, moved his hand along the curve of her body and held her tight against him. He felt a terrible hunger for her.

His hands took on a purpose of their own, moving softly over her, stroking, touching. She was naked beneath the robes, but his hands came upon the rough bulk of the braided horsehair chastity belt at her waist. She turned, reached behind her and pushed something into his hand—a knife.

"Use this. I want you to love me now, Dream-Pitalesharo, before I wake up once more," she whispered.

He put his lips next to her ear and whispered, "I am not a dream, mi Ranita Verde. If I use this knife, your father will probably kill me."

"Are you certain you're not a dream?" she whispered again, moving against him so that he shuddered involuntarily.

"It is all right if your father kills me now," he murmured.

"Who is in the lodge?" a man shouted in Comanche.

Pitalesharo and Little Green Frog tensed.

"Is someone in the lodge?" called out the voice of an old man.

"I will put some twigs on the fire," a woman said. "Perhaps it is only a dog."

"Hah," shouted Fox Shirt, "a dog that whispers with my daughter."

The robes rustled as the man threw them back, and Pitalesharo watched helplessly as the dark figure rose and lurched sleepily and angrily toward the couch where he and Little Green Frog, like a pair of guilty children, dared neither to move nor to utter a sound.

Chapter 18

Pistol in hand, Chief Fox Shirt stood above the pallet upon which his daughter lay in the embrace of a stranger.

"Grass Woman," he called out to his wife, "light the oil cups and build up the fire. I wish to know who this dog-thief is before I kill him and hang his scalp from the lodge flap. Whistling Bird, bring me my skinning knife."

Grass Woman began to shriek. But she calmed quickly, found wood to heap on the bed of coals and came to stand beside her husband. "Little Green Frog," she wailed, "you disgrace our lodge. When morning comes, everyone in the village will already know what you have done."

"The oil cups, wife," Fox Shirt repeated. "Light the oil cups." But Whistling Bird was already attending to them.

"Green Frog," the father commanded, "get out of the bed. Who is this man who has come to lie with you?"

"I will obey," Little Green Frog said. But as she rose, she dropped her own sleeping robe to her feet, snatched up

Pitalesharo's blanket and wrapped it about her nearly nude form.

"I take this warrior's robe," she said, her voice calm. "I draw it about me. Many women before me have done the same. Grandfather Whistling Bird, it was you who first explained this tradition to me. I am doing no new thing."

"She is choosing a husband," Grass Woman cried out. "Take the blanket away from her, Fox Shirt."

"What do you ask of me, wife? Shall I strip my own daughter naked in front of this stranger? I cannot do that."

Pitalesharo started to rise, but Fox Shirt leveled the horse pistol in a way that indicated he would not hesitate to shoot.

"This man has seen my body before, Father. I gave myself to him long ago because he is the one I love. Now he has come to find me. This is Pitalesharo of the Skidi Pawnee, the man who saved my life when the medicine man was about to slay me for a sacrifice."

Fox Shirt, now uncertain what to do, lowered his pistol somewhat. "Does this man speak our language?"

"I do," Pitalesharo replied. "Little Green Frog taught me many of your words, Fox Shirt."

Old Whistling Bird came close, studied the face before him and said, "This is indeed the man, my son. This is the one who brought the Little Green Frog back to us. It is hard for me to see anything by lamplight, but I recognize him."

"Pawnee," Grass Woman cried out. "He is an enemy."

Fox Shirt digested the new information. "Though you saved my daughter's life, Skidi, I owe you no debt. Your own warriors captured her and intended to kill her. Perhaps you are the one who took her prisoner, for all I know. As for torturing a woman to death, my people have no understanding of such an action. The Pawnee are worse than the white man. Not even the Spanish would do such a thing. When you brought Little Green Frog back to us, Six Feathers and his warriors spared your life. One debt cancels the other.''

"I did not come as an enemy then," Pitalesharo answered, "and I do not come as an enemy now. I have come here, even though my people and the Comanche have always been enemies, because my heart led me. Your daughter loves me and I love her. I have dreamed of her constantly since we parted in the time of late summer. Now I wish to marry her.''

"I send you to the spirit world, Skidi," Fox Shirt said, raising the pistol once again.

"No," Little Green Frog cried out, leaping between Pitalesharo and the cocked weapon. "If you kill him, Father, then I will die anyway. I will take my own life. Shoot both of us or spare him!''

"Green Frog, you are even more willful than your mother. I do not wish to shoot you. Get out of the way now.''

"I am old," Whistling Bird said, "and this is my fault, Fox Shirt. I was indeed the one who told her of the blanket ritual. But is it not true that our people have always allowed such a thing to young people who have the courage to do it? Yes, I am old, and yet I remember how desperately my heart ached within me for your mother, my son. It took three years for me to gain enough wealth to pay the bride price her father demanded.

"But see what came of it. You are now the head chief of our people. You became a great warrior, and after Red Eagle died and you defeated the Spanish at the Bluewater Mesa, the council chose you to be the new chief. If I had not persisted, my son, you would never have been born. Now my granddaughter wraps this warrior's buffalo robe about her body. And see, he sits there with her robe about his shoulders. He has risked his life for Little Green Frog."

"You are old and your speeches are very long, Father. All right, I will not kill him yet. Even though it is the middle of the night, I will summon my counselors. I will listen to their words. Perhaps they will say that I must allow this Skidi to ride away. Perhaps they will choose to spare his life since he once saved the life of Little Green Frog."

"Then I will ride away with him," Little Green Frog said.

"The daughter must not speak that way to her father," Grass Woman hissed, her eyes narrowed. "You have brought disgrace upon all of us, and now you make it worse."

"I am sorry, Mother. But I must do what my voice inside tells me."

"This man, he is the reason you have refused to marry Six Feathers, a brave and a strong leader. You have never done what you are supposed to do," Grass Woman complained.

"You are the son of the Knife Chief, is that true?" Fox Shirt asked.

"Yes, he is my father. I am Man Chief, Pitalesharo, the leader of the Red Lances. But in exchange for the hand of your daughter, I am willing to be your slave for as long as you say. I will bring you many presents. And I will become a Comanche and live here in your village."

Fox Shirt and Pitalesharo studied one another for a long moment.

"Father," the Comanche chief said, "I give you this pistol so that you can keep it pointed at our enemy. No matter what Green Frog says, you must not allow him to escape. I will go to summon my counselors to this lodge. I wish to hear what they will tell me.''

With that he handed the weapon to Whistling Bird, turned and left the tepee.

Grass Woman began to berate her daughter once again, but Whistling Bird, who had already put the pistol away, placed his hands upon his daughter-in-law's shoulders, shook his head and smiled. His old eyes were glinting in the firelight.

"It was not long ago," he said, "when you and Fox Shirt used to sneak away from the village in order to meet. Both of you thought you were doing it in secret, but all of us knew. Did I ever attempt to prevent you from meeting? No, I did not do that. All along I secretly wished that you might be my daughter-in-law, and so it happened. Sit down now, Grass Woman, and I will tell the story to Little Green Frog and her young man—"

"You and your stories," Grass Woman protested. But at the same time she gave the old man a hug.

"Children often do things that make their parents angry," Whistling Bird said, seating himself. He closed his eyes and began to doze. Little Green Frog drew Pitalesharo's robe more tightly about herself and settled next to the man she had chosen.

The counselors arrived one by one and stood silent in a semicircle about the lovers. Grass Woman brought a woven tray filled with choice portions of cold venison. The men accepted the food, chewed and said nothing.

Whistling Bird continued to sleep. He was snoring now, the cadence somewhat irregular. Only when Fox Shirt came back into the lodge did the old man come fully awake.

The chief indicated that his wife should speak first, and Grass Woman told the story of awakening to find a stranger, and an enemy at that, in bed with their daughter. As she spoke, she poured indignation into her voice.

Then Fox Shirt recounted the same tale, varying only slightly from what his wife had already said. When he had finished, he addressed Pitalesharo directly. "Tell the members of my council why you have come to this lodge."

Pitalesharo studied the hard eyes around him and sensed the futility of trying to convince the counselors of anything.

"I am Man Chief, the son of Knife Chief, leader of the Skidi Pawnee," he began, speaking slowly and sometimes having to search for the correct Comanche phrase. "I have come here because I spoke with Bear Person in a vision. He told me to follow my heart and I have done that, even though it has led me to this lodge and into the hands of those who may wish to take my life."

He gazed steadily into the hostile faces around him and squared his shoulders. "I came because I could not live without Little Green Frog. She was taken prisoner by my own people and the shaman intended to sacrifice her. I could not let such a thing happen, so I stole her away. As we traveled south into the lands of the Comanche, she and I found love together. Now I wish her to be my wife. I wish to be son-in-law to Fox Shirt and Grass Woman. If they will not have me, then they may do with me as they wish. Without Little Green Frog my life is worthless to me. These are my words, Comanche."

The counselors were silent, each man glancing from one to another of his fellows.

Among them, as Pitalesharo noted in near-despair, was the warrior Six Feathers, who now addressed Little Green Frog. "It is well known that I have long wished for you to be my wife. I believe that if you had not been captured by the Pawnee, you would have consented and I would have been son-in-law to Fox Shirt. But after this man brought you back to us, you have turned my gestures of love aside. Others have sought your hand also, and they have fared no better than I. At last we all came to believe that you had taken a vow, that you had promised Saynday or perhaps Grandmother Spider never to know what it was like to lie in the embrace of love with a man. We supposed that you intended to become a medicine woman, a healer. And yet I continued to want you, even though when we chanced to meet you merely turned your eyes aside."

Six Feathers paused, glancing from one of his fellow counselors to another, and then back at Little Green Frog. "Now I have changed what I think. Now I believe that you have already known love with this Pawnee warrior. I believe what he has told us, even though one of us would not speak so openly of such a thing. I do not like this man, Little Green Frog, and yet I think he has told us the truth. Now I ask you to tell us all. Has he spoken the truth?"

"Yes," she replied. "I have already told my mother and father that."

"And do you love this Skidi, even though he is an enemy?"

"Yes, Six Feathers, I do. Once I cared for you very much, but I did not love you. I love Pitalesharo the Pawnee. I came to love him even though I did not think I would."

Six Feathers turned his gaze to Fox Shirt, who was about to speak again when Whistling Bird interrupted him.

"Comanche," the old warrior began, "once I was like you, a member of the council. In that capacity I served Red Eagle and Big Snake before him. They are in the spirit world now, and I should not even mention their names. But I am old and will join them soon, so I do not think they will mind. Yes, I am old. And for as long as I can remember, more than eighty winters, we have always been at war with the Pawnee. We fear them even as they fear us.

"But now this young man comes to us, not only unarmed but alone—because he feels the heat of love. I am very old, and yet I still remember how that feels. When he's in love, a man will do almost anything."

Fox Shirt began to chuckle at his father's assertion, and two or three of the others did likewise.

Whistling Bird held out his hands before him as if to quiet a group of children to whom he was telling a story. "Yes, it is true—and we all know it. Some even say that women as well as men act crazy when they are in love. We have all heard the she-cougar scream in the night."

Now the chief and the counselors, even Six Feathers, roared with laughter. One man suddenly could not seem to control himself. He wiped at his eyes, shook his head and finally stepped out into the predawn darkness.

Whistling Bird removed his medicine pipe from its fur-lined pouch, filled the bowl with tobacco, lit it, and gestured to the sacred directions. He puffed slowly and waited for the missing counselor to return. Then he resumed speaking.

"Little Green Frog has been my favorite ever since she was born. My own daughters were less kind to me than she is. I tell her stories and she listens, even though I get carried away and speak for a very long time."

He glanced at her, squinted, saw that there were tears in her eyes. He winked at her.

"Yes, and sometimes she has told me what is in her heart. For nearly a full season now I have known of her love for the brave Skidi warrior Man Chief. But I do not think Little Green Frog has told anyone else. Well, I urged her to forget him, to marry Six Feathers or one of the other young men. But she could not do it. And then I began to wonder if this man, Pitalesharo, loved my granddaughter as much as she loved him. If he did, I thought, then somehow he would manage to come to her, and this he has done.

"Now he sits before us and awaits our judgment. He is willing to die for her because he could see no other way. Perhaps some of you will judge that he must die. After all, he is our enemy. But Little Green Frog has wrapped herself in his blanket, and see, Pitalesharo sits there with her robe about his wide shoulders. For myself, I am not willing to condemn a man who is wearing my granddaughter's blanket. They have chosen each other, Comanche, and we must not deny their choice."

Whistling Bird puffed once again at his pipe and passed it on to Fox Shirt. "Besides," the old man continued, "I would like to visit these Pawnee before I die. We have always been enemies, but perhaps now the time for peace has come. They do not wander across the face of the earth as much as we do, and they have gardens where they grow many things. I think it would be good for us to learn how to do this also. I will go to visit these people, and I think that Man Chief will protect me when I do. Should I speak longer? No, it is best to be brief. These are my words, Comanche."

The counselors all looked at Fox Shirt and the head chief nodded. "No one speaks briefly better than my father. There is no need to take a vote, I think. I will accept Man Chief as my son-in-law. And soon, if he will assist me, I will speak with his father about arranging a time for trade between our peoples. I will vote for peace if Lachelesharo is willing. That way both of us will be able to visit our grandchildren, wherever my daughter and her husband decide to live."

When the counselors departed, the first light of day was visible through the entry flap.

*   *   *

All morning the Comanche village was buzzing with the news of what had happened during the night. Women gathered in clusters to gossip and several of the young men, the disappointed suitors of Little Green Frog, wandered about looking hang-dog.

Before noon Fox Shirt called many of his warriors together and explained the goings-on and announced that Little Green Frog would marry Man Chief, the son of the leader of the Skidi Pawnee, that afternoon. These braves in turn quickly spread the word throughout the village.

Men and women alike discussed the matter and most were of the opinion that the warrior who had risked so much to be with the girl he loved must indeed be an exceptional person. For a Pawnee it was utterly astounding. "Even among rabid wolves, there must be one or two good ones," an old woman grinned.

Groups of curious people crowded about Fox Shirt's lodge, hoping to get a look at Little Green Frog and the mysterious Pawnee whom she would soon marry. Again and again, at old Whistling Bird's insistence, his granddaughter and Pitalesharo went out to meet one person after another.

"I would bring them into the lodge," he explained, "but the others wish to see you also. Little Frog, change into your fine white deerskin dress with the yellow braid on it. That is the dress you will wish to be married in. You must look as fine as you can. This is a very important thing that is happening."

"Yes," Grass Woman agreed, "that is what you must do."

Grass Woman had begun to take a special interest in Pitalesharo. Already she declined to speak to him, indicating that she had accepted him as a son-in-law. When she wished to ask Pitalesharo something, she would ask her daughter instead, as though the Pawnee warrior were not even present. And he in turn would answer Little Green Frog and not Grass Woman.

But the prospective mother-in-law was making such obvious gestures of deference and cautious affection toward Pitalesharo that Fox Shirt finally declared, "Wife, he is not for you. This one will belong to your daughter. You are stuck with me, even though I no longer care for you at all."

Pitalesharo grinned as Grass Woman blushed and turned away. But Fox Shirt took her in his arms and touched his forehead to hers.

"We must discuss the bride price," Fox Shirt declared. "It is only right, Pitalesharo, that the price be high, for you wish to honor the woman you marry. She is the daughter of a head chief and you are the son of a head chief. I understand that you cannot pay me now, but I wish to be able to tell my people what the price is to be. What do you think?"

"I will send you fifty ponies and a new Hawken rifle like mine," Pitalesharo said.

Fox Shirt smiled broadly. "No," he said. "Even for one so beautiful as Little Green Frog, that is too high. You would turn your father into a poor man, and then we would never be able to make peace. Let me set the price. I ask for two spotted ponies, the kind that come from the Nez Perce far to the north. And thirteen others. Also the rifle you mentioned. Is this agreeable to you?"

"It is agreeable," Pitalesharo replied. "If Grandfather Whistling Bird will accompany me to Wolf-Standing-in-Water Village, I will present the rifle and the horses to him and he can bring them back to you. Or I will bring them myself."

"It is good," Fox Shirt said. "And Lachelesharo and I will exchange presents also. If it is possible for us to make peace, then perhaps our villages will be able to visit one another when summer comes. If we cannot make peace, then at least you and I are at peace. Perhaps you will choose to live here sometimes as well as with your own people."

"My father," Pitalesharo replied, "is a man who loves peace. He seldom goes on the warpath now, even though he is still powerful. The shaman, Wounded Man, is the one who wishes for our people always to be at war."

"That is strange, Man Chief. Usually the medicine men are the ones who resist war. They wish the people to spend their time sitting and dreaming."

After the noon meal the female relatives crowded about to confer with Grass Woman. The women talked as though in fear of being overheard, and then with a great show of secret conspiracy they set off to accomplish some task.

"Now they will build the honeymoon lodge," Whistling Bird said. "It will be a small lodge, Man Chief, just large enough for a man and a woman to go into and be alone. I think they will put it on the little rise just beyond the village. Then the people may watch to see how long you and Little Green Frog stay inside. They will even be able to get close enough to listen. Is it this way among the Pawnee also?"

"Not exactly. Our lodges are larger than those of the Comanche. They are made of adobe and poles, so that an entire family may live in just one of them. But there is a permanent lodge where those who are just married may go. Sometimes others go there also."

Concern flashed across Whistling Bird's face.

"Do you already have wives, Man Chief? I have heard that some of the Pawnee have many women."

"I wish to have only one wife."

Whistling Bird glanced at Little Green Frog. "What

will you do if your husband later wishes to take many wives, Granddaughter? That is the way of his people.''

''I will not mind,'' she replied. ''Besides, it is often the way of our people also. Once you had three wives, Grandfather. That is what you told me.''

Whistling Bird nodded. ''Actually, I had but one wife always. The others were friends of hers who came to live with us. They were good women also, and I missed them after they died. But now, since I am losing my granddaughter, perhaps I should think about finding a young wife to care for me. Do you know of such a one, Little Green Frog?''

''Whistling Bird just likes to talk,'' Fox Shirt snorted. ''He is so old that his manhood has nearly vanished.''

Whistling Bird raised one eyebrow and glared at his son. ''Perhaps my manhood is a foot shorter than it once was,'' he said, ''but it is still plenty long enough. Why do you think the old women of the village make so much of me, my son?''

Chapter 19

Fox Shirt, with Grass Woman standing behind him, spoke to the assembled Comanche village. He repeated the entire story of Pitalesharo's rescue of Little Green Frog, of his risking his life to be with her again, of the possibilities for making peace with the Skidi Pawnee. Several times he matter-of-factly mentioned the bride price that Pitalesharo had offered him and the one they had settled on. The Comanche nodded in astonishment and approval. Such ardor!

And then Pitalesharo stepped forward and took Little Green Frog's hand. The Comanche women set up a loud yip-yip and the warriors applauded loudly, slapping their open hands against their chests.

Pitalesharo of the Pawnee and Little Green Frog were married.

Now a group of men and another of women came forward and husband and wife were separated. They were led off in opposite directions, but each eventually wound up at the newly built honeymoon lodge.

They were brought together once more as though in an unexpected meeting a few yards in front of the lodge. Then the two escort parties turned and ran away.

One man barred their entrance to the honeymoon bower. It was the warrior Six Feathers. He stood, arms crossed, and searched the faces of the lovers.

Pitalesharo, uncertain of the meaning of this and uncertain what to do next, placed his arm about Little Green Frog's waist and stared straight into the eyes of Six Feathers.

"I have chosen my husband," Little Green Frog said softly, declining to meet Six Feathers' eyes.

Six Feathers drew his knife and Pitalesharo reached for his. But the Comanche warrior bent forward and placed the blade on the ground.

"Man Chief of the Pawnee," he said, "if you are the one who saved her life, then it is all right. I will not block the entrance to your honeymoon lodge."

With that he turned and slowly walked back toward the village.

Hand in hand Pitalesharo and Little Green Frog entered the small, brightly decorated tepee. Inside was a comfortable bed piled with robes, several large baskets of food and two water flasks.

"I cannot believe this has happened," said Little Green Frog. "You were never absent from my thoughts, Man Chief, and yet I feared I would never see you again. Now I am your wife."

She turned away from him then and took off her white deerskin dress with the yellow braidwork. When she turned back to him once more, she was nude except for the woven horsehair chastity belt.

"Take your knife, my husband, and free me from my constraint."

* * *

We are together, locked in one another's arms after the long and all but hopeless time of denial and desolation. We revel in the good warmth of our bodies, male and female, the different kind of magic, the medicine of our touch.

Mountain Lily, beloved one, Ranita Verde, now I touch this blade to that which you have worn as a symbol of your love for me. I cut it. : . . .

My lover, my brother, iracti. . . .

Come to me woman that I love, siksa!

I am dreaming it.

Touch me. You must do this, irika-sucia.

Bashful.

I bury my face in your hair, Little Green Frog, my woman.

I touch my lips to the male game-lance. It is hard, it is long, ke-ac. *It is mine,* tati-i. Tactiriksta, *I am going to taste it.*

Ranita Verde, Mountain Lily.

Ta-tasa-a, *I am named. I am* capat, *woman,* taturicahrikse. *I am beautiful, yes, because Pitalesharo says it is so, now I am beautiful, I am with him.*

I am on fire—take me into you.

I am yours, I give myself to you, count coup upon my body, ke. . . .

It was dark and the lodge was cold. Little Green Frog roused herself from sleep, and shivering as she did, built up the fire. Then she pulled a robe about herself and watched the flames gain, dancing and flickering. Only when the little lodge had begun to warm did she wake Pitalesharo.

"Are you hungry, my husband? See all the food they have left for us. They will not be pleased unless we have eaten most of it."

Pitalesharo yawned, rubbed his eyes and sat up. "My wife speaks to me of food?"

"My husband needs to restore his energy."

They sat together next to the fire and ate, for a time taking turns at placing morsels into each other's mouth.

Then Little Green Frog reached down and felt for something. "I am still hungry."

And then they were back under their robes and the fire was allowed to die down.

They awoke with their faces pressed together, their arms still around one another.

"Oh, it is late. How long have we slept? Listen!"

Pitalesharo leaned upon one elbow, frowned.

"There are children outside," he said. "I think they're tossing pebbles at our tepee."

They heard muffled giggling.

"Go away," Pitalesharo roared.

Delighted screams accompanied the sounds of small moccasins scurrying away over the frozen ground.

Little Green Frog got up, pulled her dress on over her head and shoulders and brought a basket of buffalo meat and dried berries to her husband before she sat down beside him.

"Grey Bear," he muttered. "We will have to go to him soon, pretty one. I left him in the Sangre de Cristos. He's with Hummingbird now, the girl who was your friend when—"

"Is he married to her, Man Chief? She alone was like a sister to me."

"It is very complicated," Pitalesharo said. "Wounded Man wanted to kill her after we came back from bringing you home. Antonio Grey Bear ran away with her, but Hawk Foot found him. I was there also. She agreed to marry Hawk Foot in order to save my brother's life."

"But you have just said—"

"None of it seems to make much sense, I know. Then Antonio rode away and Hummingbird kept her promise and married Hawk Foot."

"Then why—"

"I will explain everything later, Little Green Frog."

"No, I wish to know now."

Pitalesharo stood up and pulled on his loincloth, shirt and leggings.

"All right. I left the village in order to go on a warpath with Lacheleshard. After that I did not return to the village. My heart was sad because I was in love with a certain Comanche girl, so I went back to a cave in the mountains to fast and pray for a vision. After that Antonio Grey Bear and Hummingbird and Termite Joe and Spotted Wolf's sister Broken Feather came to find me."

"This Broken Feather, she wished to be with you, Pitalesharo? You did not tell me about her."

"The Little Green Frog still has a quick tongue. She still jumps to conclusions. No, she was with Termite Joe. His wife."

"I see." Little Green Frog was obviously still suspicious. "But you said Hummingbird was married to Hawk Foot. Is that not so?"

"Yes," Pitalesharo agreed, shaking his head at the same time. "I told you it was very complicated. You see, Hawk Foot beat Hummingbird nearly to death, and after that Antonio returned to the village and may have killed Hawk Foot. Perhaps not, I don't know. I was not there in the village when it happened. Antonio and Termite Joe told me about it."

"And they are all in the Sangre de Cristos? Pitalesharo, this sounds like one of the stories Whistling Bird likes to tell."

Pitalesharo pulled on his moccasins. "Termite Joe and Broken Feather are somewhere in the mountains to the north. Joe is trapping beavers. But Antonio Grey Bear and Hummingbird are in the Sangre de Cristos, three days' ride north of here. They are guarding a herd of over two hundred horses that we stole from the Ute after they had stolen them from the Kiowa Apache. And Curly Mike, a white trapper, is with them. He's got a broken leg.''

"This Curly Mike is with the Apache?"

"Little Green Frog, you're not even trying to understand. No, Curly Mike is with Antonio and Hummingbird and the two hundred ponies. Now do you see?"

"Of course not. Not even everything we did together last night tired me out as much as this, my husband. You have made my head hurt.''

Fox Shirt's young son and daughter had gone out to fetch Red Medicine Dog, and the big horse was picketed before the head chief's lodge when Pitalesharo and Little Green Frog approached. Pitalesharo and the horse nuzzled each other for a moment.

"He wants a twist of tobacco, I think," Little Green Frog laughed. "Something to make up for being deserted.''

Pitalesharo nodded, scratched his horse behind the ears and then ushered his bride into her father's tepee.

As briefly as possible he explained to Fox Shirt the necessity of riding north so that his brother Grey Bear would know he had not been killed. He explained further the presence of Mike McCullogh, how he had found the old trapper and had taken him to the mountains where he could be cared for.

"Curly Mike," Fox Shirt mused. "For two years that one has stayed with White Hoof's people. He wishes to take a wife also, I think, but has no luck. Among the Comanche this one is known as Big Bull even though he is not large.''

"Father-in-law," Pitalesharo said, "I have been away

from my own village now for a long while. By now Lachelesharo and Raven Quill, my mother, must suppose that Grey Bear and I are both dead. It is important that I return there now, as quickly as possible, even though Little Green Frog and I have spent only one night in the wedding lodge. But I promise to return as soon as I am able to do so.''

''I will come too,'' Whistling Bird said. ''I will lead some of the young men, and they will be able to take Big Bull back to White Hoof's village. I have always liked Big Bull even though he is good for nothing. He can tell stories almost as well as I can; remarkable for a white man.''

Pitalesharo glanced at Grass Woman, in whose face disappointment showed clearly.

''When I reach my own village,'' Pitalesharo said, ''I will tell my father that he must make peace with you, Fox Shirt. And if Whistling Bird rides with us, I will send the horses I have promised back with him and his young men. I will send another present also. A Frenchman named Papin has a trading post in our village and he has many fine things to sell. I will purchase a bolt of bright red cloth and another of blue. Perhaps your wife would like to have them.''

''My son-in-law is very generous,'' Grass Woman said to Little Green Frog. ''Sometime you must tell him this: he is not only very handsome but also very generous.''

Little Green Frog embraced her mother and turned to Pitalesharo, nodding as she did so.

''It is good that my son-in-law cannot speak to my wife,'' Fox Shirt grumbled. ''Otherwise I think she would leave me and go to him. Oh well, that's the way it is when a man and a woman have been married for so many winters. I will call the warriors together to see if any of them wish to visit the village of the Skidi.''

*   *   *

On the fourth day Pitalesharo, Little Green Frog, Whistling Bird and a dozen Comanche warriors reached the box canyon in the Sangre de Cristos. Following Pitalesharo's lead, they discharged their weapons into the air as they approached the meadow where Behele, Hummingbird, Curly Mike and the horses were waiting.

Antonio Grey Bear sized up the situation immediately and broke into a wide grin. He ran forward, pulled Pitalesharo down from his horse and engaged in a moment of mock wrestling.

Introductions were made. Little Green Frog and Hummingbird flung themselves into one another's arms and then hurried off, talking nonstop, to prepare a large fire for the roasting of a full side of elk. The men would all be hungry, they knew, and it was a fine time for an impromptu celebration.

"Fox Shirt has sent me to carry the Big Bull with the bad leg back to his village," Whistling Bird announced. "Where is this famous rat trapper?"

"Right here, you damned old fool," Curly Mike snorted. "Jist try riding a damn mule down a cliffside sometime, you heathen old blabbermouth. If I was a Indian, the fall would have kilt me sure."

The Comanche admired the horses and Pitalesharo made presents of several of the Ute war ponies, including one to Whistling Bird.

"Perhaps my medicine will take me out on a warpath again," the old man said, "even though I had believed that part of my life was long over. If so, then this is certainly the pony I will ride. Perhaps I will decide to cross the mountains and make war on the Ute, for that way they will recognize my horse as one of their own."

As sunset flared crimson across the high western wall of the mountains, the odors of roasting flesh spread through the air and a pair of coyotes on the ridge above the meadows yowled long and hungrily, urging their human friends to remember them.

When morning came Curly Mike and half a dozen of the Comanche braves departed for White Hoof's village. Shortly thereafter the two Pawnee couples, Whistling Bird and the remaining Comanche drove the horses from the box canyon, onto the plains and turned north toward Wolf-Standing-in-Water Village.

The long journey was filled with almost nonstop storytelling by the old Comanche warrior.

"Doesn't he ever stop, hermano?"

"Haven't been around him long enough to say," Pitalesharo grinned. "But I'm beginning to think he doesn't."

"You must not make fun of my grandfather," Little Green Frog whispered. "Fortunately, he does not hear so well as he speaks. Anyway, it isn't necessary to listen all the time. He repeats things, so you will probably not miss anything anyway."

"Listen all the time? You must be joking," Behele snorted.

And so the days went, with the little group advancing ever northward, to the Purgatoire and finally to a ford of the Arkansas.

Two days farther on, shortly after they had crossed the Big Sandy and emerged onto the high, rolling prairie beyond, they caught sight of a lone rider atop a grassy rise in the distance. It was a white man clad in buckskin astride a big grey horse. Termite Joe Hollingback.

Joe approached, waving his rifle over his head. They rode ahead to meet the trapper, and Pitalesharo saw the trouble on Hollingback's face.

"Termite Chief, what is it? You have come looking for us?"

"That I have, Juan Pete. They's trouble in the village. Maybe real bad. Old Scar Face is at her again. Think maybe we'd better palaver and do some serious planning."

Chapter 20

Lachelesharo's victory against the Ute and his capture of five hundred ponies solidified his leadership of the tribe for a time. But the shaman, Wounded Man, continued to rave against the whites and condemn the missing Antonio Grey Bear as a white serpent. He had stolen the Cheyenne slave Hummingbird and gone unpunished only because he was under Lachelesharo's protection.

Wounded Man's influence waxed and waned with the mood of the people. For a time during Lachelesharo's absence they turned against both him and Hawk Foot. This was after Wolf Chief recounted how Hummingbird had been found nearly beaten to death and how Hawk Foot had pulled a knife on the unarmed Grey Bear. The whole village laughed when they heard how Hawk Foot had taken the beating of his life in return.

Hawk Foot was in disgrace, and the older warriors in particular laughed at his swollen face. Lachelesharo and his faction, the conquerors of the Ute, had given many gifts to the other warriors upon their return and were the heroes of the day. The chief's standing among his people was higher than it had been in a long time.

But then dysentery struck the village and many of the children fell desperately ill. Some died and Wounded Man seized on the tragedies to speak once again of Morning Star's displeasure, not only with the people as a whole, but with Lachelesharo's warpath against the Ute as well.

"It is not the scalp lock of the red man that the Great Star takes as a token in his honor," Wounded Man declared in one of his frequent fiery harangues. "No; that is why he has brought this pestilence upon us in such a way that none of our medicine men is able to quell it. The Great Star insists that the Skidi once more find the strength that is ours so that we may begin the task of driving the white men out of our lands forever!"

It was shortly after this that Joe Hollingback and his new bride returned from their venture to the headwaters of the Platte, their pack mules loaded with beaver and otter pelts. And it was then that Hawk Foot went to Wounded Man for a conference.

"I am well now," Hawk Foot said, "and I have come to my senses. I was wrong, Wounded Man. I was blinded by my desire for the Cheyenne and I did not hear your words. But now I hear them. I wish to do what is best for our people. Later, when the proper moment arrives, I will have my satisfaction on the Cheyenne and her white lover."

Wounded Man studied his nephew's face and nodded. "Perhaps this has been a test, Hawk Foot. Sometimes it is necessary for a man to learn from his mistakes. Indeed, that is what separates a leader from ordinary men. One who has the power to lead must also have the power to learn. There is great strength in such learning.

"In the days when Knife Chief was strong, he was

also able to learn from his mistakes. And he was indeed a strong leader once; you must understand that if you yet hope to lead in his place. But the white man called Red-haired Chief left the seed of his words in Lachelesharo's brain, and those words have poisoned him and weakened his medicine so that he is no longer fit to lead our people.

"This foray against the Ute proves nothing and after a time the people will realize it. What he has done has been only to gain their approval, nothing more. He will still trade our lands for a few trinkets if he has his way. But we will not allow that to happen, Hawk Foot. Morning Star has spoken, and we must follow his will or be destroyed."

Hawk Foot stared nervously at the jagged scar across his uncle's face. "You alone are able to understand the will of the gods. You are not a warrior, Wounded Man, and yet you have great power—far more power than Lachelesharo. I do not have your vision, but I have medicine of my own. My warriors follow me gladly into battle, and with me to lead them we emerge victorious over our enemies. I have been able to take many coups and many scalps because I have listened to what you told me."

Wounded Man nodded solemnly. "Together, Hawk Foot, we have the strength to lead these people. Before you gained renown as leader of the Thunderbird Lances, I had only my words and my vision. Now I have the force of your warriors just as you have the force of my thoughts."

"It would be well," Hawk Foot reflected, "if Lachelesharo were made to resign from the warpath. Perhaps it is even true that he is still able to lead, but his heart is not in it. Soon, I think, the council must select a new head chief. As things are, they will not choose me. That Cheyenne devil has caused many heads to turn against me. It's true and I know it. I am not so insensitive that I cannot feel the scorn of the people. They forget my victories and think only of how I have made a fool of myself over a slave woman.''

"That is past. The people are swayed easily. They bend like the tall grass in the prairie winds. It is true that they forget quickly. But just as they have for the moment forgotten your victories, they will forget this thing if you can count greater coups. They will see the marriage as no more than the folly of a young man. Where is the warrior who has not been ridiculous on account of a woman at one time or another?''

"You think I should draw my men together and ride the path of war? Is this what you tell me, Wounded Man?''

"Of course. The only victory that matters is the most recent one. For the moment that is Lachelesharo's, but tomorrow it may not be. The Ute are no real threat to us, but the white men are. You must decorate your lodge with the scalps of the whites, Hawk Foot. Once you have done this, Lachelesharo will not be able to make any agreements with his white friends. The Long Knives will be forced to send their soldiers against us after that, and the other Pawnee villages will join with us in order to destroy them.

"These soldiers have better guns than ours, but they do not know how to fight. They bunch together like cowards and are easily surrounded and killed. You see? I am not a warrior, but I have listened well to those who have fought against the white men. Instead of frightening them and driving them off, we should have killed all of them long ago. Now that is what we must do. English or Spanish, when their numbers grow sufficient, they attempt to enslave the red man. That is what they have done to the Anasazi and the Hopi; that is what they have done to the Kansa and the Oto and the Osage. And that is what they intend to do to us.''

"I have spoken with Mad Crow and Hairy Leggings

this day," Hawk Foot said. "They have brought me word that a party of white men is moving a supply train, more than a hundred mules and several wagons, upstream along the Arkansas River on the trail to Santa Fe."

Wounded Man grinned, his single eye gleaming with pleasure. "Where are these white men supposed to be?"

"They are probably not yet to the Blue Hills. I could meet them where the trail turns south away from the river. It is only three days' ride from here."

Red Eddie Sullivan, scouting north from Diego Blanco's pack train, pulled up his horse at the first sight of the smoke. "Damn my hide," he said aloud. Several wisps trailed up from the drainage of Whitewoman Creek, a day's ride from where he had left the pack train along the Arkansas. "Looks like I've hit onto something. It's Apache or Pawnee, one or t'other."

He wheeled his pony and began to make tracks for the Arkansas. Six smokes in December, he thought, repeating an adage he had heard years earlier, and a man's got trouble on his hands.

His responsibility to the pack train of trade goods bore heavily upon him, especially since the party also included a coach with six passengers, one of them the beautiful and cultured Señora Carlotta Fernandez, wife of Roberto Fernandez, the wealthy Taos merchant.

The fading light of sundown glinted from patches of snow on the rolling and desolate prairie over which he led a pack mule. There would be no campfire this night, he realized, no hot coffee or food, no rest. He would have to drive his tired animals until dawn. Thirty miles to the river, as he calculated it, due south. And if Blanco hadn't run into any difficulties during his absence, the supply caravan ought to be somewhere close to the mouth of Mattox Draw, the little stream that inexplicably turned back westward, running almost parallel to the Arkansas for nearly ten miles before finally giving up and draining into the east-running river.

It was nearly dawn when his horse began to limp. Red Eddie cursed, drew the creature to a halt and inspected its hooves. A broken shoe would force him to leave the pony behind and continue his ride on the pack animal. But luck was with him; it was only a shard of slate jammed into the frog of the left front hoof. Sullivan teased it out with his knife and was on his way once more. The limp was much less noticeable, but the horse was tired. He kept talking to it, leaning forward and whispering into its ear for encouragement.

He drew up atop the long crest between Mattox Draw and the Arkansas at dawn, took a chew of tobacco and watched the yellow-white globe of the sun appear from far down the tree-lined course of the river.

There was no sign of Blanco.

Sullivan pushed his exhausted horse on toward the river, where he found no fresh tracks. He crossed through the shallows to the southern bank and finally saw what he was looking for: mule sign, horse tracks, and more important, the marks of the iron-rimmed wheels of the Spaniard's coach.

"Come on, horse," he cajoled it, "they can't be far ahead of us now."

Four miles upstream he found them, the animals strung out and grazing freely over several hundred yards, taking forage as they might. There was no sentry posted and everyone apparently was still asleep.

"Son of a bitch," Sullivan growled, "I swear to my father's God in old Erin, this is the absolute last time I ever undertake to string along with a passel of damn fool greenhorns." He approached the caravan undetected, let out a yip and fired off his Hawken.

A dozen men leaped from their sleeping rolls.

Diego Blanco shot straight up, pistol in hand, then relaxed.

"*Madre de Dios,* Red Eddie, is that you? What is wrong, amigo?"

"Nothing much," the scout drawled, spitting tobacco juice. "Spotted a little war party to the north of here. Goddamnit, Blanco, this ain't no way to run a pack outfit. The whole Apache nation might have come down on you and scalped you in your sleep. Why ain't there no sentry posted?"

"If there's no danger, then I let the men sleep. Why not?"

"Old friend," Red Eddie replied, "I tell you—I've told you—aw, hell, it don't do no good at all, does it? But I'll say it again: *there is always danger.*"

Blanco shrugged. "Come. We fix the fire. We have coffee and something to eat."

"Food, by the buttocks of Jesus! Man, I'm telling you we've got troubles on our hands. Get them horses hitched up and the mules brought in. I've done rid all night to get here. Ain't you never heard of wild Indians, you dumb-ass Mexican?"

"*Calmarse, calmarse,* Señor Sullivan. Be easy. Where are these *indios*?" But Sullivan was fuming and cursing at the drovers and rousting out the male passengers to get the caravan organized for travel and self-defense.

Señora Fernandez emerged from the rough-hewn coach in which she had been sleeping. She was already fully dressed, as was her habit, not in clothing appropriate to the trail but in a full skirt of intense blue, fringed at the bottom with gold lace and beadwork, with a slim black leather belt drawn tight so as to accentuate her ample hips and breasts. Her silk blouse was cut low, the sleeves puffed and fringed with more lace. Tiny pointed-toe shoes, bracelets on either wrist and a gaudy striped bandana over her black hair made up the rest of her outfit.

Red Eddie closed his eyes, shook his head and cursed silently. What in the name of God, he wondered, had possessed an otherwise sane man such as Roberto Fernandez to send this empty-headed primping woman north to St. Louis to conduct business for him? To be sure, she could read and write English as well as Spanish, and she was reputed to be good with figures and a shrewd bargainer, but there it ended. In Sullivan's mind she had no sense at all, absolutely none.

"Edward," she called out, "*bienvenido*. But why did you frighten us all by shooting off your rifle and shouting so?"

In spite of himself Red Eddie pulled off his battered black felt hat as he went before her.

"Indians, ma'am," he replied. "Don't know for sure that they're headed this way, but it's a war party north of here, near the head of Whitewoman Creek. Apache or Pawnee, and in either case, if they run across us the best we can hope to do is buy them off."

Carlotta Fernandez smiled and shook her head.

"I do not see why it is that the *norteamericanos* cannot control their Indians," she sighed.

Brown and Blackwood, a pair of Missouri merchants, came huffing up to Red Eddie to demand to know why they had been so roughly awakened. "Foolishness, Mr. Sullivan," Brown said. "You were highly recommended; otherwise we would never have suggested that Señor Blanco keep you on."

"You'll die of a heart attack before you're forty," Blackwood added. "Furthermore, you've frightened the lady and given me an upset stomach. You don't really think there's any danger, do you? Thirty miles from here, you say? I should think we're safe enough, then."

Give me strength, Lord God of the potato-eaters.

"Gents," Sullivan said, carefully keeping his voice in control, "I'd suggest that you help get the horses hitched to the coach. The Pawnee put under a party of bluecoats a couple of months back, and those boys would dearly love to cut off your peckers and use them for medicine. And I just might trade you two to them for safe passage on to Santa Fe."

"Barbarian," Brown muttered.

"The government has given us assurance that the road to the Spanish settlements is quite safe," Blackwood insisted. "I really don't see what all the hullabaloo's about."

Red Eddie grinned and spit out a stream of tobacco juice. "Hell, gents, if it was my pecker in question, I guess I'd be a bit more concerned about it. You boys do have peckers, don't you?"

"Unseemly conversation, Señor Sullivan," Carlotta Fernandez complained. But she was smiling and her brown eyes glittered with strange little lights.

Sullivan ate a quick meal of cold beans, corn cake and buffalo jerky. He washed this down with two cups of Diego Blanco's hot coffee, then instructed the rotund little Mexican to keep the stock moving and to insist that the drovers keep their pistols and rifles loaded, primed and ready. He mounted, snapped the reins and swam his horse across the Arkansas to the north bank. *Best I keep an eye on those boys, whoever they are,* he thought.

From across the river he looked back at the little caravan that was now beginning to make signs of getting under way.

He saw the blur of a full blue skirt, the flash of a

braceleted arm. Carlotta Fernandez was actually waving to him. "I'll be damned," he said aloud. He raised his Hawken and waved back.

One fine-looking female animal, no doubt about it.

Then he turned his horse and was gone.

Chapter 21

Diego Blanco was not really concerned about Sullivan's warnings, for the big Irishman had shown this nervousness on several other occasions. Nonetheless, the scout knew the trail and was a good hunter. Whether Red Eddie had ever actually found himself in combat with the indios, Blanco did not know. He claimed so, but who was to say?

Blanco still saw to it that his men kept their weapons at the ready and that the passengers were armed. Even Señora Fernandez had with her, as Blanco knew, a very nice and relatively compact little Owen & Evans flintlock pistol. He had seen her husband press it into her hand before they left Taos to go to St. Louis nearly three months earlier. All in all Blanco was not particularly worried about the danger of hostile Indians.

The day's travel progressed smoothly enough. Blanco was not at all worried that Red Eddie Sullivan was still away from the caravan. The scout, having overreacted in the first place, could hardly be expected to admit his mistake. So without doubt he was spending the day hunting, and certain it was that some fresh buffalo or antelope meat would be a welcome addition to the larder.

Inside the coach the five American men were talking the usual politics and other small concerns with which such individuals occupied their time. At times Blanco was able to pick up scraps of their conversation.

They seemed to be discussing problems concerning black slaves and the agreement in the legislature to allow Missouri to enter the Union as a slave state, while the District of Maine, in Massachusetts, would enter as a free state. It seemed Arkansas might also enter as a slave state.

One man expressed worry about whether certain court decisions in Kentucky were constitutional. Whigs and Democrats, bank failures, economic and financial relief measures came up next. Only two had voted for President James Monroe, whom the Electoral College had almost unanimously elected, with only a single vote to John Quincy Adams. Daniel Tompkins had been kept on as Vice President.

Diego Blanco grinned, shook his head and slapped the traces across the backs of his matched greys. The norteamericanos, he thought, they spend much time worrying about things that do not matter at all. En verdad, my own people are much the same. But what does it all come to at last? The Mexican system, it is much better.

And what was La Fernandez doing? Mostly she ignored the chatter of the Americans, even though she could tell the men hoped to impress her with the intelligence of their arguments. Probably she was ignoring them and reading, insofar as that was possible with the coach creaking and thudding along a few faint tracks upon the frozen earth. Blanco had noticed one or two books among her things, a Bible and a couple of novels.

She sure is pretty, he thought as he envisioned her face.

Then he heard rifle fire. As he turned, an arrow pierced his throat and he was thrown backward, his hands vainly grasping at the wooden shaft that had cut through his windpipe and lodged against his spine. He fell, crying wordlessly, into a pool of blackness. . . .

The Pawnee war party, nearly a hundred mounted warriors in all, struck the supply caravan with deadly efficiency. A single marksman, Mad Crow, had concealed himself among the willows and young cottonwoods near the river, close by where the whites would have to pass. With one pull of his bowstring he had dispatched the coach's driver.

At that moment Hawk Foot shouted the loo-ah and the Thunderbird Lances poured in from their place of concealment beyond the rise to the south of the river.

Rifles roared and arrows whistled. The two matched coach horses, feeling their reins go slack, pounded forward, dragging the coach faster and faster behind them.

Men cursed, pistols exploded and a woman screamed.

The coach veered. One of its wheels struck a boulder and the wooden spokes tore from the rim. The coach toppled and skidded across muddy, half-thawed earth. A corner of it caught on something and it spun, snapping the leather traces of the horses. One of them pitched forward, snapped its neck and lay dead, while the other continued running. Meanwhile, the drovers were wasting firepower by shooting at the advancing Pawnee before they were within range.

The Pawnee, with Hawk Foot at their head, thundered past, launching arrows and rifle balls at the caravan, then swung back for another pass.

Hawk Foot shouted to his warriors to stay back out of rifle range. Victory was already his, but it would be a bitter one if he lost any men in the battle. Lachelesharo had returned from his raid on the Ute with many horses and had lost none of his men; only a few were wounded. If possible Hawk Foot intended to accomplish his end with no casualties at all.

Some of the mules were down, a few of them slain by rifle fire but others butchered by the drovers, who used the bodies as cover, firing across the tops of the bulging grey bellies.

Bad Ankle, Sits Alone and Laughing Dog approached the wrecked coach, moving cautiously first on foot and then on hands and knees, keeping low and making good use of whatever protection the nearly level land afforded them. When they detected movement from within, they poured lead into the shattered remains of the vehicle.

Finally Laughing Dog ran forward, pulled open the door from above and pointed his fusee into it. ''We have scalps to take,'' he shouted.

A few of the Pawnee were already tired of the waiting game with the drovers and the dead mules and rode forward now. Hawk Foot and Mad Crow were among them. They approached the coach and Mad Crow leaped from his pony and ran ahead. He pushed Sits Alone to one side and clambered up onto the coach with Laughing Dog.

''Let us pull these dead white men out so we can take their hair,'' he laughed. ''How easily they die, these English. We have been fools ever to fear them.''

They had dragged three of the white men out and hurled their limp bodies down when Laughing Dog stared in surprise.

''A woman,'' he cried out, ''and she is still alive!''

He reached down for her and was pushed aside by Mad Crow just as the barrel of an Owen & Evans flintlock pistol came up and discharged with a muffled crack and a puff of smoke.

Mad Crow slumped forward into the carriage, his face shattered and the back of his skull blown away.

The Pawnee shouted with rage and Hawk Foot, cursing the stupidity of his chief warrior, called out to the knot of men near the coach. "Take her alive! She must pay for what she has done."

The larger force of Pawnee, perceiving the great excitement about the wrecked coach, left the mule drovers to their own devices and came at a gallop with much whooping and yelling.

They saw Hawk Foot scramble up among his warriors. They watched silently as the Thunderbird Lance leader and Laughing Dog lifted out the dead body of Mad Crow and then a moment later the feebly struggling woman. A woman, yes, but like no other they had ever seen, with gold bands on her arms and beautiful clothing, almost like what they imagined a goddess might wear.

But she had killed Mad Crow.

Hawk Foot grabbed at the bandana and pulled it away, revealing the coiled loops of her long black hair.

"It is a Spanish woman, that is all. Beneath the bright cloth, she is like any other woman. And she has a cunt between her legs, just as they all have. Warriors, this one is deadly. She has killed our brother Mad Crow.

"Go now and kill the men who hide behind the bodies of their mules. Do not let any of them get away, but take no chances. I do not wish to bear any more of my men home to Wolf-Standing-in-Water to be buried.

"Later, when you have scalped all of the white men, I will give this woman to you. She will cry and scream, but she will give you pleasure. Then when we have finished with her, if she is still alive I will give her to Wounded Man. He will make her cry out for him to kill her."

The Pawnee whooped and charged back toward the pack mules. Two of the drovers tried to escape on the mules, but they were easily ridden down and dispatched. Despite several charges the remainder of the men held out until nightfall. But then they were taken from behind by a dozen braves who slipped up on them under cover of darkness.

Carlotta Fernandez was bound hand and foot and left in the company of Hairy Leggings while the battle raged in the darkness. She tried to speak to him, first in Spanish and then in English. But his face, dimly illuminated by firelight, remained impassive. Indeed, for a time she wondered if her guard might not be deaf, for he responded not at all to anything she said. Not even crying or screaming seemed to stir him.

When the massacre was over, Hawk Foot and the others returned to where she was being held. The chief of the Thunderbird Lances glared down at the bound woman and spat on her.

"*Puta,*" he said, "Spanish whore. I cannot speak your language well, but I can speak the tongue of the English. Do you understand what I am saying?"

"Yes, I understand you."

Hawk Foot grinned. "Good. Then I can tell you this. Later I will give you to my men so that they can take pleasure of you. You will not like it, but they will. Perhaps I will do it to you first. It will be enjoyable to hear you scream."

He turned and gave an order to his men. They put her astride a horse, looping rawhide from one ankle to the other beneath the horse's belly. Her wrists were tied behind her back.

Then, laughing and yipping and waving the fresh scalps, the men lit torches and rummaged through the storage compartment of the coach and the two drayage carts. They broke open crates and pulled out bolts of cloth to wave in the air. They found a crate full of rifles and yelped in glee. They picked over the contents of the pack saddles on the dead mules and took what they wanted. The rest they strewed all over the battle site.

The mules that had escaped death were added to the remuda, and within a short time Hawk Foot gave the order to cross the river. He would take no chances on a larger, better-armed band of whites happening on the scene of carnage while he and his men were close by.

The river water was icy cold, and Carlotta Fernandez was barely able to stay on the horse. For a moment she contemplated sliding over sideways to drown herself as her horse began to swim the deeper portion of the river.

But her legs were bound around the horse, she realized, so it probably wouldn't work. So she clung as well as she could and remained upright as the horse emerged from the water and onto the bank.

Suddenly a pistol roared and the brave who led her horse sagged sideways. His pitch-pine torch fell into the weeds. She saw the face of a white man, a weathered, bearded face beneath the brim of a battered black felt hat.

Red Eddie.

He made a desperate attempt to slip a coil of rope about her horse's neck, but another shot echoed and he spun, falling to hands and knees. One more shot and he toppled backward and splashed heavily into the river.

Hawk Foot turned his pony and shouted directions to the Thunderbird Lances. Several leaped down and attempted to assist her escort, but the brave was already dead. Cries of rage went up. Torches were brought to the edge of the river and men moved quickly downstream, searching the bank with flares held high.

The search went on for perhaps an hour, but without success. Only when the Pawnee had convinced themselves that the white man had been killed and the body sucked

under or caught on a snag in the river did they finally
resume their night ride.

As she waited out the search, Carlotta Fernandez
shivered violently. Beads of ice were forming on her wet
skirt and petticoats. She tried to rub her bound hands
against one leg and then the other. But the warmth of the
horse's body was far move effective than anything she
could do.

At length Hawk Foot shouted his warriors forward
and they departed from the river.

He was hurt bad, and he knew it. He had taken a
pistol ball in the shoulder and another in the lower belly.

That's the one what kills me, he thought dimly,
allowing the current to take him, unable to do anything else.

*If I get out of the water they'll find me, sure as
thunder. If I stay in I'll go numb and drown. But I'm a
dead man anyhow.*

The wounds were strangely painless. Shock and the
ice-cold Arkansas River combined to eliminate nearly all
sensation.

*A dumb-ass thing to try, but there wasn't no choice. I
tried because that's what I had to do, and now I'm finished, something for the catfish to nibble at if any of 'em's
awake this late in the year. Just close my eyes, breathe in
the darkness. . . .*

He figured he had only a little while longer.

*Poor goddamned empty-headed little Carlotta. She
ain't never going to see Taos again, that's for sure. Those
red devils will rape her every way from Sunday and she'll*

*beg them to kill her, and damn them, even then they won't
do it. They'll cut her fingers off and gouge out her eyes
and still find some way of keeping her alive and conscious.
I had to try, damnit, I had to.*

Darkness swirled about him, but at the last instant he
sucked in and found air, cold air, and his mind began to
work once more.

*Busted up and dying, and goddamn it, I cain't die,
not even when I want to.*

He drifted to a little island, a mud bank with young
willows growing from it. His head struck something hard,
a drift log, and it took him a moment to realize what it was
and another to realize he had lost his hat.

A man ought to be allowed to have his consarned hat
on when he dies, he thought. But he struggled up out of
the water, barely able to move his limbs. The left arm was
useless, the right nearly so. He cried out and rolled onto
the frozen mud.

"Bleed to death, damn you," he said. "At least let
me die right."

He sucked in his breath, groaned and drew up his knees.
He huddled against a mat of twigs, leaves and dead branches.

When morning came, he was astonished to find he
was still alive.

All night and into the middle of the following day the
Pawnee warriors rode, bearing their booty and their two
dead. They were back in the sparsely wooded area of the
rolling hills to the north of the Arkansas now. No longer
concerned about the possibility of pursuit, they put their
ponies to graze in a marshy meadow. The men ate quickly,
a meal of pemmican and corn cake, and when they were

finished, Hawk Foot cut Carlotta loose from her pony. Exhausted and only half awake, she slipped sideways and hit the earth face down.

The fall jolted her back to her senses. Hawk Foot stooped over her and held his skinning knife to her throat. He saw a flash of defiance. He lowered the blade, nicked one of her breasts and cut the bindings from her wrists. He spat in her face, laughed and tossed some scraps of food on to the ground beside her.

She wiped at her cheek, realized how badly swollen her hands were and forced the fingers to move. It was necessary to use both hands to lift the bits of food to her mouth.

Hawk Foot and the other Pawnee seemed to have lost all interest in her, and she wondered if it was possible to slip away. The warriors, having finished their meal, were putting their robes down in sunny spots on the grass. Soon all but two were sleeping and once again the thought of escape flashed in her mind. But escape to what?

No, her only chance for survival lay in staying with the Pawnee. They could kill her, but they hadn't done so yet. So long as she obeyed them, there was a slim chance that she would survive. Exhaustion took her and she fell into a deep sleep.

Rough hands seized her and she tried futilely to protect herself. "Puta," Hawk Foot laughed, "I wish to fuck you now." She was not yet fully awake when he grabbed her blouse and tore it away from her.

Several men stood behind him staring in wonder at the strange undergarment that encased her torso and cupped her breasts—the corset.

"What is this?" Hawk Foot demanded. "Are you stuffed with the feathers of a prairie hen, like a child's doll?"

The Pawnee warriors, silent until now, burst out laughing. She glanced from one face to another but saw no hint of mercy or compassion.

Hawk Foot reached to grasp her skirt and she screamed and slapped at him, missing entirely. "Hold her arms," he commanded. Two warriors grabbed her. Hawk Foot yanked away her skirt, pointed to the petticoats, laughed. He drew his skinning knife and cut the foundation garment away from her.

"Now I will show you that what I said is true," he growled in Pawnee.

She understood nothing, but screamed.

He ripped away her remaining garments. She looked up at him, pleading with her eyes, but saw only the way his loincloth bulged with his excitement.

And then he removed it, revealing himself to be fully erect.

"Puta," he said. "Now I will show you what a man can do." He dropped to his knees and covered her, forced her legs apart, thrust into her. She tried to lash out, but her hands were pinioned. She bit her lips at the pain. As she closed her eyes, the warriors were making strange yip-yipping sounds.

By the time Hawk Foot was finished, she was moaning and crying, unable to control the sounds that issued from her throat.

And then another mounted her.

And after that another.

And another. . . .

Chapter 22

Pitalesharo restlessly paced up and down the gully where he and Termite Joe had concealed themselves and their horses to await sundown before entering Wolf-Standing-in-Water Village. His buffalo robe was drawn up over his hunched shoulders, but he was barely aware of the hard freezing wind. His narrowed eyes were angry.

"Might as well set down and relax your bones, Juan Pete," Joe remarked, sitting back in the shelter of a group of boulders and blowing out thin clouds of smoke from his briar. "She's awhile yet to darkness, and you know—"

"Yes," snapped the chief's son. "Well, to me it is a sad thing, a shame, to have to sneak into my own village after dark like some thieving Sioux."

Termite Joe tapped at his knee and squinted up at the sun. "Give it another hour, lad, and we'll move. Still some five mile, give or take, to the town. It'll be dark enough, time we get to where anybody's likely to be out and around. Course, you could always go charging in there. They's probably someone willing to take on your widow.''

Man Chief dropped down cross-legged beside the trapper and pressed the heels of his hands against his forehead.

''Three days ago I was happy, Termite Joe. I had my new wife, the woman I loved for so long a time. Grey Bear and I had a fine herd of horses and we were coming to our village with our wives and our horses to make peace within the tribe. Today I am hiding in a gully with my friend because the village has become an enemy village. Perhaps Wounded Man is right after all. Perhaps Morning Star does hate me. Maybe I should turn back and go to live with my wife's people.''

''And leave your pappy and ma and everybody else what cares for you to get driven out or killed by that old fraud and his scum of a nephew? Hell no, you wouldn't be doing that. Besides, we don't know that it's all that bad. Could be Lachelesharo's got everything calmed down since I left. Knife Chief ain't never caved in yet to that scar-faced shaman. Jist practicing a leetle caution, is all. It don't hurt.''

''It hurts me,'' Pitalesharo muttered, but he remained sitting.

Twilight had already faded into darkness when the two men approached the village, circling and coming in from upstream, near the chief's lodge. Something was going on across the settlement near the medicine lodge. They could see the reflected glow of fires and hear rhythmic chanting and the accompanying thud of drums. Most of the people were gathered near the great fire pit, and the remainder of the village seemed nearly deserted.

''Wonder what new deviltry old Scar Face is up to

now?" Termite Joe grumbled. "Sure he ain't about to roast someone else?"

Pitalesharo shook his head and the two glanced about to make certain they were not observed before slipping to the entry of Lachelesharo's lodge.

Raven Quill jumped up startled as the two entered, and Broken Feather, who sat tending a pot of meat that hung over the flames, ran to fling herself sobbing into her husband's arms.

"Termite Chief," she cried, "I am so glad you have come back. Now you and I must go away again at once."

Raven Quill touched the young woman's arm and signaled her to be silent. "Termite Joe has nothing to fear in this lodge," she said sternly. "A good wife should control herself better. We have much to tell my son and friend Termite."

Raven Quill turned to Pitalesharo and embraced him tightly. He could feel her trembling and knew she was controlling her own emotions only with effort.

"My son," she said at last, "I feared you were dead. That is what many people have been saying. Even Wounded Man has been speaking of your death."

"Mother. . . ."

She stepped back and looked at him, tears starting in her own eyes, and then embraced him again.

"Tirawa has given us at least this one great happiness," she said. "Man Chief, I wish you had returned to a village at peace with itself. There is great trouble."

"My father . . . ?" Pitalesharo was afraid to frame the question that was in his mind.

"Lachelesharo is well. I must let him tell you what has happened as soon as he returns to the lodge."

"Please, Mother, you must tell me now," Pitalesharo cried.

"I do not know everything. Your father has gone to

the medicine lodge to try to bring the people to their senses, but I am afraid it is too late. They are dancing over there right now, and Wounded Man is probably driving them to frenzy with his visions and his twitching and his spitting of blood. He has seized Pierre Papin and the white woman who was captured when Hawk Foot massacred the mule train. Termite Joe has told you of that?''

''Yes, I know about that. What will Wounded Man do with Papin and the Spanish woman?''

''He has been crying for death to all the whites,'' Raven Quill answered. ''If your father cannot stop it, I am sure he will have the young men crazy with his dancing and his trickery, and they will sacrifice these poor people, our friend the trader and the woman as well. My son, everything is falling apart. This is not the village I was born in.''

''The shaman will try to take Termite Chief also,'' cried Broken Feather. ''My husband, we must go away. I have all our things packed. I have been waiting for you. Hawk Foot said that he would kill you and force me to be his wife. But I would kill myself if that happened.''

Hollingback stroked his wife's hair and stared into space. ''Don't you worry about her, leetle gal,'' he soothed her. ''Young Bird Droppings ain't going to do a thing to this child, you can count on her. I should of put lead into him a time back, and now I guess I will. There ain't nobody, ever, that's run the Termite Chief off before he was ready to go on his own account.''

''Perhaps Broken Feather is right, Termite Joe,'' Pitalesharo put in. ''Perhaps it would be best if you took her back to the mountains for a while.''

''Wagh,'' Joe snorted, ''and miss out on this leetle tea-dance? Not on your gizzard, Juan Pete.''

''You must not talk of such things,'' Raven Quill said, her eyes wide. ''You speak as if there will be a war within our own village, and that must not even be thought of. If Wounded Man makes all the people crazy, we must go away. We cannot fight and kill our own people!''

''I know it is a horrible thought,'' Pitalesharo said wearily, ''and I know that my father thinks as you do. I have agreed myself. But it may be that there is no other way. We cannot always control what happens.''

Raven Quill fought against tears, took a deep breath and smoothed her hair back with both hands. When she spoke again, it was in a completely different tone, as if none of it had been said.

''Well, women do not decide these matters. Where has my mind been? You must be very hungry and tired. You have had a long trip. Sit down, both of you, over there. I will get you something to eat.''

She moved to the fire and served them both bowls of the meat and vegetables that had been bubbling in the pot. The two men ate quickly and in silence for a few moments. Broken Feather sat curled against her husband's side and Raven Quill settled across the fire, both politely waiting until the men were finished with their meal before speaking. But all the while Pitalesharo noticed that his mother's eyes were focused on nothing, or rather on some inner vision.

''Are you not going to ask me my news, Mother?'' he suggested, putting his bowl aside. He spoke teasingly, trying to break her out of her painful abstraction. ''You have not even asked me about my brother, Grey Bear.''

Raven Quill looked at her son and smiled with an obvious effort of will. ''I knew that my son would tell me what we wished to know,'' she replied. ''Grey Bear is well, is he not?''

''Yes, Mother, Grey Bear is very well. He and Hummingbird are disgustingly happy with each other, and he has a herd of over a hundred horses now. So do I.''

Pitalesharo paused and took a deep breath. "I was also very happy until Termite Joe found us and told us of what was going on in our village. I am a married man now, Mother."

Raven Quill uttered a little cry and put her hand to her mouth.

"It is true," he continued. "It is a very long story. I will tell all of it later, when my father is here too. Anyway, Mother, I am married to Little Green Frog now, the one I rescued from Wounded Man. Her people have accepted me, and they have agreed to be at peace with our village if we will keep peace with them."

Raven Quill rose with a cry and embraced her son again. This time she was unable to keep the tears back. "My son, I hardly know what to say. This is such happy news, and everything else is so sad. I have known that your heart wept for her ever since you took her back to her people. I am very glad for this thing."

At that moment they heard sounds outside the lodge and Lachelesharo came in. Close behind him were the Red Lance warriors, Pitalesharo's society, as well as several members of the Wolf Lances. The men appeared weary and subdued. Lachelesharo's face lit up as he saw his son, however, and the two men embraced affectionately.

"My son," the chief said, "this was a very black day, but now there is something to be glad for." They stepped apart and gazed at one another.

"Grey Bear is not with you, Pitalesharo?"

"He is not far away now. He is well."

"That is good, my son. But do you know what is happening in this village?"

"I have heard."

Lachelesharo nodded, turned away to put his weapons in their places. Pitalesharo noticed now that none of his

friends had stepped forward to greet him. He turned to
them, puzzled.

"Two Boulders. Spotted Wolf. Buffalo Runner. Do
not any of the Red Lances remember their leader?"

"Greetings, Man Chief," said Buffalo Runner. He
still hung back uneasily, as did all the warriors. But they
also uttered cautious salutations.

"What is happening?" Pitalesharo cried out. "Are
you not glad to know that I am alive and home?"

The warriors didn't reply until at last Two Boulders
spoke up. "We are very glad if you are truly alive, Man
Chief. It is just—"

"Just what?" Pitalesharo nearly shouted.

"Well . . . how can we be certain that you are truly
alive? The shaman has told us that you were taken away
into Awahokshu, the spirit world, that you are now one of
the chixu. Maybe you have come to take your friends into
the spirit world to be ghosts with you. Or maybe you are
here to work mischief; that is what the chixu do when they
come back, even if they were very good people when they
were alive."

"Wounded Man had a vision in which you were
dead," added Buffalo Runner. "I do not believe Wounded
Man's visions, but . . ." The warrior's voice trailed off.

"You are all a bunch of silly children," Raven Quill
scolded them. "You should believe what you see with
your own eyes and not what is said by that evil old man
who wishes to destroy our people. Did you not see Knife
Chief embrace his son? Did he die? Did I not embrace my
son before that? Pitalesharo is solid. He is muscle and
bone, just as you are. And he is stronger than all of you
together. I will not have you in my lodge if you are so
foolish. Go away! Go on, all of you."

The warriors took a step backward before the indignant advance of Raven Quill, who was waving her soup ladle at them all.

"Please, Raven Quill," Two Boulders cried out, "I would rather be killed by your son than by your ladle. I am not really afraid. I am very glad to see my friend Man Chief, and that is true. I will embrace him because I am so happy to see him that I don't even care if he is a chixu."

Two Boulders strode forward and placed his hands on Pitalesharo's arms, looked carefully into his face and wrapped his arms around him in a bear hug. Then he stepped back, rolled his eyes up into his head and clutched at his throat, staggering backward. The assembly gasped, but Two Boulders miraculously recovered and bent double with laughter, whooping and pointing at his comrades.

Termite Joe burst into great baying guffaws, rolling about on the floor of the lodge and in obvious delight. "By God," he gasped, "that were the best leetle dumb show I ever saw, better'n the ones in St. Louis even, maybe even in New York, though I ain't never been there. Be even funnier if you was actually dead, Juan Pete."

Broken Feather was staring at her husband in consternation. "How can you laugh like that, Termite Chief? I do not understand men at all. You are all laughing! Our village is being destroyed by the shaman's poisoned words and my husband will be killed because he will not go away with me. How can you laugh?"

"Aw, pretty face," Joe grinned, getting up from the ground, "she'd be a sorry world if nobody what was going to get killed anyhow ever laughed once in a while, now, wouldn't it? But I ain't fixing to go under jist now. Me and Lachelesharo and these fine braves there are going to take care of the matter at hand quick and easy, you'll see."

The trapper winked, pulled his wife close with one arm and pinched her bottom at the same time. Spotted

Wolf grinned and gestured, but Lachelesharo sat gravely in his place, not eating the bowl of stew before him.

"I wish that were true, Termite Joe," the chief said slowly, "but I cannot see what to do. I went to where the young men are dancing to try to talk to the people, but they are almost all crazy with what Wounded Man has stirred up in them. I could not speak to them at all. They did not hear me. Wounded Man danced over to me and vomited blood at my feet so that it spattered my leggings, and he cried out in the voice of Morning Star that I was the enemy of my people, that I was a weak man and not to be feared. One warrior leaped at me with his knife raised, but my friends stood before me. They are not quite crazy enough yet to start a full war between the societies, but it will come."

The head chief paused and glanced at Termite Joe again. "Wounded Man and Hawk Foot say that I am the friend of the white man who will bring misfortune upon us. And yet it was I who traveled to the villages of the whites and saw how many there are. I am the one who talked to Red-haired Chief and refused to give away any of our lands. It is I who know that the only way we can continue to live is to get along with these white men, who may be as many as the flies that come during the summer moons. What Hawk Foot has already done will bring the soldiers upon us."

"The chief does not need to convince his friends that his heart is good," Spotted Wolf said. "We have always known this, and that is why we are here. Now we must decide what we can do to stop Wounded Man from destroying the people."

Lachelesharo sighed and put his head down upon the palm of his hand. He did not speak for some time. "I cannot think of anything, my friends, that will not split apart the Skidi." He was nearly inaudible.

"You must call your council together," Buffalo Runner said.

"And say what to them? Some will stand with me and some will demand that I step aside so that they can select Hawk Foot as the new chief. I would do this, but what would it accomplish? He would immediately set out to kill yet more whites, and finally Red-haired Chief would send all his soldiers against us."

"It would take many bluecoats to defeat us," Two Boulders insisted.

"Perhaps that is so," Lachelesharo said, "but always they would send more. They have much better weapons than we do, and they would bring their cannon and destroy our village and all the Pawnee villages. Time would always be on their side."

"Then we must go away from here," said Buffalo Runner. "That is what happens when people can't get along together. Long ago we were one people with the Arikara, and then we came here. That is the story we have all been told."

Lachelesharo looked up. "Maybe so, but Wounded Man and Hawk Foot intend to kill Papin and the Spanish woman very soon. That is what Morning Star was crying for in Wounded Man's mouth. They will sacrifice them tomorrow night when the dancing is over. How can I go away and allow my people to kill my friend Pierre Papin, whom I have known for many winters, who has been a friend to all of us? And this poor woman who has already been raped and beaten, though she did nothing but try to defend herself?"

"Nope," Termite Joe agreed, "that jist ain't acceptable."

"But if we try to save them the way we did the Comanche," Lachelesharo continued, "most of the village will be against us. We could not hold off the warriors who will fight for Wounded Man this time. He now controls twice as many as I do. And even if it were not so, I do not wish to make the blood of my own people to run in this village."

"Where are Papin and the Spanish woman now?"

"In the medicine lodge, my son. There is no way of spiriting them out, I am afraid. The dancing is going on both inside the lodge and outside as well. And the Thunderbird Lances and the Dog Soldiers are armed."

"Seems like what we needs here is a truly devious plan," remarked Termite Joe. "Any ideas?"

"Perhaps we could stampede the horses through the village and take them out during the confusion," ventured Two Boulders. "That is the most devious thing I can think of, but it is probably not enough."

Termite Joe stared fixedly at Two Boulders, thinking intently. No one spoke for several minutes.

Finally Pitalesharo glanced at Joe and then at Two Boulders and the other Red Lances. "So Wounded Man has told the people of a vision in which he saw me in the spirit world?"

"Yes," agreed Buffalo Runner. "And he has said that this shows Morning Star's displeasure with Lachelesharo."

"Ah," nodded Pitalesharo. "But if the people see that I am alive, will they not know that the shaman is a fraud or that his visions lie?"

"Now we're getting somewheres," Termite Joe beamed. "That's starting along the line of the devious. Let's think about her some more. You and Juan Antonio both showing up with all them horses is a good idea, and the Comanch too. But they's a good chance of you getting killed afore those crazy-ass red niggers get it figgered out about Wounded Man's visions. Old Scar Face will see through her first, and he'll scream for his warriors to kill you, sure as buffalo dung."

Another prolonged silence fell. Termite Joe pulled out his briar pipe and filled it, dropped a coal on the tobacco and puffed. He passed the pipe to Lachelesharo.

"I think I have thought of something," Raven Quill ventured hesitantly. "I am only a woman and I should not speak. But—"

"Speak, wife. Anyone who can think of anything must speak."

Raven Quill nodded. "I saw how these warriors acted when they thought our son was one of the walking dead. Would not the other men, who are not Pitalesharo's friends, be even more afraid?"

"Wagh," shouted Termite Joe. "There she is, the very thing!"

He sprang to his feet and planted a noisy kiss on the center of Raven's Quill forehead.

"But it would be very dangerous," she pleaded. "I do not wish to lose my son—my two sons—again. Husband, Pitalesharo is now married to the Little Green Frog, the Comanche woman. He has not had a chance to tell you yet. I am not certain how this thing happened, but our son has told me Fox Shirt's people wish to be our friends now. Maybe it is better for us to return with Pitalesharo and his new wife. We could go to live among her people. Papin the Frenchman is my friend too, but sometimes it is not possible to save everyone. And in that case it is better to save those we can."

"Woman of my heart," Lachelesharo responded, "I understand what you are saying, and yet I cannot do as you wish. No, I must lead the Skidi as long as I am able to do so."

Raven Quill lowered her eyes and sat in silence.

"If Wounded Man himself can be made to fear the

chixu," the head chief continued, "I think my people will lose their respect for him."

"Damned right," Joe laughed. "It's getting better and better. We get Old Scar Face and his nephew Bird Droppings scared out of their war paint, even make the people laugh at 'em, and they'll turn on the old fraud for sure. That's what this white nigger's thinking. Got to make her good and dramatic, though. Something to beat twitching and roaring and puking blood."

They spent the next hour or so working out the plan in detail. Wolf Chief and Buffalo and a few of the older warriors who were faithful to Lachelesharo were brought into the lodge and advised of what was afoot.

When the men departed late in the night, they took with them strong warnings about keeping the meeting secret, even from their own families. Termite Joe and Pitalesharo stayed on a little longer so Man Chief could recount for his parents the strange circumstances under which he and Antonio Grey Bear had managed to take the Ute horses as well as how he came to win Little Green Frog.

"I reckon we'd better be getting back to find Antonio and all them Comanch," Termite Joe suggested at last. "Must be nearing dawn, and we got a lot to do before the sun comes up out of the east a second time."

Pitalesharo nodded and reached to embrace both his father and his mother again. He held Raven Quill tightly and whispered, "Don't worry, my mother. I am not going to die now, not when I have more than I ever had to live for." She didn't reply, only pressed her cheek against her son's.

Chapter 23

Termite Joe and Man Chief cautiously stepped out into the bone-searing chill of the late-night air. Near the medicine lodge the reflected light of the fires still danced against the trees and the lodge mounds. The singing and drumbeats continued, frequently punctuated by shrill yells and gibberish as the hysteria increased, the half-nude bodies gyrating through shadows and firelight despite the subzero cold of midwinter night.

Pitalesharo briefly remembered Papin's face—the comical wrinkles on either side of the mouth like long furrows in the earth, yes, and the kind brown eyes. He thought of the man bound inside the medicine lodge, imagined his terror as the frenzy of the dancing increased and he heard Wounded Man calling for his death. And the beautiful Spanish woman of whom Termite Joe had told him—brutalized by the enraged Thunderbird Lances, despised by the Pawnee women who saw her in the tatters of her finery, her pride broken. What was she feeling?

"We're coming for you, Frenchy," Termite Joe whispered, apparently thinking along the same lines. "You got to hang on, 'cause we'll get you out of this fix, sure as God's backside. Hang on, old partner, damnit."

Just as the sun appeared like a point of white fire on the horizon, Pitalesharo and Termite Joe spotted the distant moving mass that was the horse herd.

"Now ain't that a purty sight," Hollingback exclaimed. "Closer even than I'd hoped. We'll make her back to Wolf-Standing-in-Water some hours before sundown. We might even be able to catch a couple of hours of shut-eye, Juan Pete. Not that I exactly remember what it feels like, but I recollect it were a pleasurable thing."

When Pitalesharo and Termite Joe met their compañeros, they called a rest by common consent. Behele had been pushing the herd north with only brief pauses, a stratagem the Comanche had agreed to somewhat unwillingly and with a good deal of grumbling. Only Little Green Frog had not questioned the need for haste, eager as she was to rejoin her new husband.

Termite Joe and Pitalesharo explained what they had learned in Lachelesharo's lodge and described the plan that had been conceived there.

The Comanche warriors were appalled at what was going on in the Pawnee village. They looked at one another in dismay. But Grandfather Whistling Bird laughed in pure delight as the details emerged, his nearly toothless gums showing pink.

"This is good," he chortled. "This is very good. How do you say it, Pitalesharo? Tu-ra-heh. Maybe you need a very old Comanche from the spirit world to accompany you? I am very good at chanting and shaking the horse-hoof rattles, and I look dead enough without any paint. Is that not true, Little Green Frog?"

"It is true that you are a very good, loud singer, Grandfather," she smiled. "I like this plan too, Man Chief, though I am horrified about what is happening in your village. Some of the Pawnee are very evil people. But it is a good plan. May I be a ghost also?"

"And I will be one," said Hummingbird. "I left with you, Grey Bear my husband, so they will think that I am dead as well."

"Too dangerous, Hummingbird, too dangerous," Behele said quickly. "There is no certainty that the plan won't backfire, and if that happens, I want you to be somewhere safe. These Comanche warriors will take care of you and get you back to their village, and that is what I want."

"Do you not know yet that I would kill myself if you died?" she replied quietly, looking straight into Behele's eyes. "I am a good woman and I will always obey my husband, but in this one thing I will not obey. I will stand by your side when you face Wounded Man. Perhaps I will get the chance to kill Hawk Foot myself. I have the right."

"I wish to stand beside my husband also," added Little Green Frog. "I think Wounded Man will be surprised to see me. The people will not believe that you could have brought me back unless I were in the spirit world too."

"Ranita Verde," Pitalesharo exclaimed with some agitation, "there may be fighting. There probably will be fighting. How can I fight when I am worried about you?"

"For Chrissake, Juan Pete," Termite Joe blurted out, "let 'em come. Ain't you got no sensitivity? The ladies don't want to be setting off in some gully waiting to hear whether you young fools got your heads blowed off. They want to be there with you. Wouldn't you want to be there?"

"That is different, Joe, and you know it," said Grey Bear. "They are women; we are warriors."

"They's human, ain't they?"

Pitalesharo turned to the two women and looked at them closely.

"Is this truly what you both wish to do?" he asked.

"Yes, Man Chief," Hummingbird answered. Little Green Frog nodded, staring steadily at her beloved.

"I would feel much happier in my mind if I knew that you were safe, Ranita mia, and I am sure that Grey Bear would wish the same for Hummingbird. And yet perhaps what Termite Joe has said is true. I will consent to this thing if my brother will."

Antonio didn't speak, didn't move for some time. At last he stepped forward and took Hummingbird in his arms. "Very well," he murmured against her hair. "But you must leave Wounded Man for me. That is an order a wife must obey." The young Comanche warriors grinned and whistled, and even Grandfather Whistling Bird laughed.

"I propose that we all catch a leetle shut-eye before we push on to the village," Termite Joe suggested. "She's going to be quite a night."

When Whistling Bird translated this remark for the Comanche braves, they all whooped their approval.

"I will sit up and guard these fine horses," the grandfather declared. "I am very old, but there are still some things I can do. And I do not need so much sleep as those who are younger. Anyway, soon I will have a very long sleep, and after that Old Man Coyote will wake me up."

"You've been sleeping on your horse all night, Whistling Bird," Antonio Grey Bear said. "I heard you snoring."

"Not everyone can ride a horse in his sleep," replied the old one as he turned away with great dignity.

*　　*　　*

Man Chief and Little Green Frog walked up a ravine carved by a small creek until they were out of sight of the others. Here they spread their robes and lay down, clinging to one another. Little Green Frog pressed her cheek to her husband's.

"I do not think that we will die this night, man I love. But I am glad that you will let me be with you," she whispered. They coupled quickly, fiercely, with an urgency made more intense by the danger that lay before them, and then they fell into a deep sleep in each other's arms.

They awoke with Whistling Bird standing over them laughing. Pitalesharo raised his head and saw that he had gone to sleep half on top of Little Green Frog and that the edge of the buffalo robe had pulled back so that his bare buttocks were exposed. Little Green Frog blushed and began to giggle like a child as Pitalesharo pulled the robe around himself and pretended to throw a stone at his grandfather.

The old man scuttled off a few paces, then turned back to call, "Don't *sleep* too long, newlyweds. It will tire you out." He walked away chuckling loudly.

It was late morning by now and they got under way fast, pushing the ponies north at a good speed. Even so, it was after sundown when they reached a little valley about three miles from the village. This was where they had already decided to leave the horses. At Whistling Bird's command the eight young Comanche warriors were designated to remain with the animals.

"There is no danger that they will be found this night," Pitalesharo reasoned. "Everyone will be in the village to attend the sacrifices. Five thousand Cheyenne warriors could come down upon the Skidi tonight and no one would know about it until they actually attacked."

"That's a fact," Behele agreed. "Even so, I think it would be a good idea for Juan Termite to stay with the Comanche and the horses."

"Blue balls of hell," replied Joe, "I done said there ain't nothing going to keep this child away from being in on the fun—or at least watching it."

"I feel the same as the buckskin person," Whistling Bird added. "I think it will make a very good story to tell my great-grandchildren."

Behele threw his hands up. "Does anyone else wish to come? Maybe the whole Comanche nation and their Kiowa friends as well? Maybe the President of the white men? The King of the Spanish?"

"No," replied Whistling Bird. "My warriors do not think it would be a good way for them to make peace with our Pawnee brothers. It would not be good, they say, to be involved in a war among these people."

Behele tapped his head. "They are very wise warriors, then."

The two young couples, in company with Termite Joe and Whistling Bird, set out for the village. They tied their mounts to trees along the river and sneaked to Lachelesharo's lodge.

Broken Feather sprang forward to embrace first her husband and then Hummingbird, making little cries of gladness and concern. Raven Quill hugged both her sons.

Lachelesharo greeted the party also, formally welcoming Whistling Bird to his lodge, and then went on to sketch in what was happening in the village.

"Hawk Foot's warriors have tied Pierre Papin and the woman to the trees near the medicine lodge, and the wood for the fire has been placed about them, ready to light. It is all happening as we knew it would, Pitalesharo. Wounded Man will not light the pyre until Morning Star has risen, so there is still time for you to eat and rest before you prepare yourselves.''

"Is Pierre holding up all right?" Hollingback asked.

"Yes," Lachelesharo replied. "Hawk Foot has almost ignored him so far. He has placed all his attentions on the woman. She is without clothing. He has burned her on the belly with a torch. The others laugh and applaud. When I approached the sacrifice trees, my good friend Papin saw me. He did not speak, but he looked at me with such eyes that I had to turn away. It made my heart so heavy that I felt as if I had swallowed a stone of fire.''

"Heathen red devils—pardon me, gents. But they ain't no god what believes in torture, no sir," Termite Joe burst out. "Might be better if I jist moseyed out and put some lead in both of 'em.''

Lachelesharo looked a little brighter as he thought of something else. "One thing I have discovered: many more warriors remain loyal to me than I had thought. They will follow Wounded Man and Hawk Foot if they must, but they would prefer me. When the conflict comes, it will be more nearly equal than I had hoped. The Wolf Lances and the Red Lances are all with me, and it is possible that we should confront Wounded Man directly and not wait any longer.''

"Chief of the Skidi Pawnee," Whistling Bird said, "I am a stranger, an old man who comes in peace in the hope that the long-standing wounds between our peoples may be healed. For that reason I should remain silent and not interfere or add my words to the confusion. But I am more than eighty winters old and I will go to the spirit world soon anyway. So I will speak my piece.

"Lachelesharo, I have observed your son carefully and I have taken him as one of my own. He is a very brave man and a very powerful warrior. The buckskin man and Grey

Bear are no less capable. As it is, if the forces are nearly equal you may be able to rescue the man and the woman but your people will be split in half. No, something must happen that will change the balance of things. Then the result will be more certain. I do not wish to see either my granddaughter or my new grandson slain, or any of my new friends. But I think it will work, what has been planned. If a shaman can be bested at his own game of magic, then he is obliged to retire in shame. It is that way among my people and I think it is that way everywhere. Is it not so, Lachelesharo?''

The head chief of the Skidi squinted at the old man and then turned to his son. "Man Chief, where did you find this ancient wizard?''

The tension was broken, and they all relaxed in a new sense of camaraderie. They ate a little of the food that Raven Quill had prepared for them, taking care to be polite, but no one had much appetite. They sat talking quietly around the fire. The men had no desire for sleep, but Hummingbird and Little Green Frog dozed against their husbands' shoulders.

After several hours Lachelesharo went out to join the Red Lances and the Wolf Lances and the other loyal warriors in front of the medicine lodge.

Pitalesharo and the others began their preparations. Raven Quill and Broken Feather had already assembled everything that would be needed, baskets of fine white clay from the riverbank, ocher and various other paints.

Little Green Frog thinned the clay with water and began to slather the slimy mixture on her face and hair, unbraiding her tresses with muddy hands and twisting them into grotesque, snaky strands. The others did the same, covering themselves with the pale yellow substance.

Broken Feather, arranging Hummingbird's hair into wild peaks and clumps, broke into giggles. Hummingbird turned with a handful of mud and smeared it down Broken Feather's face and neck, dropping a cold glob into the front of her dress. Broken Feather squealed and the solemn preparations turned into a wild mud fight, with all three young women smearing clay on each other and laughing hilariously.

Little Green Frog suddenly turned on her grinning husband and dropped an oozing handful of slime inside his loincloth. She gave it a quick rub and then ran shrieking as he came after her.

"Nice to see the children enjoying themselves, now ain't it, Whistling Bird?" Termite Joe drawled.

"I would not mind having a mud fight with a pretty woman," the old man grinned. "What do you say, Raven Quill? Your husband wouldn't mind, would he?"

"Huh," she snorted, "he would kill you." She straightened her back and pretended to be insulted, but she couldn't hide the smile that pulled at the corners of her mouth.

"Now I wish to be turned into a ghost also," Whistling Bird announced. "I am a very good ghost."

"Why not?" laughed Pitalesharo. "Come here, Grandfather, and get smeared with mud."

When the entire group was a uniform ghastly yellow-white, they allowed the mud to dry. Then they applied paint to their faces and hands, making black hollows under the eyes and cheekbones and smearing bright vermilion on their hands and around their mouths. Once finished, they studied one another critically. Antonio added a touch more black to Hummingbird's cheek and burst out laughing.

"It is true, what Old Screeching Bird has said," he chortled. "It even frightens me."

Whistling Bird had given himself a gory wound around the edge of his scalp in front, with rabbit blood dripping down his forehead. He let his mouth hang open, a black cavity displaying only three teeth. He did indeed look like death itself.

Chapter 24

To both captives, it was almost a relief to know that the end of their ordeal was near. Neither knew precisely how long they had lain bound on the floor of the medicine lodge while the dancing went on around them. They had been fed nothing but a little meat broth, and neither had been taken out except twice a day to relieve themselves.

Carlotta Fernandez, who had been in considerable pain and shock to begin with, had passed a good deal of the time in uneasy sleep, from which she would awaken with a wild cry. Now and again Pierre Papin had tried to whisper some word of encouragement when she seemed to be conscious, more often than not being rewarded for his efforts by a kick in the head from one of the braves who stood guard over them.

Papin, who had been in good health to begin with, was able to sleep hardly at all, and in a way came to envy the woman even as he pitied her. Even when awake, she seemed hardly to be aware of what was going on around her, while Papin was unpleasantly alert.

A great fire was kept burning at the center of the lodge at all times, and the chanting and the drumming never ceased, nor did the dancing. The bare-chested warriors leaped and gyrated in the orange glow, casting eerie shadows on the walls. When occasionally one dropped in exhaustion, another immediately took his place.

Occasionally a warrior would fall down in twitching convulsions. Another might stand, arms raised and gesturing spasmodically, and in a horrible unearthly voice begin to pour out babble. Or a brave might leap from the line of dance and rush toward the bound captives, hatchet or knife raised and eyes gleaming with insane fury. Others took pleasure in kicking and spitting on the captives.

Finally they were led outside. It was a relief to breathe the crisp night air after the smoky interior of the lodge, but it was bitter cold. A pair of warriors tied them back to back, spread-eagle between two trees.

"What will they do now, Señor Papin?" The woman's voice was clear, oddly devoid of emotion, but apparently she was now wide awake and rational.

Papin sidestepped. "There is still hope, madame. Do not give up yet. You are *chrétienne*?"

"*Sí, Catolica.*"

"We will pray together, then, oui?" Without waiting for her answer, Papin began the Ave Maria. Her voice joined in on the second line. He counted off a decade with his tongue on his teeth and led her into the Gloria. The feminine voice seemed to gain strength with the recital, and Papin, who had not troubled himself about his religion in years, found some comfort in the Latin words recalled from his distant childhood. He wondered if they would live long enough to finish the rosary.

The chanting and dancing of the Pawnee continued

with ever-increasing frenzy, and the ghastly figure of Wounded Man remained near the great central fire. He writhed convulsively, sometimes exhorting the people about the evils of the white devils and spurring their hatred, at other times speaking in tongues. He drew a bird, a dead snake, some rocks from his mouth. He vomited blood.

Women and children had gathered at the edges of the circle, their eyes glittering with excitement. At one point Wounded Man, jerking as if propelled by forces other than his own, moved around this circle, crying out in a great voice, *"I am Morning Star, the Great Star. I smell the blood of these offerings already, and I will come soon to shine upon my people. My people will walk in my way forever. I am well pleased!"*

Wounded Man gave a strangled cry then and spun about, whirling himself through the line of dancers, through the fire and out again. Several women screamed and the children began weeping and shrieking. One woman stood up trembling, rolled her eyes back in her head and fell to the ground in convulsions.

Hawk Foot grabbed a brand from the fire and used it to ignite a pitch-pine torch. He ran toward the captives, shook the torch before Papin's face and laughed.

"Enfant de Dieu, Hawk Foot!" the trader cried out, but the warrior only stood grinning at him, shaking the flaming wand.

"I am Papin! I have always given your people good value. I have given you provisions for nothing when you needed them. I made gifts to you and your warriors when Hummingbird was taken from you. How can you do this thing?"

Hawk Foot shoved the flames directly at Papin's face, then dropped the torch into the pile of sticks and sagebrush at the trader's feet. He laughed when the Frenchman's eyes widened in terror before he stamped out the small blaze he had started.

"Later," he gritted, putting his face next to Papin's. "Now I will play with the pretty Spanish, the puta."

The leader of the Thunderbird Lances moved around to face Carlotta Fernandez, held the torch up for her to see and flicked at one of her nipples with his finger.

"Por Dios," she whispered, "just kill me."

Hawk Foot laughed and shoved the sputtering flames against the woman's side. She screamed as he continued to sear her flesh with flames. At last she fainted, her head falling sideways as she sagged against the ropes binding her wrists.

Papin rolled his head back and forth at the sound of her screaming. Lachelesharo stood off to one side with a group of Red Lances, watching with set, unemotional eyes. Papin stared at the chief, whom he had considered one of his staunchest friends. Papin knew the chief had argued against this sacrifice. Perhaps there was still hope. He searched the chief's face for a clue, but Lachelesharo showed no sign of recognition. After a moment he turned on his heel and walked away, several of his warriors following.

The night wore on, another kind of eternity, measured by exhaustion and cold and unrelenting pain.

And sheer animal terror, the terror of not knowing when the fire would be lit. The fire might be kept low enough to burn for long hours before the captives succumbed. Eventually their injuries would be irreparable, so that rescue would not save them, and agonized life might continue for hours or days.

The morning star would appear just before dawn, but Pierre Papin was tied facing west, so he would not be able to see its first glow.

Wounded Man had moved to the eastern edge of the

fire and stood tense, gazing toward the horizon. The yelling and the singing increased in pitch, and several of the women stood up and began to shout in tongues, writhing and whirling. One woman fell into the edge of the fire and then rolled out. She went running wildly around the circle, flames licking at the fringes of her skirt, until another woman tackled her and managed to extinguish the flames.

Wounded Man continued to gaze fixedly toward the east, his arms raised and head thrown back, praying fervently. Pierre Papin knew that the moment of the star's rising must be at hand and that in the moment of the rising, the shaman himself would bring a torch and set ablaze the tinder under his feet.

"Soon, señora," he lied but hoped it was the truth, "soon it will all be over." There was no reply. Carlotta Fernandez was unconscious.

Lachelesharo and his warriors were once more standing near the edge of the circle and looking on, but they made no move. Papin's heart sank. If the chief wished to save them it must be now, and still they stood impassively watching the others.

Then suddenly behind Wounded Man apparitions appeared near the fire, four bizarre creatures with ghastly dead-white faces and white clothing, gaunt-cheeked with great black hollows under their eyes and bloody smears around their mouths. A fifth appeared a short distance away, facing Wounded Man. It was the most hideous of all. Demonic eyes glared at the shaman. A bloody gash marked the forehead at the scalp line. Papin was unable to repress a superstitious shudder, but he assumed that this must be some part of the sacrificial ritual.

Women screamed in real terror, and most of the brave children who had withstood the other frights of the ceremony fled shrieking and sobbing into the woods or through the village toward their own lodges.

"Waku!" shouted Wounded Man. "Speak! What is this blasphemy?"

But the shaman, uncertain precisely what it was that confronted him, involuntarily backed up a step from the apparition before him.

The grim figure did not speak but pointed behind the shaman. Wounded Man glanced around to see the other four advancing upon him.

"False magic! Warriors, seize these people!" But no man stepped forward.

"Wounded Man, hear the words of Morning Star!" Pitalesharo called out, his voice loud and deep with authority. "I was called Man Chief while I lived, but now I am chixu. People of Wolf-Standing-in-Water Village, hear the words of Morning Star. Look at this man!" He pointed a quavering finger at the shaman.

"This one, Wounded Man, is the enemy of the people, just as he is the enemy of Great Star. Morning Star throws back his gifts. They stink in the god's nostrils. No, Wounded Man, Morning Star wishes you yourself to go to the spirit world. I have come back to take you there."

"Hawk Foot," the shaman called out, "this is some trick! Take these people. They are not chixu. Do not be afraid of them." Despite his words there was an edge of panic in the magician's voice.

Hawk Foot took a hesitant step forward, but Hummingbird writhed toward him, her arms outstretched invitingly, and the warrior dropped back. She pursued him until Hawk Foot stumbled against a woman at the edge of the circle and fell to the ground. He continued to back away on all fours as the people nearby scattered screaming.

When Hawk Foot regained his feet, he broke and ran.

Several of his warriors, glancing frantically at one another, followed their leader's example and ran toward the woods.

"Come, Wounded Man," Pitalesharo kept repeating, "come with me to awahokshu, the spirit world. . . ."

The other apparitions took up the phrase and turned it into a chant, with Whistling Bird dancing and gyrating his way to join the group and Hummingbird walking backward and moving her head from side to side. Then all five advanced upon the demoralized shaman, slowly shuffling their feet and reaching out with their hands, repeating in eerie tones, "Come, Wounded Man, come to awahokshu, come, come, come. . . ."

Wounded Man inched away, still calling for his warriors. But when Pitalesharo suddenly leaped at him, the shaman gave a terrified cry and stumbled into the fire pit.

He shrieked again, tried to leap away from the flames, staggered and fell among the embers. He howled curses as Pitalesharo and the others pressed forward. The shaman scrambled out of the fire and the chixu bent over him, their blood-red hands reaching for him.

Wounded Man managed to regain his footing and then he too fled into the dark woods, his clothing smoldering and sending up wisps of smoke around him.

To the utter confusion of the villagers who remained—most simply too paralyzed by fear to move—the five apparitions erupted into loud laughter. They slapped each other on the back and whooped, and the figure of death was crying out in the language of the Comanche. The five began to scrub at their faces, removing enough of the paint so that patches of skin showed and they began to take on a more nearly human appearance.

While the attention of all the people had been riveted on the performance, the Red Lances had quietly moved to surround the captives, and now at a word from Lachelesharo they encircled the two trees.

Termite Joe Hollingback, who had been observing from the shadows, stepped among the warriors and cut the bonds of the prisoners. Carlotta Fernandez slumped forward and it was all Joe could do to catch her and ease her to the ground.

The two young couples and Whistling Bird continued to rub at their paint, but with not too much success until Raven Quill stepped into the firelight carrying a container of steaming water and some soft bits of leather. The clay and paint came off at once then and the five were revealed as ordinary people.

The Skidi began to make puzzled sounds, exclaiming and questioning one another. An old warrior stood up and ran to the fire, where he began to mimic Wounded Man's undignified departure, holding his hands out pleadingly, pretending to stumble into the embers and then to turn and flee, looking back fearfully over his shoulder and rolling his eyes. Several of the men began to laugh and some of the boys repeated the old man's performance, vying to outdo one another in outrageous exaggeration.

Lachelesharo stepped forward looking very stern and held up his hands to quiet the people.

"Skidi! I have been your head chief now for a long time, many winters. I have tried to lead my people in good ways, in ways that would make all hearts glad. Yet if you wish me to resign, that is what I will do. But right now I want you to look at your own actions and decide whether what you have done is a good thing.

"I think you are like grass, or the gnats that follow the wind and have no sense and no will of their own. You have seen Wounded Man disgraced, and now you will probably wish to follow me for a while.

"But the next time something bad happens, the next time a child gets sick with the running bowels or someone doesn't take many buffalo in the spring hunt, then your ears will open to the shaman's poison once more and you will forget this night when you saw him fleeing in shame. You will forget that he brought you a false vision in which he said he saw my two sons dead. He lied when he said that Morning Star had taken Man Chief and Grey Bear because he was angry with me. Now you can plainly see that my sons are both quite alive, and yet you will forget everything.

"Perhaps you will once again allow yourselves to be convinced that the star wishes you to kill someone like our good friend Pierre Papin or a helpless woman who has fallen into the hands of Wounded Man or Hawk Foot. I do not think I wish to lead such a people, Skidi. The council may choose someone else as soon as it can. But for now I say that the Red Lances will lead away these two who were captives. They are not to be abused any further. These are my words. Lachelesharo has spoken."

The chief turned and went to join the Red Lances and the Wolf Lances, the two societies that had remained loyal to him. Pitalesharo and his fellow chixu, their faces fairly well cleaned by this time, did likewise.

The Skidi sat in silence, none speaking or looking at his neighbor. Some rose and quietly disappeared from the circle.

At last there spoke a Dog Soldier, one who had participated in the incantatory dancing. "Wait, Knife Chief. I do not know about these others, but I do not wish you to stop leading us. You are the only one who can make us see wisdom. I am ashamed of this night, but I am not so ashamed that I cannot say this: I will do whatever I can to help you now and I wish you to be head chief always."

Many of the others now concurred. "Yes, that is true for me also."

"We will follow Knife Chief."

"The sorcerer stole our wits from us even though we knew better."

"We wish to tell the Frenchman and the Spanish that we are sorry for hurting them."

"Tell us what we must do now, Knife Chief."

"What has happened to Wounded Man? Where has he gone?"

Lache.lesharo turned, his arms folded across his wide chest, and stared at his people. Those about the fire were utterly silent now, no one wishing to speak while the chief was looking directly at them. The only voice was that of Pierre Papin, cursing at Joe Hollingback.

"Enfant de grace, I wish to forget all of this. *Merde alors,* take me to where the rum is, I must drink. No, Joe, help Carlotta, get Raven Quill to help her. This night, *c'est incroyable.*"

The Red Lances began to move away with Papin and Señora Fernandez in their midst. Termite Joe joined them.

Suddenly a rifle shot rang out from the shadowy trees.

Chapter 25

"Hummingbird," Grey Bear cried. He reached for her as she slumped to the ground at his feet, a bright blossom of blood forming at the base of her neck.

Another shot kicked up the frozen earth next to Behele's foot. He pulled Hummingbird out of the way and bent over her as the Red Lances surged about them.

Little Green Frog knelt beside her brother-in-law and put a hand to Hummingbird's throat. "She is still alive, Grey Bear. I will take care of her. There is nothing you can do here."

Behele nodded, stunned. He touched his wife's hair, looked helplessly up at Little Green Frog.

The eastern sky had begun to lighten. The morning star, clearly visible, had risen while no one noticed.

"It is Hawk Foot and perhaps some of the others. Do you not wish to kill them? Go after them, Grey Bear."

A mad cry issued from Behele's throat, a roar of murderous rage. He grabbed a rifle from Two Boulders and strode past the Red Lances toward the trees, from which more rifle fire was now coming.

Pitalesharo motioned to Two Boulders and together they plunged after Grey Bear. They caught up with him and threw him to the ground just as another volley sang through the air.

"Let go of me, Man Chief! I have business up there," Behele growled, fighting against the strong arms that held him.

"Think, my brother, *think*. Wounded Man and Hawk Foot have a dozen warriors up there, perhaps more. Can you kill them all? You do not know which one fired that shot."

"You mean the one that killed Hummingbird? Let go of me, Pitalesharo, damn you."

"Listen to him, Grey Bear," Two Boulders urged.

Behele relaxed and Pitalesharo released him.

"Now what?" the tall Spaniard demanded. "Are we going to let them get away? That one owes me a death, whoever it was. And that murdering Hawk Filth is responsible no matter who fired the shot."

"First," Pitalesharo said, "we get our ponies and our weapons. Two Boulders will need his rifle back. He's coming with us. And Joe, he'll come. That makes four of us, and it'll be sufficient, I think."

"And Big Prairie Dog, Spotted Wolf, Buffalo Runner, Thin Cloud also," Two Boulders added. "We all wish to stand with the sons of Lachelesharo."

The trail led, predictably enough, toward the Pitahauerats village. Wounded Man and Hawk Foot obviously hoped to find friends there. But the shaman and the warriors were on foot. There had been no opportunity for any of them to get to their horses, for soon after the shooting began Lachelesharo had dispatched the Wolf Lances to secure all the animals.

* * *

"Looks like they's going straight north to the Arikaree, gents," Termite Joe said, having examined the sign by the full light of early morning. "Might be they could set to running and keep ahead of us that way, but not unless they figger to leave old Scar Face behind 'em. Don't figger him for being up to no seventy-five mile jog."

"They might leave him at High Boulders and return on horseback, probably with a few of White Cougar's Thunderbird Lances with them. White Cougar may not be able to control his warriors, not if the leader of the Skidi Thunderbirds calls for their assistance. If Hawk Foot gets to the Pitahauerats village before we do, he's free to tell whatever story he wishes."

"That may be it, hermano," Behele said. "They are headed in the direction of the boulders. There's water there, and good protection. Wounded Man and one or two warriors up among the rocks would cost us much time. If we move northeast across the open prairies, the way to Pitahauerats is shorter but there is little water for us and our ponies."

"Guess this nigger knows where they's two, three springs if they ain't froze solid. One way or t'other, boys, we can do her."

Pitalesharo studied the faces of his companions for a moment and then said, "Joe, you and Two Boulders and the others ride on toward Pitahauerats. By pushing your horses, you can arrive there before Hawk Foot and his men. But don't enter the village. Come down to the creek four or five miles from the village and then ride back upstream. Once you've done that, be careful; keep to cover as much as you can. The Thunderbird Lances are on foot, but they have their weapons. Pin them down if you can. Do not allow them to reach White Cougar's village.

Whether the shaman is with them or not, you will get there before they do.''

"And what will you and Grey Bear do?" Two Boulders demanded. "Do you wish to attack these men all by yourselves?"

"What Pitalesharo's saying, amigo," Behele nodded, "is that we wish to see who may be hiding among the rocks. If Wounded Man is there and we can capture him quickly, then that is what we will do. Otherwise we will continue to follow Hawk Foot and the others. Have I read your mind, hermano?"

"That is it," Pitalesharo replied.

The blood brothers parted company with their friends and rode directly north, pushing their horses hard. Within an hour they had come within sight of the peculiar formation of granite slabs they sought. In this high, open, desolate region there was no cover available. The only way of approaching undetected was to wait until nightfall, something neither Pitalesharo nor Behele wished to do.

Instead they rode directly forward, following the trail of Hawk Foot's party. The moccasin prints were faintly visible on the half-thawed earth, bare where it was not splotched with the stubble of winter-dead grasses. They did not stop to observe the fortress of boulders, did not even bother to look up, but were careful to remain beyond the range of any rifle that might be trained on them from a fracture in the stone.

"Here they have stopped for a time," Grey Bear said. "And look there; two sets of tracks move off toward the rocks. It looks as if your intuition is correct, Man Chief. Do we pass on by or—"

"Hawk Foot is not there; he has to go on to Pitahauerats in order to accomplish anything. So it's the shaman and one other. They can see us right now and they know what we're thinking. It's two against two, but they have the advantage of position.''

"They have no advantage at all," Grey Bear answered. "They are afraid and we are not. And my hatred is great enough to kill fifty men.''

"All right, then. Let us ride on by, no faster than before, just as though we had decided to stay with the main trail. When we reach the far side where the big dead cottonwood is, we double back. Then we ride fast and crooked, as the jack rabbit runs.''

"The big split that goes up under the rim—the one we climbed when we were still boys?''

"I think we can get to them that way," Pitalesharo said.

They rode to the cottonwood, then turned their horses and set off for the base of the boulders.

A shot rang out, followed by another. Then after a pause for reloading a third shot echoed. Lead spattered against a broken shelf of granite at the base of the formation.

They tied Red Medicine Dog and Behele's big paint below an overhanging verge of stone. They worked their way around the talus slide and climbed up the big chimney in the granite, wedging backs opposite hands and feet against the cold hard stone.

"Hairy Leggings knows this is here," Grey Bear puffed. "If he's the one up there with Wounded Man, he'll be waiting for us at the top of the chute, just where the fracture turns sideways.''

"He can't get both of us," Pitalesharo grunted.

But the top of the chute was empty. Pitalesharo and Grey Bear, pistol in one hand and knife in the other, silently moved around between the high lichen-spattered piles of granite.

Grey Bear's hand touched his brother's arm.

"I see them," Pitalesharo whispered. "Should we try to take them alive?"

Grey Bear thought for a moment. With the shaman at the edge of a cliff was a young warrior named Antelope Tail. "The two of them together are worth less than one man," he sneered. "The shaman cannot fight and Antelope Tail will piss on the rocks when we jump down at them."

"Grey Bear still has his sense of humor," Pitalesharo muttered. Then he stood up.

They screamed out the Skidi war cry and leaped.

Wounded Man spun, his elbow catching Antelope Tail and knocking him off balance. The young warrior grabbed at the shaman's leg, but it was too late. He went screaming over the edge.

Wounded Man seemed hardly to notice. He stood pistol in hand, facing the two sons of Lachelesharo.

"You will not kill me. Your only chance is to trade me to Hawk Foot for your own lives when he returns with the Pitahauerats Thunderbirds. A Spanish slave and the son of a weakling—"

The shot reverberated from the ancient walls of granite and a cloud of blue-grey powder smoke belched from the barrel of Antonio Grey Bear's pistol.

Wounded Man, his scarred face twisted in disbelief, dropped his pistol and stared down at the blood that covered his stomach. He looked up again, mouth open, wordless, and crumpled backward, plunging over the cliff face to join Antelope Tail on the jagged rocks below.

Pitalesharo and Behele pushed on after Hawk Foot and his Thunderbird Lances. They would return later for the two bodies.

Each would be buried by Skidi tradition in accord with his rank and status. Wounded Man would be given full honors and his bones later removed to a sacred place, while Antelope Tail, as one who had not taken coup, would be tended to unnoticed by his mother and father.

The blood brothers drove their horses on to Arikaree Creek, then turned east the direction of the Pitahauerats village. Although by nightfall they had covered more than sixty miles, Hawk Foot and his horseless warriors were still ahead.

They rode on through the cold darkness for a time and were nearly ready to stop for food and sleep when Pitalesharo smelled wood smoke. "Hawk Foot," he said.

Grey Bear nodded. He glanced up and realized no stars were visible. The smoke was hanging low. A storm was approaching. "Do we fight in the darkness, hermano?"

"Night is a river that flows both ways," Pitalesharo answered. "Hawk Foot has a fire. It will blind him. He will not be able to see out into the brush and trees that grow thick along the creek. He will not know if we are two or a hundred and two."

"Yes," Grey Bear answered. "Whatever happens, Man Chief, that one is mine. Perhaps I will never know who fired the shot that has killed my wife, but it will not matter. Hawk Droppings is responsible, and no one else. Even before this happened I vowed to kill him as soon as Old Coyote Man gave me the chance to do it. Or perhaps he will kill me, but that doesn't matter either."

"Hummingbird may not be dead at all," Pitalesharo said softly. "It was bad, where she was hit, but others have survived such wounds."

"A skinny little thing, that's what you called her, hermano. What chance did she have? But we had happiness together, even if it was for only a short time. Now she is watching from the Path of Stars on her way to the spirit world. We will meet there, my brother. Coyote-Jesus will see that it is so."

Pitalesharo did not answer.

"All these clouds—it will rain very soon. Do you think she will be able to see through them, Man Chief? I would like her to watch me when I drive my knife into Hawk Carrion's throat."

"Spirit people can see through clouds," Pitalesharo assured him, "just as they can see into our minds and know our thoughts. That is how the spirits are able to come to us in dreams."

They sat silent for a time then, holding the reins slack, waiting for nothing in particular. They already knew what they were going to do next.

A warm gust of wind found its way up the narrow valley between the low sandstone ridges. It brought with it the smells of sagebrush and dry sweet grass and the first drops of rain.

"It is almost like spring tonight," Pitalesharo mused. "It is a good night to die. The brush will be wet with rain as we crawl through it."

"A better night to live," Grey Bear answered. "Are you ready, Man Chief?"

They tethered their ponies and moved ahead on foot as the rain increased. Hawk Foot's warriors were huddled around the fire eating.

"They have run far today," Pitalesharo whispered. "They must be very tired."

"One of them at least will not have to run any farther," Grey Bear answered. The two men moved apart then, one to either side of the nine men.

A rifle roared and the lead cut into the coals of the campfire. A pistol shot sounded from the opposite direction, followed by another rifle blast and a second pistol shot. Once again the rifle roared, this time from a point several yards removed and arrows came in from both directions.

Hawk Foot and his men scrambled for the protection of the low growth of trees along the creek. Some fired back into the darkness.

"Pitalesharo speaks to you, Skidi!" came a loud voice from the darkness. "My Red Lances and Buffalo's Wolf Lances have you surrounded. Throw down your weapons. Throw them into the water. I do not wish to spill the blood of my own people."

A Thunderbird Lance named Red-shouldered Hawk, dimly visible in the firelight from where Grey Bear lay hidden, fired his rifle toward the sound of Pitalesharo's voice.

Grey Bear aimed his rifle carefully, squeezed the trigger and fired. Red-shouldered Hawk flopped forward, crawled a short distance and lay still.

"Throw down your weapons," Pitalesharo called out again. "It is foolish for all of you to die. Do you not understand me? There is no way for you to escape, but I will harm no one who throws his weapons into the creek. I will even allow you to retrieve them in the morning. Skidi! Many of you have been my friends. I wish you no harm now. It is only Hawk Foot that we want. Grey Bear wishes to fight him, one man against the other. Hawk Foot killed Grey Bear's wife back at the village, and he demands his right to combat."

"It's a trick," Hawk Foot cried out, but already splashing could be heard as his warriors threw their weapons into the stream.

"Now move away from Hawk Foot," Pitalesharo called out. "Come out to the edge of the darkness and stand in a line."

The Thunderbird Lances did as they were told and

Pitalesharo and Grey Bear emerged from the darkness, pistols leveled.

"I told you it was a trick," Hawk Foot screamed. "All these two know is tricks. It is only these two, no others."

"For once Hawk Foot speaks the truth, brothers. But my Red Lances would have found you in the morning anyway. They have ridden directly to the Pitahauerats village and will come back up the creek in the morning. White Cougar and his warriors will be with them, I think."

Suddenly one of the Thunderbird Lances, knife in hand, lunged toward Pitalesharo, but a shot from Grey Bear's pistol stopped him in midstride. He was dead when he struck the ground.

"You could all rush us at once," Grey Bear said, leveling his rifle at the remainder of the men, "but then others would die without cause. What Pitalesharo has said is true. I have come to challenge this coward Hawk Piss to a contest with knives. I could have killed him from where I lay concealed, but I would have received no pleasure from it.

"Look at him there! He alone still holds his rifle, but you see that he does not use it—no, not even to protect his men, though they are willing to die for him.

"Let these Thunderbird Lances judge, Hawk Foot. You have slain Hummingbird, my wife, the woman who was your wife until you beat her and left her for dead by the stream near the village. Do your men know about that, or did you give them some lie?"

Two of the warriors lay dead. The remaining six now turned their gaze toward the one who had led them. When he returned their stares, Hawk Foot saw anger in their eyes.

"It will be as you say, Pitalesharo," one of them

said. "I will build up the fire, for otherwise the rain will put it out. Hawk Foot has been challenged. He has no choice. He must fight."

The gentle rain continued to fall, but the fire blazed up, feeding on dead juniper boughs. The warriors formed a circle around it. To one side two men stood stripped to the waist, knives in hand.

Cautiously they moved toward one another, circling, looking for an advantage. Both moved somewhat clumsily, exhausted from physical effort and lack of sleep.

Then Grey Bear stepped back and tossed his knife to the ground. "I am tired. I do not wish to play this game of feinting and dancing any longer. You have killed my wife, Hawk Foot, and now I am going to kill you. I do not need the knife to do that. I will use my hands. Do you remember when we wrestled as boys? Once I caught hold of you, you could not get away. Now I am truly chixu, the ghost. Now I do not need to paint my face with white clay, for I will very soon go to the spirit world so that I can be with the woman I love. Do you hear me, Hawk Foot? I am chixu."

Hawk Foot grinned, the firelight glinting in his eyes.

"I will help you to go there, Spanish. My heart is heavy when I think of how lonely you must be."

"Use your knife, Antonio," Pitalesharo cried out. "Mi hermano, pick up the knife!"

"Grey Bear has chosen," one of the Thunderbird Lances said. "We must not interfere."

Grey Bear crouched, his big hands out before him. Hawk Foot moved in, feinted to one side and then drove his blade toward Grey Bear's throat.

But Grey Bear grasped the wrist and gave it a terrific wrench. Hawk Foot cried out in pain and fell forward. His

arm was broken at the elbow. His knife skittered across
the ground.

Grey Bear lunged for him, but Hawk Foot managed
to twist and send a kick to Grey Bear's chest. The blow
had no apparent effect. Grey Bear landed knee first on
Hawk Foot's chest.

Then the strong hands of the man who claimed to be
chixu clutched his enemy's throat. Hawk Foot's eyes bulged.
His voice box was crushed. His head flopped about like a
broken doll's.

Pitalesharo stepped forward, wrapped his arms about
his brother's shoulders and pulled him to his feet. "It is
done. You are avenged."

Termite Joe Hollingback and the Red Lances rode up
Arikaree Creek. The day was strangely springlike after the
brief rainstorm and the sky shimmered translucent blue.
Despite the seriousness of the matter at hand, Termite Joe
had an urge to go fishing. The dark, slow-moving creek,
he was certain, was filled with hungry fish.

It was nearly midday when Two Boulders discovered
the campsite and hurried back to rejoin the others.

The men approached cautiously, their weapons at the
ready. But they found only eight men sleeping peacefully
and the remains of a large fire, now nothing more than wet
ashes. Nearby were the bodies of three warriors lying on
their backs, arms folded across their chests. Two of these
bore bullet wounds; the third had been strangled.

"Wal, Bird Droppings," Joe Hollingback drawled,
"it looks to this nigger like you ain't going to be taking no
more bad advice from the one-eyed magician."

The sleepers awoke slowly, rubbing at their eyes and
yawning. The Red Lances gestured with their weapons,
but the men did not seem particularly concerned.

Pitalesharo strode toward Hollingback. "Termite Chief, did you think to bring your bag of coffee beans?"

"By the grace of God's left buttock, Pitalesharo, what the hell's happened here?"

The Skidi, bearing their dead with them, arrived at Wolf-Standing-in-Water Village the following day to find the place strangely subdued.

Lacheleshara, Buffalo and Wolf Chief met them. The head chief glanced at the five bodies, closed his eyes and nodded.

"The thing has been accomplished, Father," Pitalesharo said. "Wounded Man and Hawk Foot have come home to be buried, as is their right."

"Where is Hummingbird's body?" Antonio Grey Bear asked, his voice quavering.

"Her body?" Lacheleshara asked, raising one eyebrow as he spoke. "Oh, it is in the lodge with all the other bodies."

"Juan Antonio wants to see his leetle lady buried proper," Termite Joe added. "I think he may want to take her back to her own people. We've tried to talk him out of it, but—"

"Well," Lacheleshara said, "it isn't time to worry about that just now."

Behele cast a puzzled look at the head chief. He dismounted, walked to the lodge and entered.

Little Green Frog looked up, her eyes questioning. She rose from beside the pallet in the corner of the earthen lodge.

"Pitalesharo—" But then Grey Bear saw a sight that he could not believe—a skinny little woman, her neck bandaged, looking at him and grinning broadly.

Epilogue

There were weeks of blizzard and intense cold. At first the smaller streams and then the river itself froze solid. On good days the children would wander about on the ice and search down into the clear semiwhite crystal to see if they could detect any fish trapped in the freeze.

The time of sickness had passed. The stored produce of harvest time and the great quantities of buffalo, dried, cured and turned into pemmican, made for a well-stocked larder. Only occasional hunting forays for fresh meat were necessary.

The death of Hawk Foot and Wounded Man and a handful of their warriors had come as a great shock to the Skidi, but in the aftermath all agreed that life was now much better in Wolf-Standing-in-Water Village. A few of the Thunderbird Lances had taken their families and gone to live among White Cougar's people in the Pitahauerats village, but most returned within a relatively short time.

Bad Ankle had been selected as the new leader of the

Thunderbird Lances, and that warrior had been quick to renew his boyhood ties with Pitalesharo and Grey Bear and others among the Red Lances and the Wolf Lances.

In accordance with custom, the names of the dead were never or very seldom mentioned again, and new tribal unity was established. The dysentery had vanished, a sign that the favor of the gods had been restored, and peaceful prosperity had returned.

Those who had doubted the ability of Lachelesharo now gave him their full support, and his wisdom and vision were praised.

Pïerre Didier Papin, whose first impulse on release from captivity had been to pack up and leave, was dissuaded by Lachelesharo and Termite Joe Hollingback. As a result he went back to the business of being agent and trader, and profits soared. The braves, realizing the great injustice that had nearly been perpetrated upon their old friend, brought in piles of furs. Some of these were left before the post entry at night, as presents.

"War reparations, Pierre," Termite Joe laughed. "Old Pilcher ain't never going to believe all the pelts you've got, and some without even trading for 'em. Our stock's going to go way up in the company offices, sure as God's big blue pecker."

The problem of Carlotta Fernandez was quite another matter. The Spanish prisoner had been hysterical for days after her release, given to fits of screaming and sobbing. Even the sight of the benign face of Lachelesharo or Whistling Bird was enough to send her cowering into a far corner of Papin's lodge.

Termite Joe, however, spent long hours talking with her, and Broken Feather brought dishes of specially prepared foods for her. Raven Quill, Hummingbird and Little

Green Frog set to sewing dresses and moccasins for her, and these things, at first out of fear, she accepted.

When the cold finally broke and the first signs of spring appeared, Carlotta Fernandez, in company with Joe Hollingback and Pierre Papin, made her first ventures about the village and was gratified to realize that the people bore her no malice. In fact the children, sent by their elders, would approach her bearing small presents of one sort or another.

At length she was brought to visit Pitalesharo at his own lodge and was pleased to realize that Lachelesharo and his family all knew enough Spanish to be able to communicate with her in her native tongue. The tall man called Grey Bear also could speak it quite fluently. She listened in fascination as he told the story of how he had been found and adopted into the Pawnee community.

"Soon," Behele told her, "it will be time to take you back to your own people. Perhaps we will all go to visit Taos. For myself, it is possible that I still have relatives living there. I do not know."

After that Carlotta took a particular liking to old Whistling Bird, and the two spent much time together talking. The old man knew a little Spanish, and Carlotta undertook to improve his diction and his vocabulary, to the old man's obvious pleasure.

Having adopted the clothing of the Pawnee and something of their language as well, Carlotta Fernandez was seen often in the company of the old Comanche warrior whose mission among the Pawnee, as the people understood very well, was one of peace. They spent much time wandering about almost like children, studying and commenting on the ways of the Skidi.

When the meadows were green with the first new grasses of spring, Whistling Bird made preparations to return to his own people. He bore with him and his young warriors the ponies, cloth, weapons and other goods that Pitalesharo was sending to Fox Shirt as a bride price. Lachelesharo was sending nearly as much as a gift-giving in recognition of the state of peace that was now to exist between the two villages. But Carlotta Fernandez declined to accompany the old warrior south, even though he assured her that she would be given safe conduct from the Comanche village back to her own people and her husband in Taos.

"There is no understanding the nature of women," Whistling Bird confided in Pitalesharo. "But it may be that she no longer wishes to rejoin her husband. I do not know. But what will happen to her if she does not do that? It is very puzzling, grandson."

"Did she tell you anything of the sort?" Pitalesharo asked.

"She has said that her husband, Roberto Fernandez, he will no longer wish to have her. Yes, she said that. But I do not think so. I think it is something else."

"Is she falling in love with Pierre Papin?" Little Green Frog asked.

"Ah," Whistling Bird answered, his own status in the eyes of Carlotta having been questioned, "that is not the case. No, she would come to live with me before she would marry Papin the Frenchman, even though he is very generous to her."

"What is it, then?" Pitalesharo persisted.

Whistling Bird wrinkled his forehead even more and shrugged. "Perhaps Carlotta does not wish to be a Spanish anymore," he said.

Nor was Carlotta willing to accompany Termite Joe Hollingback and Antonio Behele on their trip down the Republican, the Kansas and the Missouri to the little cluster of houses, the military post and the field office of the

Missouri Fur Company in the town of Kansas. Despite numerous entreaties and the waste of much logic on the part of Lachelesharo and his son, it was clear she as yet had no intentions of leaving Wolf-Standing-in-Water.

It was late in April when Joe and Antonio returned from the excursion of nearly a thousand miles with news that word of Hawk Foot's massacre of the Diego Blanco caravan had long since reached Governor William Clark in St. Louis.

"Things is buzzing," Joe told Lachelesharo and Pitalesharo. "Weren't nobody at the outpost except a damn fool sergeant and two privates, and I couldn't get no information at all out of them niggers. Young feller was running the fur company post, though, and I did better with him. A half-greenhorn named Buttermilk Thompson, of all things. Nice feller."

"Grey Bear," Lachelesharo said in exasperation, "you tell me. The termites have finally gotten into this man's brain." Behele started to speak, but Joe cut him off.

"You want a full report or don't you? Wal, listen then. Thompson told us the word was a full goddamned battalion was being sent out to deal with the Pawnee. By the Blue Christ's breeches, Knife Chief, that's three hundred soldier boys, maybe more. And old Colonel John Moorehead's leading 'em. I served under that loony son of a bitch for a year when we was having Indian trouble in Kaintuck. The man's a fighter, I'll say that much for him."

"This is not good, Father," Pitalesharo said. "But even that number of bluecoats is no match for us."

"The last thing I want to have happen," Lachelesharo sighed. "But if we have no choice, then we must fight. Then after we have driven these soldiers away, more will come."

"Funny thing," Termite Joe mused. "Leetle Buttermilk said he'd been told that Josh Pilcher was coming along with Moorehead and his troops.''

"What does this mean?" Pitalesharo asked.

"God turn me into a damned German or some such if I know," Hollingback shrugged.

The Skidi had already begun their initial preparations to move upcountry to the foot of the Shining Mountains for the spring buffalo hunt, but all the customary ceremonies were called off. Instead small bands were sent out to bring in meat.

Pitalesharo and Behele set out north to the Pitahauerats village to alert White Cougar to the danger, but before they could reach the forks of the Republican, where White Cougar and his people were hunting, the brothers caught sight of the long, thin blue line of troops in the distance. They turned about and rode steadily until they reached Wolf-Standing-in-Water.

Lachelesharo called the warrior societies together and explained his plan for driving the soldiers away with as little bloodshed as possible.

"The bluecoats must already have passed through White Cougar's people," he said, "but I have received no word as to what may have happened. Perhaps the Pitahauerats chief simply took his people back to Arikaree Creek in case he should have to defend his village." The warriors listened solemnly as Lachelesharo, backed by the members of his council, explained the plan.

The following day all of Knife Chief's warriors were positioned and ready. Scouts had been sent out to keep track of the movements of the troops. These returned well before noon to say that the bluecoats were riding up the south branch of the Republican and had already reached the mouth of the stream the whites called Landsman Creek, some fifteen miles below the village.

* * *

Colonel John Moorehead was having second thoughts about the entire matter. The fact that he was in the company of Joshua Pilcher and Governor William Clark and even Chief White Cougar and fifty of his warriors didn't alleviate the officer's fears. Although they were deep in Skidi country now, there was no sign of Indians—curious, hostile, friendly or otherwise.

"Governor, my intuition tells me that we're falling into a trap. Perhaps it would be best to dig in and send an emissary or two on ahead."

"I shouldn't think there's anything to worry about," Clark responded. "The troops aren't going to turn and run no matter what happens. In any case it's altogether possible that the village has already removed itself to the hunting grounds. White Cougar's of that opinion. Relax, Colonel. Look at old Josh here. He's not looking for Indians; he's looking for beaver dams, and not seeing too many of those either, I might add."

At that point Indians began to appear along the low rim to the south of the little river.

"Holy Jesus," Pilcher murmured, pointing.

Now another long line of warriors appeared along the northern rim.

"I've never seen so damned many Indians all at once, not in war paint, I haven't," Pilcher moaned.

More Indians appeared at their rear.

Moorehead turned in his saddle. "Hold your fire!" he commanded. "Stand at the ready, but hold your fire!"

Another two hundred warriors, perhaps more.

"How in blazes did they manage to get behind us?" Moorehead barked at Clark.

"We're in their lands, Colonel. They know the lie of the country and we don't."

As the regiment came to a halt, supply wagons and

all, Red Eddie Sullivan came riding in from upstream, driving his pony at a breakneck clip. He drew rein and pulled to a halt beside Colonel Moorehead.

"More troubles ahead, sir. Must be two, three hundred of 'em up there. And from the looks of things their big chief's with them. Enough damned war bonnets to scare the bejesus out of an elephant-eating grizzly."

Moorehead looked around him, made quick calculations.

A thousand Pawnee warriors, give or take a hundred. And I'm pinned down, all but helpless. The pride of the western army, and unless Clark's got big medicine with the savages, I'm going to go down in the history books as the officer who got an entire regiment wiped out.

"Sullivan," the governor snapped. "That chief, you get a good look at him? A big man with broad shoulders, my age maybe?"

"Sounds like the red devil that's leading them, all right."

"Good. With any luck that's Lachelesharo, gentlemen, old Knife Chief himself. Colonel, you're damned lucky you didn't come here to fight. There's one Indian that would bring out the best in you, but I guess you've got that figured out already. Keep your men under control. Sullivan, you come with me. We're riding ahead to pay our respects. Josh, you come along too. I don't expect any trouble."

White Cougar and his Pitahauerats warriors had ridden up and now came to a halt beside Clark, Pilcher, Moorehead and Sullivan.

"What do you think, Chief?" Clark asked.

"I think my brother Lachelesharo will be glad to see his old friend," White Cougar replied.

*   *   *

A great feast was prepared and the village of Wolf-Standing-in-Water was more than a little inclined toward celebration. Blue coat soldiers, still a bit intimidated by so many Indians, stood and watched the dancing. Older women brought them baskets of steaming meat and they ate hungrily, wishing only that the meat were more fully cooked and that younger, unattached Pawnee women had brought it.

While this was going on, a meeting was taking place in Lachelesharo's lodge.

"We spoke earlier of the idea of taking some of the Plains chiefs east to meet with the Great Chief of the Whites, President Monroe," Clark said. "I have not changed my mind on that matter, and the officials in Washington, even the President himself, are willing. Several Pawnee chiefs, including White Cougar here, are willing to go. The same with Kansa, Osage, Oto, Sioux and Missouri. I wish to make that venture this summer, Lachelesharo. Are you willing?"

"We will return in time for the fall hunt, Red-haired Chief?"

"Yes. Up the river by boat, and then by coach to Washington City. It will be well for you to understand more about white men, Lachelesharo. And it will be well for the leaders of the United States to understand more about you."

"You will wish me—all of us—to sign our mark to an agreement with your Great Chief?" Lachelesharo asked.

"Yes, that is what we're hoping for."

"You are my friend of many winters, Red-haired Chief, but I must tell you something honestly."

"That is how friends must speak together, Knife Chief."

"Yes, it is so. Then this is how it will be. I will pledge no more raids on those who travel the trail between Santa Fe and St. Louis. The one who led those raids has now gone to the spirit world of my people, and there will be no others. But I must tell you that I will never agree to anything that will cause my people to weep and to say that I have led them falsely. Do you understand this, my friend?''

Clark nodded.

"Then I will be happy to meet with your chief of the white men.'' Lachelesharo reached for his medicine pipe. "But I wish my son Pitalesharo to accompany me. Yes, and Little Green Frog, his wife.''

Clark nodded in turn.

"Antonio Grey Bear,'' Lachelesharo said as he tamped tobacco into the pipe, "you have proven yourself a great and brave warrior. For this reason I will tell the council that I wish to have you act in my stead while I am gone. You must be the head chief until Pitalesharo and I return from our journey. Will you do this for me, my son?''

Hummingbird's eyes had come wide open at the head chief's words, and now she squeezed her husband's arm.

"I will do as you ask, if that is what the council wishes also,'' Grey Bear replied.

"Good.'' Lachelesharo was about to light the pipe.

"Before we smoke in friendship,'' Clark said quickly, "there's one other matter that I have to take care of. Mr. Sullivan here tells me that a certain Carlotta Fernandez was taken prisoner by the Pawnee at the time of the Blanco massacre. The caravan was Mexican, so the matter's actually out of my jurisdiction, pending the treaty that we hope to create. But is she still alive, Lachelesharo? What can you tell me of her? I must make my report to Washington.''

"The Spanish woman is here,'' Pitalesharo said. "She's with Papin in the trading post. We have wished to send her back to her husband, to her own people.''

"Shall I send for her?'' Lachelesharo asked.

"Señora Carlotta Fernandez' husband is dead,'' Clark

replied. "Killed in a barfight in Santa Fe, if my information is correct. But yes, send for her. I'll arrange for her to be taken back to Taos or wherever she may wish to go."

"Carlotta's alive?" Red Eddie asked, the words suddenly registering upon him. "By the God of my father, I never hoped that—"

"This one sounds almost like Joe Hollingback," Lachelesharo laughed.

"Naw, he don't neither," Termite Joe growled. "The coon's half greenhorn, and besides, he don't talk very good."

"Termite Joe," Clark chuckled, "I'd heard that you were dead."

"Cain't kill no real mountain man," Joe said, settling back in his seat.

Lachelesharo lit his pipe, gestured to the four sacred directions and to the earth and the sky, and then puffed. He was just passing the pipe to William Clark when Broken Feather, who had been sent on an errand to Papin's trading post, returned with Carlotta Fernandez.

It took her a moment to recognize Red Eddie Sullivan, and when she did, she started toward him, then stopped.

Sullivan rose, folded his arms across his chest and cleared his throat before speaking. "I done told the lot of you to keep on the lookout, didn't I? You and Diego, none of you *ever* listened to this coon."

Carlotta Fernandez tilted her head and smiled. "What have you done with that ugly old black hat of yours, Señor Sullivan?"